Utah

Not a gentle first kiss. It was a kiss filled with tangled emotions he thought he'd need a lifetime to unravel—the savagery of his beast, the anger at her rejection of his soul, and the desire to please her.

His raptor wasn't good enough for her. But even as he dived into all the sensory pleasure enhanced by his animal nature, he knew it could never be about only one thing with her.

Tracing her lips with his tongue, he tasted her. As he deepened the kiss, fighting his soul's demand that he abandon human behavior in favor of ripping her clothes from her luscious body, he felt something waken in her. It stretched, flexed its claws, and looked at him.

She wrapped her arms around him and met his ferocity with her own. Opening her mouth, she welcomed him in.

And all the reasons in the world why he shouldn't be doing this went to hell.

This was what *he* wanted, what his *beast* wanted.

And neither one would be denied.

ETERNAL PREY

NINA BANGS

AVON

An Imprint of HarperCollinsPublishers

AVON BOOKS
An Imprint of HarperCollins*Publishers*
10 East 53rd Street
New York, New York 10022-5299

Copyright © 2010 by Nina Bangs
ISBN 978-0-06-201895-3
www.avonromance.com

First Avon Books paperback printing: January 2011

Avon Trademark Reg. U.S. Pat. Off. and in Other Countries, Marca Registrada, Hecho en U.S.A.
HarperCollins® is a registered trademark of HarperCollins Publishers.

Printed in the U.S.A.

10 9 8 7 6 5 4 3 2 1

To my readers,
This book is for you.
Thanks for embracing my characters,
from zany to dark.
Love ya, guys.

ACKNOWLEDGMENTS

U tah and Lia would still be wandering aimlessly through Portland's Shanghai Tunnels without the guidance of several people. Mega thanks go out to Cindy U'Ren for all her help in making Portland come alive for me. She was the next best thing to being there. And I have no words for how much I appreciate Gerry Bartlett's input. She has critiqued every one of my Gods of the Night books and not once said, "You have to be kidding."

ETERNAL PREY

CHAPTER ONE

Trapped. Freaking *trapped*. In the wrong time, in the wrong place, defending a bunch of dumbass humans. Utah leaned on his horn to signal the crappy driver in front of him that when the light turned green you were supposed to *go*. Maybe he should free his beast and eat the guy. A protein snack would perk him right up.

And to think he'd really believed he could fit in here. Out of all the Eleven, he'd been the happiest, ready to put the past behind him and embrace 2012. Then the vampires had killed Rap, and he'd realized this time was no different from the last. It was just a different kind of jungle. Killing was still the only answer.

So let him kill. He was good at it. But Fin was trying to put him in a box, make him follow *his* rules. Damn it, Utah was used to leading, to going where he wanted, to slaughtering what he wanted. And what he wanted to slaughter was vampires. To emphasize his independence, he slammed shut the door in his mind that connected him to Fin. Didn't want to talk to anyone right now.

He whipped around the car in front of him. Too slow. After tonight, someone else would control the speed, but for now, he'd tear up the road if he wanted. And he didn't care if the immortals they were chasing *did* find him without his human shield. To hell with them.

Everyone was right. He was a maniac behind the wheel. To prove it, he skidded around a corner, straightened out, and gunned it. Did he care? Not much. This would be his last shot at mindless speed for a while. He'd shackled himself to his brother Rap's soul and a hired human driver who was trying to catch him right now. Too bad Utah had pulled out of the condo's parking garage just as his driver was pulling in. Utah knew his smile was all kinds of evil. He didn't know who Fin had hired to shuttle him around Portland, but they weren't starting their job tonight.

He demonstrated how pissed off he was with the situation by jamming his foot down on the accelerator. Immature, but it felt good. He looked in the mirror. Still there. Okay, so the guy could drive. Utah would have to try harder.

Good thing it was so late. There wasn't much traffic, and he hadn't seen any cops. Utah glanced at a city park. If he took a detour across the grass and around a few trees, would the human stay with him? Might be worth a try.

While he was busy mulling over ways to escape from the guy riding his back bumper, his cell rang. He punched the button on his steering wheel. "Yeah?"

"Pull over, you prehistoric jerk. I've been trying to catch you since you left Fin's. Let me guess, you had to dump all the Cracker Jacks from the box to find your driver's license. No wonder Fin wants me to drive you around. You're a menace."

Shock made him slow down a little. He didn't know what surprised him more, that his tail was a woman or that she'd had the guts to call him a prehistoric jerk. Men had died for less.

"Look, lady, I don't need a babysitter tonight. Go back and tell Fin you lost me."

"Not going to happen. And you absolutely need me. A human has to stay close—like *inside* your car—to keep this Seven guy from tracking you. Just an aside, but I feel stupid calling anyone Seven. Give him a human name like Bill or Tom. Anyway, that's me, your designated human. Now pull over."

"Immortals don't have names like Bill or Tom." She intrigued him. She knew more about him than the ordinary humans Fin hired to drive them around. But that didn't matter. No one, not even a female with a sexy voice and a bossy attitude, would interfere with his last wild ride.

"Sure, pulling over now." Utah flipped on

his blinker and coasted to the curb. He kept the engine running. Then he waited until she parked her car and climbed out.

He had a brief glimpse of long jeans-clad legs before he jammed his foot down on the accelerator and took off. Utah laughed as he glanced in the mirror and saw her flinging herself back into her car. Too late.

Utah was so busy wondering what went with those legs that he almost didn't see the man standing in the middle of the dark street. Only the lightning-fast reflexes of a born hunter kept him from hitting the guy. The street was too narrow for this kind of crap, and Utah almost plowed into a light pole as he jerked the wheel to the left. The man didn't even flinch as he came *this* close to getting his dumb butt flattened.

Utah slid on the wet street—didn't it ever stop raining in Oregon?—as he corrected for his sudden turn. Once the car was pointed in the right direction again, Utah paused. What he wanted to do was get out of his car and knock the idiot onto his ass. Jeez, he was still standing in the same spot.

But Utah had to get back to Fin's in an hour. The Eleven were meeting to talk strategy. And since Utah had decided to rejoin the team, for now, he wanted to be on time. Reluctantly, he pressed down on the gas . . . and listened as the motor cut off. Wonderful.

The human mind is slow. His hadn't even

begun to make sense of the situation. Good thing he had a soul with a primitive instinct that simply *knew. Danger. Don't get trapped in the car.*

Utah listened to his instinct. Shoving the door open, he launched himself from the car . . . a second before it burst into flames.

He automatically scanned the area. No other people on the street, no one sticking his head from a window. There was a car on fire, for God's sake. Where were the rubberneckers? But everything remained silent except for the crackling of the fire. He backed away from the burning car as he flung his hand in front of his face to block the heat. Then without warning, the fire died, leaving nothing but a blackened frame. What the . . . ?

Utah shifted his gaze to the man still standing in the street. Night shadows cast darkness across his face. All Utah could see was a tall man dressed in black. Except for his hair. Even without light, Utah could see the dark red sheen of it. Long, the guy's hair seemed to have the same glitter going as Fin's hair. His imagination? Could be. Utah narrowed his eyes in an attempt to see the man's face. He had a predator's vision. Even with no light, he should have no trouble seeing. But he still couldn't make out the guy's features.

Wait, where were the streetlights? And there should've been lights coming from some of the buildings on either side of the street. There weren't. Shit.

It didn't take many brain cells to put things together. Utah didn't have a human with him, so Seven could track him. Seven and Team Evil had all kinds of crazy power. Was this Seven?

Thought became action in his mind. He crouched, ready to spring. But in the second before his beast would have exploded from its cave buried deep in his soul, he staggered and almost fell.

It felt as though someone had put hands of steel on both sides of his head and squeezed. Utah swore he could feel his brain turning to mush. He expected it to shoot out of his ears at any minute. Then there was the voice in his head.

"You'll be so easy to kill, Utah. The fire didn't get you, but all I'd have to do is to keep squeezing that hard head of yours until your brain really did squirt out your ears. Love the mental picture. Should've listened to Fin and hung around a few humans."

Utah froze, unable to move forward no matter how hard he tried. He fought to fling the intruder from his mind.

"Now, now. Trying to kick your guest out so soon? And I have so much to say to you." His mental laughter echoed eerily. *"Hate to tell you, but if I want to stay, I'll stay. Right now, I'm trying to decide the most entertaining way to kill you."*

Utah gave up on the mental eviction attempt, and focused on releasing his animal. But his beast, always eager to taste freedom, crept further back into its cave. *No.* This couldn't be happening. Utah concentrated harder.

"Your predator is sleeping in tonight. Sorry." He didn't sound sorry. *"Fin isn't the only one who can control your beast. Let's see now, will it be spontaneous combustion or an exploding head? Both are lots of fun to watch. Oh, and if you want to give Fin a mental shout-out, feel free. I'll even get out of your mind so it won't be too crowded in there. After all, it doesn't seem fair for you to die when Fin was the one who brought you here."*

This was about Fin then. If Utah called for help, Fin would come. Utah wasn't going to be the bait used to draw his leader into an ambush. So he kept the link between them closed.

Utah struggled against the invisible whatever keeping him from the bastard. All his effort got him was a cold sweat and shaky legs.

The guy had to be Seven. Only Seven would know this much about the Eleven. But if this *was* Seven, then they were all in lots of trouble. Utah had fought Eight, but Eight's power hadn't felt like this—a heavy pulsing in his veins that threatened to burst them, a drumbeat of energy that kept getting stronger and stronger and stronger.

Utah knew when to retreat. He couldn't touch whoever or whatever this was, so he needed to escape. Fast. He had to lose himself in the dark, maybe run down one of the side alleys where he might be able to slip away or free his beast. Not that he had much of a chance. If this was Seven, he could follow Utah anywhere. Utah had to try, though. Because once his opponent realized he hadn't sent Fin a distress signal, he'd have no reason to keep Utah alive.

But his feet wouldn't listen to his brain. He was stuck to the street, held there by something that pressed in on him from all directions. This was bad.

Utah didn't find out exactly how bad because at that moment a car came roaring around the corner. The driver sped up instead of slowing down and laid on the horn. Then he swerved around Utah and hit the red-haired bastard, bouncing him off the car's right fender. The man lay there for a moment, and then began to rise.

Utah felt whatever force had been holding him snap.

He stayed in human form and ran like hell. His beast might move faster, but it made a larger target. He didn't sense anyone in his mind, so he opened his connection to Fin. No one else could get in now.

"You cut me off." Fin, sounding annoyed. *"Now you're back. Explain."*

"Missed you."

"Smartass."

"I have a situation. Talk later."

He sprinted toward the car that had finally stopped. The driver switched off the headlights and jumped out. Even in the darkness he recognized those long legs. She'd found him.

She held a gun and looked as though she expected him to leap into the car so they could escape. A mistake. Even rattled by the impact, Seven or whoever that was could incinerate it before they drove out of sight. And if she managed to shoot the guy, he'd be extra pissed. Because Utah figured it would take more than a few bullets to put him down. They had to hide.

The street had lots of narrow alleys. He chose one at random and led her into darkness so complete that only his predator's eyes could see objects. He grabbed her hand and guided her around boxes and trash bins. When they emerged from the other end of that alley, he led her down another and another. Seven couldn't track him while he was with her, so as long as Utah could keep him from getting a visual, they might have a chance. Finally, he crouched with her in the shadow of a truck and waited. Nothing.

She'd remained silent the whole time. No screaming, no demanding explanations. Smart lady.

He answered her unspoken question. "We couldn't take your car. You saw what he did to mine. He would've gotten us before we reached the corner." Utah stood, looked around, and then leaned against the truck.

She nodded. "Who *was* that?" She rose in one lithe motion and moved away from him.

"Seven, maybe." Since awakening to this time a few months ago, Utah had fought his share of nonhumans and had loved every minute of every battle. *Except for the one where Rap . . .* He shoved that thought aside. None of them had felt like this man, though.

"I can't take the chance of going back for my car tonight even if he left it in one piece. And by the time I show up for it in the morning, the cops will have had it towed." She snatched the cap from her head, freeing a riot of short blond curls. She narrowed her eyes and tightened full lips that he decided would never be described as thin no matter how ticked off she was. Her expression said this was all his fault.

It was, but he damn well wasn't . . . Wait. Utah did some eye narrowing of his own. Now that he'd gotten a good look at her, he recognized the curls and those blue eyes drilling a hole through his forehead. They'd never met, but he'd seen her twice back in Philly when they'd been hunting Eight. She'd worn the same glare back then. He wondered what would make her smile and then discarded the thought as unimportant. Because no matter how tempting she was, she had one fatal flaw.

"You're Lia, Katherine's daughter." Katherine, the regional leader of the Northeast vampires— cruel, power-hungry, and thankfully, dead. Lia had taken over that leadership. "Still human, huh?" She wouldn't stay leader long if she didn't become vampire soon. Right now her mother's reputation along with a rigged fight Lia had won over a powerful vampire kept her afloat. She'd sink the first time another vampire challenged her.

"Still filled with primal rage, *huh*?" What an

understatement. Lia was glad she'd put some space between them.

His rain-darkened blond hair framed a face that shouted dangerous predator. He was gorgeous, with the kind of savage beauty you would only feel safe admiring from behind the bars of a very strong cage. If she could see his eyes through the dark and rain, she was sure they'd gleam with hate for all things vampire. He pushed away from the truck and walked toward her.

Utah was over six feet of toned muscle, and he moved with the fluid grace of a hunter. "I lost my brother about a month ago, so yeah, I'm still a little resentful." He stopped about a foot from her and then leaned in.

Startled, she lifted her gaze to his eyes. He'd stepped into her personal space. Close enough to see his eyes clearly. Blue. And so cold they made an Arctic ice floe seem cozy.

"I know vampires murdered your brother. But all of them are gone now. So why the killing frenzy?"

"I enjoy it. And how did you know about my 'killing frenzy'?"

"News travels." Her mother would've loved this guy, but he gave Lia chills. Lia did what she needed to do, and if killing was involved, so be it. But she never enjoyed it.

Utah was one with his soul, and his soul was nothing more than a killing machine. No softer human emotions would ever clutter up his psyche.

His human form was only a convenient cover for what he really was.

She didn't have a clue how to forge a connection with him. Speechless for a moment, she found herself staring at the hard planes of his broad chest clearly delineated by the wet T-shirt clinging to every powerful muscle beneath his open jacket.

"What're you doing here, Lia? Portland is a long way from Philly."

Lia refused to back up an inch. "I came here to kill you."

He tensed and glanced at the gun she still held.

She'd surprised him. Good. "And I still carry a sword." She pushed her long coat aside to reveal her weapon. "The gun might not kill you, but it'll put you down long enough for me to take your head." Left unsaid was that Superman wasn't the only one faster than a speeding bullet.

"An armed and dangerous woman. Always a challenge." His eyes remained cold and wary, no hint of playfulness in their depths. "You can explain this sudden urge to fly across the country to kill me after I've called for a ride back to Fin's." He started to reach for his cell phone and then cursed. "Can I borrow your phone? Mine went up with the car."

After handing him her phone, Lia left him to it as she tried to organize her thoughts. Things were happening too fast, and Utah was a lot more everything than she'd expected. She'd gotten a glimpse of him twice in Philly, but he'd been in his animal form both times. It looked like she'd have to improvise on the fly, because they'd be spending some quality time together in the next few weeks, or at least until they got rid of Seven.

He returned her phone. "Tor will be here in a while. While we're waiting, you can fill me in." He walked to the mouth of the alley and looked up and down the street.

He didn't fool her by turning his back to her. She'd seen the Eleven in action. In the time it took her to bring her gun up and shoot him, he could rip her head off. She slipped the gun into her coat pocket. "All the regional leaders got a call from Adam."

"And Adam is?"

"Our boss, leader, biggest toad in the puddle, whatever." She didn't like Adam. "He told us to get our butts to Portland because someone was slaughtering vampires. The local clan wasn't having much luck hunting you, so Adam decided to bring in mid-management."

"And now you're my driver?" His tone suggested she'd better make this good.

"Adam changed his mind after meeting with Fin. He wants to be on the winning side in this battle between you and the number guys. Fin asked for a little time to talk to you. In the meantime, Fin mentioned that you'd need a human driver. Adam volunteered me."

"Why?"

Because if you won't listen to reason, I can still kill

you. "Because I straddle two worlds. I'm human, but I understand the supernatural. I can fight, and I can help you track down Seven."

Utah nodded, but Lia couldn't tell if she'd convinced him.

He looked over his shoulder at her. "How did you know I was in trouble tonight?"

She grinned. "I didn't. When I came around that corner, I was just trying to catch your ass. As soon as I saw your car, though, I knew something was up." Lia shrugged. "You know the rest."

"You made a helluva distraction." He smiled.

For a moment, she was mesmerized by the raw masculine beauty of that smile. The moment allowed him to close the distance between them.

He grabbed her arm and pulled her close even as she used the hand that wasn't fumbling for her sword to try to push him away. So close that she was pressed against his chest and stomach. Heat spread from every contact point. She was surprised steam didn't start rising from their damp clothes.

Her gun hand was firmly trapped between their bodies, and she couldn't free her sword with her left hand. Great. Just freaking great. She brought up her knee.

He deftly stepped aside and bent his head to whisper in her ear. "Don't ever try to kill me, sweetheart. It wouldn't end well for you." Then he released her.

Lia shoved him away from her. She was furious with him but just as mad at herself. She'd allowed his closeness, his warm breath feathering her skin, her total *awareness* of him to slow her reaction. A fatal mistake when dealing with the Eleven. Lia was so angry she wanted to draw her sword and skewer him in his oversized ego. "I wouldn't be too sure about that. And *never* grab me again without my permission."

His smile widened, fueling her temper. *Control it.* She hadn't survived growing up around her mother by giving in to her emotions. Taking a deep, calming breath, she changed the subject. "So is all this 2012 stuff I'm hearing about true?"

He shrugged. "Depends on what you've heard. Cliff's Notes version. Time is cyclic. This particular cycle began millions of years ago. At the end of every cycle, ten immortals are given access to Earth. They destroy the dominant species using the excuse that out of death comes life. Dumbass excuse if you ask me."

"So they've done this before?"

"Yeah. The last time they came was sixty-five million years ago. The dinosaurs went extinct then. Now it's humanity's turn."

"Who gives them access?" She'd cooled her temper with a cold splash of reality. Humans were in big trouble.

Utah shrugged. "There's always a higher power."

Translation: he didn't know. Or maybe he was just avoiding answering the question. Lia figured with Utah you could never tell.

"And all this will go down on December 21?" Guess the Mayans really did know their stuff.

"Exactly at 11:11, winter solstice. Unless we can get rid of all the immortals. Nine and Eight are gone. We still have to deal with Zero and the other seven."

The sound of a car slowing down ended her questioning. Utah went to look and then beckoned to her.

She made sure she got the passenger seat. Lia didn't want to chance Utah sitting beside her. He bothered her in ways she didn't understand, didn't *want* to understand. Utah slid into the backseat.

"Lia, this is Tor. He's my brother."

Tor looked exactly like Utah, except that Tor had short, spiky hair and a better attitude. He grinned at Lia. "I remember you from Philly. Eight kidnapped you and Jenna. Took you to the Museum of Art. We saved your butts."

"My butt thanks you." Lia figured she sounded as grumpy as she looked because Tor left her alone. Instead, he pried the night's story out of Utah.

While Utah and Tor discussed things, Lia worried about her car. If she found a burned-out hulk tomorrow, she'd use the insurance money to buy a car with a big engine. For a human, survival

in this shadow battle going on right under the
world's nose depended on speed and smarts. And
the smart needed speed to escape.

She came out of her funk in time to notice that
Utah and Tor had changed the subject.

"So how did Fin draw you back into the fold,
bro?" Tor didn't take his eyes from the road while
he talked. And he was driving under the speed
limit.

Ah, the careful brother. If she had to hang with
one of the Eleven, then Tor should be the one. Instead, all she could remember was her adrenaline
rush as she'd chased Utah across town.

"Fin pointed out that we need the vampires.
Without them, it'll take longer and be a lot tougher
to get rid of Zero and his bunch. And that means
he won't be able to bring Rap back anytime soon.
He's right." Utah didn't sound as though he liked
admitting Fin could be right about anything.

Tor nodded. "And with you killing off the vampires, they won't be signing on to our team."

Lia turned to look at Utah. "You took out
Adam's top enforcer two nights ago. Don't expect
an invite to any vampire parties."

"Yeah?" Utah's lips tipped up in a half smile
that made her swallow hard. She stomped on the
reaction.

Lia had to know something. "Bring Rap back?"

Utah didn't say anything for a moment, but
then he shrugged. "We'd gone to a little restau-

rant in South Philly for cheesesteaks. Vampires ambushed us. Rap didn't get a chance to free his beast before one of them took his head."

"And?"

"His body died. His soul didn't." Utah met her gaze, his eyes almost black in the darkness. "Fin can remove souls from bodies. That's how he saved all of the Eleven. He sends the souls to a safe place near a strong natural power source until he can return them to a body. Rap is tucked away underground somewhere near Sedona, Arizona, right now."

"What's stopping Fin from bringing Rap back now? Lord knows you need all the help you can get."

Utah looked frustrated. "Fin needs his power to keep Zero off our backs. Hard to believe, but Fin says Zero is stronger than he is. Fin tries to distract the bastard with a constant barrage of psychic attacks. A soul transfer would drain too much from Fin. Besides, Fin needs the right body. So Rap will have to wait."

What kind of being could manipulate souls? The word "god" popped into her mind, but she shoved it aside. "What if something happens to Fin?"

"Then Rap's soul sleeps forever."

Utah might sound casual, but there was nothing casual about his clenched fists.

"I'm sorry." And she was. She studied his face,

for the first time seeing just a man. A man who was hurting for his brother.

"Yeah." He seemed to give in to weariness as he rested his head against the headrest and closed his eyes.

She took the hint and turned away to stare out the window. It seemed to take way too long before they pulled into the condo's underground parking garage. No one said anything as they took the elevator up to the top floor.

Stepping from the car, Utah covered the distance to Fin's door in a few long strides. He pounded on it. Lia would have rung the bell. She wondered if they had even one thing in common.

He'd raised his fist to pound again when the door swung open. A tall, dark-haired man stared at them. As doormen went, he looked a little intense.

"Lia, this is Shen, Fin's assistant." Utah stepped past the man into the condo.

Shen smiled and stood aside for Tor and her to enter. His smile didn't exactly transform him into Mr. Relaxed, but at least he seemed welcoming. "Hi, Lia. Follow me. Everyone's in the dining room."

As she followed Shen, Lia tried not to let the total awesomeness of the condo impress her. Walls of glass overlooked the city and river. And Fin definitely didn't shop for furniture in the same places she did. Mega cash outlay. Where had Fin scraped that kind of money together? But she figured if you had your own pack of predators working for you, people gave you what you wanted.

Shen stopped in front of a closed door. Lia could hear men's voices behind it. She steeled herself as Tor swung the door open.

They were all seated around a long table. Everyone stopped talking. They turned and looked at her. These were the Eleven then. No, ten, since Rap was missing. All big, all lethal, and probably humanity's best chance to survive the end of this year. She'd seen some of them in Philly, but in very different forms.

Lia straightened her spine, tipped her chin up at a confident angle, and walked with Utah and Tor into the room. She felt their stares follow her as she chose a seat between Utah and Tor. Then she met each of their gazes.

She'd lived around vampires her whole life. Lia understood predators. Never look nervous, never look away, and always send a message that you're the biggest badass in the room. She saved the man at the head of the table for last.

This, then, was Utah's boss, the leader of the Eleven. And no matter that she'd heard descriptions of him . . .

There were no words.

He had to be at least six foot seven, but it wasn't his size that riveted her.

Long silver hair spilled over his shoulders and

down his back. Not gray. *Silver.* The glittery glow of it raised goose bumps along her arms.

"I've been waiting to meet you, Lia."

Fin's voice, sensual or threatening? Lia came down on the side of threatening. But who would ever care about his voice when he had that face? It was a face carved from shadows and dark places where normal people never dared go. It was primitive force, sexual power, and unearthly beauty all stamped with an aura so ancient it took her breath away.

"We need to have a long talk soon." Fin smiled.

Lia decided Fin's smile wouldn't fool anyone. Transfixing like the rest of him, the smile somehow didn't ring true. Maybe because she sensed that no emotion lay beneath it. Fin's smile would be the last thing you'd see as you died, and it wouldn't make the dying easier.

"Sure." She tried to sound casual, but she absolutely did *not* want to be closed into a room alone with this man.

"I don't think you've met most of the Eleven."

"Not in their human forms."

Fin introduced all of them, a string of names attached to unfamiliar faces. But it wasn't their faces she saw in her mind, but their beasts. She didn't think humanity was ready to accept what walked among them. Lia wasn't sure she was either.

Fin leaned back in his chair and shifted his attention to Utah. "What happened tonight?"

Utah told his story, straightforward with no apologies.

Lia found herself holding her breath, waiting for Fin's anger to explode. It didn't. His expression remained neutral.

"You have to control your anger, Utah." There was no condemnation in Fin's voice. He was simply stating a fact.

Lia surprised herself by speaking up. "He lost a brother he loved a month ago. Anyone's emotions would still be raw."

Utah's look said her defense had shocked him. She frowned at him so he'd know that this didn't make them friends. Lia just thought someone should keep things fair.

Tor leaned close. "Thanks. Not many outsiders would dare disagree with Fin."

Lia *was* an outsider here. She had to remember that and maybe keep her mouth shut more.

When he spoke, Utah's voice sounded calm, but she could almost feel the tension rolling off him.

"You knew what you were getting when you woke me four months ago. My last memory? A kill that Rap, Tor, and I made a lot of years ago. But that kill felt as though it'd happened only minutes before I woke. None of us have had much time to adapt. I'm still what I was back then. One of those online research sites called my beast cunning, savage, and ruthless. That's me. I'm a killer. Deal."

"You *will* overcome your animal nature." Fin

stood and strode to the bank of windows. He stared out at the city lights.

Lia sensed an or-else attached to that order.

"You made a big mistake, O Glorious Leader."

Fin didn't turn around.

"When you put my soul into a man's body, you didn't allow for human emotions. Now you have mindless savagery married to human feelings. I hurt. And my soul is big and bad enough to do something about it."

Everyone in the room went still, waiting. From the tense glances the rest of the Eleven were sending Fin's way, she got the feeling most of them trod a little more carefully around their leader.

Fin turned and walked back to the table. He sat and then looked at Utah. When his lips turned up in a rueful smile, Lia could hear the collective sigh of relief.

"I know what you're feeling. You have no idea how much I know." He tapped one finger on the table as his expression turned thoughtful. "Did you say the man who attacked you had red hair?"

Utah nodded. "Yeah. I figure it was Seven."

Fin's thoughts seemed to turn inward. "I think congratulations are in order for both you and Lia."

Utah looked puzzled. Lia had a bad feeling about this.

"Because you both met Zero tonight."

Beside her, Tor sucked in his breath.

"And survived."

CHAPTER TWO

Utah heard Lia's small gasp, felt the shocked ripples circling the room.

"I wasn't the target." Utah was certain of that. "Zero didn't want me to die in that car. He could've killed me anytime he wanted. He did want to scare the crap out of me, though, so I'd call you." He met Fin's gaze. "Zero wanted to draw you out. He even told me to call you."

"And you didn't." Fin finally looked annoyed.

"No."

"If there's ever a next time, call."

"No." Utah saw Fin's annoyance turning to anger and decided to explain. "You're the only one who matches up with Zero. Sure, the rest of us might get lucky and manage to kick the rest of his gang back out into the cosmos, but then Zero would wipe us out. The way I see it, *you* need to survive."

"And *you're* not expendable." Fin's expression said the discussion was closed. "Now we need to talk about how to find Seven."

Utah subsided.

Lia leaned toward him. "He's right. Fin needs you guys as much as you need him. Don't underestimate yourself."

Utah didn't want anything she said to make him feel good. It was bad enough that he was imagining those legs . . . No, he wasn't going there. Ever.

"Does anyone have any leads on Seven?" Fin looked around the table. His question got no response. "Let me rephrase that. Has anyone heard of unusual events in Portland lately?"

"Homicides are way up. I checked the city crime stats." Q kept up with things like that.

Fin nodded. "Right now Seven is recruiting from the paranormal population, from *your* people." He glanced at Lia. "He's promising them power and wealth, promising that they can kill at will. The killings serve a purpose. Terrorize the population and the battle is half won."

"Adam's mad because almost a third of the Portland clan has gone missing. He thinks there's a rogue vampire out there luring them away to join a new clan." Lia looked at Utah. "Then there're the ones you killed."

"Interesting." Fin didn't seem concerned with

the dead vampires. "We can assume the missing vampires are with Seven."

"That doesn't help us find the bastard." Car stated the obvious.

"We need the local vampires. They know Portland and all the places nonhumans gather." Spin looked ready to tear the city apart to find Seven.

Lia leaned forward. "If you want the vampires' help, then Adam is your key. As he goes, so goes the whole vampire nation." She smiled. "Except for a few regional leaders with the guts to stand up to him."

"Like Jude." Fin went back to tapping the table with his finger. "He helped us in Philly, and he's passed on some helpful information here in Portland. We're lucky Adam called for all his regional leaders to help hunt Utah or else Jude would still be back in Texas."

"Adam won't like that. What's his is his forever. He doesn't share, and that includes information." Lia looked worried for Jude.

"I explained to Adam how upset I'd be if any harm came to Jude." Fin's eyes turned glacial.

"One thing you need to know about Adam. He can't be trusted. Sure, he seems to be leaning your way right now, but that could change in a second. Power motivates him." Lia didn't sound as though Adam was her leader of choice.

Utah let the conversation flow around him as he built a plan he thought might work. When he had everything straight in his head, he spoke.

"We need Adam, and Adam needs a new enforcer to wipe out this rogue vampire and any vampires who follow him."

"A new enforcer?" Ty was starting to look interested.

"I killed the old one."

A few of the Eleven congratulated him, but Fin's stare stopped that.

"I'll volunteer to be Adam's enforcer."

Lia laughed. "Adam hates you."

"What do you have in mind, Utah?" Fin sat forward.

"He needs an enforcer who can hunt down and eliminate this rogue vampire and his followers, and I like killing vampires. Tell him that I'd be doing what I like to do and at the same time atoning for my random kills. Both sides win."

"Why would he believe you'd go for that idea? You're already destroying vampires at a record rate." Fin didn't look happy about the thought.

Utah shrugged. "Tell him the truth with a twist. Explain that you need the vampires' help, and offering my services is sort of a goodwill gesture." He grinned. "Hell, tell him you threatened to kill me if I didn't agree. He'd love that."

"It might work." Lia had stopped laughing. "Adam is all about intimidation. He'd respect someone who ruled through threats."

Spin spoke for the first time. "Once Utah's on the inside, he can feed us information even if Adam doesn't feel like sharing."

Fin turned his silver gaze on Utah. "Understand that once you're working for Adam, you'll be in constant danger. And not from Seven. Adam doesn't seem the type to forgive and forget."

Utah nodded. "Understood."

"I'll run it past Adam now. Dawn isn't far away." Fin glanced around the table. "That's all for tonight. Keep searching. Oh, and never go anywhere without your human driver."

"What about Zero?" Utah could still see the immortals' leader standing in the middle of the freaking street.

Fin's eyes suddenly swirled with purple, a rare display of emotion. "I'll take care of Zero." Without a backward glance, he strode to the door and left.

He didn't slam the door behind him. Maybe if Fin slammed a few doors, Utah could connect with him more. There was something about Fin that always felt . . . wrong.

"So where are you heading now?" Lia watched the others leaving.

"Back to my apartment." Good thing that Fin believed in spreading the Eleven around the city. They each had their own apartment. He needed alone time tonight.

"I'll drive you."

He surrendered to the inevitable. "Fine."

She disappeared for a minute, and when she returned, Lia had a set of car keys in her hand. "I got us a loaner for the night."

Once out on the street, he gave her his address and settled back for a quiet drive across town. God, he'd miss the rush he got from shoving the accelerator to the floor and feeling the car surge.

"I have a few questions."

Utah groaned silently. Scratch the quiet drive. "Shoot."

"Why do you talk about tossing Zero and his pals back out into the cosmos? Why not kill them so they don't show up again to hassle you?"

He rested his head against the headrest and closed his eyes. "Vampires can be destroyed. I can be killed. These guys are true immortals. They *can't* be killed. I could tear them into bite-sized bits, then feed the bits into a wood chipper, and their essence would still exist. They'd just come back in a different form. The best we can do is to send them home with no return address."

She lapsed into silence for a few minutes, and he hoped she was done with the questions.

"I don't understand your attitude about vampires. Hey, I don't blame you for hating the ones who killed your brother, but the rest of it . . ." She shrugged.

This he wouldn't mind explaining. If she was going to spend time with him, she'd have to know how he felt. "You have to understand pack. It might seem a long time to you, but it's only been a few months since Rap, Tor, and I hunted together. Fin saved all three of our souls and brought us here so we could once again walk the earth, hunting as one. *Pack*. Now one of us is gone. Without pack, something big and empty sits right here." He fisted his hand against his chest. "I might look human, Lia, but my soul is animal. And my beast screams for revenge."

"I still—"

"Look, a fire ant bites you, you don't just kill that one. You go in and wipe out the whole hill along with their queen. Make sure they don't bite anyone else."

She firmed her lips and kept her eyes on the road. "That's a lot of hate you're carrying around. Does Tor feel the same way?"

He laughed. Tor and he might have the same human faces—and how the hell had Fin managed that?—but they didn't react to things in the same way. "I released my need for revenge in the most violent way I could. Tor holds things in. All that repression can't be a good thing."

Lia knew he saw her unease.

"Yeah, Tor is the good brother. I'm his evil twin." He seemed to find that amusing. "I've answered your questions, now I have few of my own."

Lia gripped the wheel tighter. She didn't want to talk about her life.

He chose to ignore her wall of silence. "Last I heard, you wanted to become vampire like your mother. Still planning on it?"

"I want to be vampire, but not like her. I want to lead my people in a direction that doesn't involve draining humans in dark alleys." And wouldn't Katherine hate that.

Lia figured that Jude had allowed her to win their battle for leadership of the Northeast vampires not just because he had his hands full with his own territory. He didn't want to be bothered ruling a bunch of vampires that Katherine had terrorized for so many years. Her mother had never allowed independent thought, so they had none.

"Then why not get it done?" His voice seemed carefully neutral.

"Dad doesn't want it to happen until I've experienced what he feels is the full joy of human life."

"I remember him. He's a good man."

"Yes, he's a wonderful father." With issues. Katherine made him and then treated him like she treated everyone. She was in charge and never let him forget it. He didn't mourn her passing. And there was something sad about that. "So I'll give him the time he wants."

To forestall any more questions about her life, she changed the subject. "If you hate vampires so much, why do you tolerate Jude being around? I'm surprised you haven't torn *him* apart."

Good. They'd reached Utah's apartment building. She quickly pulled into an empty space and turned off the engine. Not a minute too soon. The inside of the car had been shrinking with each question.

He opened his door, but before climbing out,

he leaned across to whisper in her ear. "Jude is an ally, sweetheart. Loyalty is my *only* redeeming quality. Remember that." Then he got out. But he hesitated before striding away. "You have your own apartment?"

"Sure. Don't worry about me." She waved him away.

Lia watched him stride toward the building. She should have told him, but she wasn't in the mood to listen to his complaints. Once he was inside, she got out, locked the doors, and followed him.

Her apartment was on the fifth floor, so she took the elevator. Amazing how having a dustup with the biggest bad on the planet could wear you out. When the elevator doors opened, she walked down the short corridor and . . . saw Utah standing outside his apartment fiddling with his lock.

Oh shit. Before she could turn around and run back to the elevator, he looked up and saw her. With a resigned sigh, she continued on to her apartment right next to his.

"Having trouble getting in?" Lia knew her smile reeked of insincerity.

"You've got to be kidding." He didn't even try to hide his disgust.

Now she was mad. "What? Are you afraid I'll keep you awake at night with wild vampire parties, maybe knock on your door to borrow a cup of blood, or—"

"Just be quiet." His voice came as close to a roar as she'd ever heard it.

Lia took a deep breath. It had been a tough night, and they were both tired. She kept her mouth shut.

"I don't care if ten vampire wannabes live next door. What I do care about is bringing my work home with me. That's what it'll be like living next to you." He raked his fingers through his hair.

Vampire wannabe? That hurt. "I don't know what your problem is. You had a driver back in Philly. That driver lived next to you because, hello, the Eleven need to have their humans ready to drive them anywhere at a moment's notice." Lia threw up her hands. "Oh, this is ridiculous."

She unlocked her door and left him standing in the hallway. A few minutes later she heard his door slam shut. Good thing. Because she didn't take *her* work into her apartment and allow him to sleep on her couch.

Her annoyance kept her buzzing long after she should have fallen asleep. Finally, she started to doze. No bad dreams, she hoped. At least she wouldn't have nightmares about her mother's death, because she hadn't been there when it happened. And she'd never asked which one of the Eleven had killed her.

Lia woke to pounding on her front door. She struggled out of bed and pulled on her robe.

Light slipped in around her blinds. She'd have to get blackout curtains once she became vampire. Glancing at her clock—how had she slept till four P.M.?—she ran her fingers through her hair and hurried to the door. Lord, she hoped Utah didn't want to leave right now. She didn't function without coffee.

She pulled open the door just as he raised his fist to do some more pounding. "See the little button? It's called a bell. Use it."

He looked puzzled.

Lia sighed. She was being bitchy because he'd dragged her out of bed. *Get used to it.* This probably wouldn't be the last time it happened. The apocalypse waited for no woman. She stood aside so he could come in.

"Sorry I got you out of bed." He carried a duffel bag that he set by the door. Then he settled himself on her couch.

Dressed in jeans, boots, T-shirt, and brown suede jacket, he looked ready to take on an army of immortals. His hair was shaggy and a little overlong, but it shone with a blending of shades from pale blond to dark gold. Gorgeous.

And her? She was standing there in a cotton robe, bare feet, and a bad case of bed head.

"No, you're not sorry." She padded into her token kitchen and then paused. "How long?"

"A half hour."

Damn. She reached for the instant coffee. Any caffeine was better than none. "Coffee?"

"Not if it's instant."

"Elitist." Lia made her coffee and then took it into her bedroom to drink as she got ready. Fifteen minutes later, she emerged dressed and minimally functional.

He'd opened the blinds and was staring out the window.

"Who're you looking for?" She sat on her one easy chair.

"Jude."

She glanced at her watch. "You have a few minutes. Explain what's happening."

"Fin called me about an hour ago. Adam accepted the deal. He's sending Jude to pick us up and take us to where Adam and his vampires are staying."

Lia refused to admit that her stomach did a slow roll at the thought of being in Adam's presence. He might not be a beloved ruler, but he was certainly a feared one. He'd starred in her monster-under-the-bed nightmares since she was a child.

"Why have Jude pick us up? I can drive my car—"

"Flattened."

She winced.

"Don't worry, Shen called your insurance company and reported it stolen."

"We have the one Fin loaned—"

"He needs it back. Oh, and I forgot to tell you, Adam wants us to stay at his place, so you'd better pack a few things."

What a crappy start to her night. She didn't have time to argue with him. She raced back into her bedroom, and when five minutes later he yelled that Jude was down in the parking lot, she had her bag ready.

They were silent on the ride down to ground level. She'd swear the walls were closing in on her. And somewhere during the short trip, she admitted that what had started in the alley last night hadn't gone away.

Utah made her nervous, but not in an I'm-scared-of-you way. He made her *aware*. Of all six-feet-plus of him filling the small space. Of his hair with its shining strands tempting her to touch, to smooth, to *feel*. Of those predator's eyes softened by ridiculously long lashes. Of his mouth . . . She did a mental head shake. Oh no. Recognizing the problem was one thing, encouraging it was another. Thankfully, the elevator door opened and she was free. For the moment.

By the time they stepped from the building, dusk had fallen. Jude was parked at the curb. He didn't climb out to greet them. Not that she'd expected it. He released the trunk latch, and Utah loaded their stuff inside.

Then Utah glanced at her. "Front or back seat?" He'd already opened the rear door.

Lia hesitated. She wasn't ready to revisit what she'd felt in the elevator, so she pulled open the front passenger door and slid in. She didn't look back at Utah because Jude had captured her complete attention.

The vampire's flow of dark hair was a tangled mess, and she could see blood in it even in the dim light. His jacket was open, and as she leaned in for a closer look, she saw that the front of his white shirt was soaked in blood. Already fading cuts and bruises marred his face.

"Ohmigod, what happened to you?" If he were human, she'd be calling 911. But he was vampire. This wouldn't kill him, and hospitals were dangerous places for the undead.

"Adam isn't happy with me helping Fin. He explained that to me at length. Then he sent me here to pick you up." He didn't look at her as he prepared to pull out into traffic.

Utah leaned forward and put his hand on Jude's shoulder. "Stop."

Jude obeyed, but he didn't even glance at Utah in the mirror.

Utah opened his door, climbed out, and then opened Jude's door. "Get out."

Jude finally looked up at him. "If I stand up, I'll fall over. Give me a half hour, and I'll be as good as new."

"Why did he do this?"

Utah sounded mildly interested, but Lia knew body language. And Utah's clenched fists signaled barely controlled anger.

Jude shrugged, wincing as he did so. "Adam

felt I was getting too cozy with you guys. Afraid I might pass on the wrong information to Fin. He used his considerable powers to make me an example. Probably would've taken my head, but he didn't want to stir up trouble with my people." His smile was a pained grimace. "Especially the five vampires you saw me with in Philly. Even Adam would think twice about setting them off."

Lia saw the humiliation Jude was trying so hard to hide. "Look, Adam is millennia old. He has insane power. I don't know any vampire who could stand up to him."

Jude nodded, but he didn't seem convinced. "He made a mistake tonight. You don't embarrass one of your own in front of a packed house." His voice dropped to a whisper, all the scarier for its quietness. "I'll remember."

Lia got out and walked around to the driver's side. "Utah can help you into the backseat. I'll drive. Oh, and I'd get those five vampires here as soon as possible." She glanced up at Utah to get his support. Uh-oh.

Utah's eyes almost glowed, and she didn't need anyone to tell her his soul was close to the surface.

"When I'm finished working for Adam, I'll kill him."

"Why?" Jude seemed sincerely puzzled.

"Adam punished you for helping us. The Eleven take care of their own." Utah's fury was contained, but that didn't make it any less impressive. "Did you show Fin what he did to you?"

"No." Jude rested his head against the seat. "Fin needs the vampires' help. Adam holds ultimate control over all of us, and he doesn't like Fin. Your leader is too powerful, and I think Adam sees that power as a challenge. Before he began his teaching session, he said something about Fin threatening him if anything happened to me. Adam wanted to thumb his nose at Fin's threat by letting Fin *see* what he'd done. I didn't want Fin to be forced into doing something that would jeopardize whatever agreement he made with Adam."

With no further comment, Utah helped Jude into the backseat while Lia took his place behind the wheel. Utah then joined her in the front seat.

Lia followed Jude's directions, winding through the Portland streets until they got to what he identified as Old Town. Finally, he had her park in back of what looked like an art gallery. It had an "Under New Management" sign in the front window. It was closed.

She started to retrieve her bag, but Utah stopped her. "Leave it here until we know we're staying."

"Good idea." After seeing what Adam had done to Jude, she figured they'd better be ready for a fast escape.

She watched as Utah helped Jude out of the backseat. At least Jude was steady on his feet now.

A dark figure detached itself from beside the

back door. Huge, hulking, and probably a seven on her oh-shit scale—he'd never outrank Utah, Fin, or Zero—he moved between them and the door. Vampire.

"This is Reed. He's one of Adam's guys." Jude sounded weary. "Reed, meet Lia and Utah. Now move aside."

For a moment, Lia thought Reed would refuse, but after glaring at Jude and then giving Utah the once-over, he moved away from the door without a word.

Once inside the darkened building, Jude limped across the room, pulled open a door in the far wall, and led them down rickety stairs that were almost as scary as Reed.

"There's nothing here." Utah glanced around the basement.

From the little she could see, it looked like an ordinary basement. A few boxes and other things were nothing but dim shadows in the almost total blackness. Zero along with all his crummy numbers could be crouching in the far reaches of the room, and she wouldn't know. This wouldn't be a problem if she were vampire, with a vampire's enhanced vision. *Soon.* Lia continued to follow Jude closely as he wound his way around the boxes to a side wall where a large display case stood.

Jude, with Utah's help, moved the cabinet aside, revealing a brick, arched doorway with a heavy wooden door. "This leads to the Shanghai Tunnels. Legend says that back in the day, men were drugged, then dragged through these tunnels to waiting ships where they were forced to work for years. Talk about cheap labor. The tunnels go under the streets of Portland all the way to the Willamette River. They connect the basements of a lot of old buildings. Most of the entrances have been closed up, though."

Jude raised his hand to push at the door, but someone opened it before he had a chance to touch it.

A woman stood in the doorway. Framed by the brick archway and backlit by the glow of distant light, she looked beautiful and otherworldly. Okay, undead. Utah knew a vampire when he saw one. No amount of long dark hair, big brown eyes, soft mouth, and killer figure could hide it. The long white dress that floated around her did *not* make her look innocent.

She didn't even glance at Jude or Lia. "I'm Tania. And you're Utah. Adam said to expect you." She widened her eyes and parted her lips to show exactly how much she expected him.

And from the hungry gleam in her eyes, she was evidently not disappointed. But Utah didn't fool himself. That gleam meant she wouldn't mind fucking him right before she drained him to the last drop.

Personally, he thought Lia was a lot sexier. He almost grinned. She'd hate that. All she wanted from him was respect for her fighting skills and almighty toughness. But the urge to grin died an inglorious death. She'd soon be vampire, and he never wanted to find a vampire tempting. All he wanted to do was kill them. Except for Jude. He was okay. He'd proven himself.

"Adam has me walking around in case some dumb human wanders down here. Like that's going to happen at this time of night." Tania was a great pouter. "There's this story about the ghost of a woman in a white dress haunting the tunnels. I'm supposed to scare everyone away." She shrugged. "But I'm bored. Tours don't go where we are, so I don't know why I have to do this."

"What if someone *does* go into the tunnels? And what if they don't scare?" Lia peered around Tania.

"Then I eat them." She looked excited by the thought.

"Way to get rid of a problem." Lia edged past Tania, but stopped to allow Jude to take the lead.

Utah brought up the rear as they walked toward the distant light. Only the mesmerizing sight of Lia's small round behind swaying ahead of him kept him from feeling claustrophobic in the musty tunnel.

Finally, they reached the light source. A vampire sat in a folding chair in the middle of the tunnel. Must be Adam. He was about Utah's height, with black hair and weird-looking gold eyes.

About ten of his people lounged around him. To his left and right were what looked like small cells. There were no doors on the cells, so the space felt a little more open than the rest of the tunnel. The vampires stopped talking and stared at him. Not friendly stares. Probably hadn't liked his keep-Portland-vampire-free campaign. Tough.

Adam smiled. Utah didn't.

"So, my newest employee has arrived. Welcome." Adam's eyes didn't say welcome.

"Why are you down here? Seems to me you could afford somewhere classier." Fin wouldn't like him poking at the bloodsucker, but right now Utah didn't give a damn.

Adam's smile never slipped. "Ah, but these tunnels offer something a fancy condo never could." He swept his hand to encompass the tunnels that branched off in many directions. "They have exits into all kinds of basements. Sure, most of them are closed off, but that wouldn't stop one of us. Easy ins and outs can be important."

"Fine, I get that, but this is pretty primitive." Lia glanced around at the cots that had been set up in the small cell areas.

"We won't be here long. Now that I've brought Utah to heel, I only need one more job completed before I head back to California. You, my beast, and your new partner will take care of that."

Brought him to heel? *My* beast? Utah wanted to rip the jerk's head off. Adam was enjoying Utah's humiliation in the same way he'd probably enjoyed Jude's. That kind of attitude deserved payback. Utah glanced at Jude. Yeah, they had the same thought.

It wasn't Adam's leash that kept Utah from exploding into violence. It was the still-fresh memory of what his previous loss of control had almost caused, along with the realization that it would be tough to free his soul in these tunnels. No maneuvering room.

"Besides, I have another reason for setting up camp in the tunnels."

Utah was barely listening. He'd just digested the second part of Adam's message. *New partner?* What partner? Wasn't Lia shadowing his every footstep enough? Apparently not. He already hated this new person. Lia's expression assured him she was on the same page where new partners were concerned.

Adam blabbed on, uncaring that he was the focus of some totally pissed-off "employees." "When I was newly made, I hired wizards to do any magic that needed doing. That became counterproductive because I kept losing my temper when they failed to produce the desired results. I tended to express my displeasure with violence. I got tired of replacing wizards, so I decided to learn what needed learning so that I could do things myself."

"Umm, about this new partner." Lia was staying focused.

Adam paused to glare at her. Damn, he was good. That stare raised the hairs on Utah's arms. He'd make sure never to underestimate this guy. A vampire with a variety of skills had lots of options when it came to killing. Utah didn't think Adam would resort to brutality just because Lia had interrupted him. He'd count on intimidation to cow her.

She calmly returned Adam's stare. Utah tensed, ready to act if he had to. But Adam simply continued his spiel, ignoring her comment.

"So why are we in these tunnels? Down here we're surrounded by stone, close to water, and in a place that saw lots of death and misery. All elements that make for strong paranormal activity. Perfect for my summoning spells."

"Summoning spells?" Utah couldn't keep his mouth shut. "What would you need to summon?"

Adam's smile was slyly triumphant. "Your new partner."

CHAPTER THREE

Utah felt a slow cold creep up his spine and knew something was standing behind him. He forced the tension from his body and pasted a neutral expression on his face as he turned. Utah didn't want his new partner to think he was anything special.

Utah didn't by so much as a blink show his surprise. Lia had turned with him. She tensed, but nothing more.

The face was familiar. Hell, no one would ever forget that face. He'd seen it a month ago in Philly.

"Don't react. Pretend you don't know me. I'll explain later."

The face might be familiar, but the voice in his head wasn't. He'd never talked to the guy. But he did know one thing. Kione, unseelie fae prince, would make a lousy partner on many different levels. He turned to face Adam again without saying anything to the prince.

First, Utah didn't trust Kione. Yeah, so he didn't trust many people outside of the Eleven. And even the Eleven were iffy except for Tor. Utah was too close to his past to trust anyone but pack. Besides, he sensed that Kione was a loner. No pack would ever hold him.

Second, Lia's glazed expression bothered him. She was staring at the guy with unblinking intensity. Utah didn't like that. And he refused to analyze his dislike.

Finally, the fae prince made him . . . feel things. Not things he had time to examine right now.

Adam laughed. "Once I knew you'd be joining us, Utah, I decided to give you a worthy partner."

Lia dragged her attention away from the dark fairy long enough to protest. "A *worthy* partner? What am I, day-old blood?" It seemed to take an effort of will for her to turn her back on Kione.

"Face it, you're human, Lia." Left unsaid was: *therefore useless.* "I wanted someone with Utah who'd complement his physical power, someone with supernatural skills."

Utah drew in a deep calming breath. *Keep your mouth shut.* Strange how much more he hated Lia's humiliation at Adam's hands than he had his own. In the end, he had to say something.

"Lia will make a great partner." Where had that come from?

"I will?"

It was worth the lie to see her lips tip up in a grateful smile. Utah realized he wouldn't mind seeing those lips do any number of interesting things.

"Not a doubt in my mind. If we're hunting vampires, then I want someone with me who can tell me how they think." He grinned. "And someone who can drive like hellfire is singeing her ass."

Adam frowned. "You work for me, Utah, so Kione is your official partner. Lia is just there to keep this Seven guy from finding you. I went to a lot of trouble to get him. The summoning spell was . . . troublesome."

For the first time, Utah noticed the circle drawn in the dirt behind Adam, along with the candles and the blood.

Adam saw the direction of his gaze. "Human blood. Only the best to get the best." His expression was shadowed for a moment. "I was summoning a demon." He shrugged. "Just as good."

Utah wasn't sure. He'd felt the wash of power coming from Kione. Pretty heavy stuff. Could Adam control that?

Lia jumped in with a question. "What're you hunting? You wouldn't need all this firepower just to go after one of our own." She tried to concentrate on Adam's answer, tried to ignore the man behind her.

Fine, so calling Kione a man understated what he was by a few light-years. He was over six feet, but she couldn't tell much about his body because he'd wrapped himself in a dark cloak. But that was okay, because Kione was all about his face. And his face was all about sex. From the perfect lines of his jaw and cheekbones, to the curve of sensual male lips, to intense forest green eyes framed by thick dark lashes, he oozed erotic promises. A woman might die from the pleasure of what he did to her body, but she'd die happy. And if he chose to trail his smoke-dark hair across her bared flesh, he'd leave first-degree burns behind.

But his danger wasn't in his fae beauty. He made her *want*. Beyond her power to resist. Her instinct was screaming for her to turn and run, because to get any closer to him was to become nothing more than a panting, heated lump of female dough ready for him to mold into any sexual position he chose. As if that weren't bad enough, she wanted to jump whoever was closest to her. That would be Utah. If she wasn't holding on to her control with fingers, toes, and teeth, she'd leap on him with a primal scream and take him right in front of every vampire here.

Because . . . Lia tried to look like she wasn't staring at Utah. God, if she wasn't determined to become vampire, and he didn't hate vampires, she'd think he was the hottest thing with a heartbeat, all smoldering threats and dangerous promises.

No, those weren't her thoughts. Kione had generated them. She pushed them away.

Yeah, she knew exactly what Kione could do, because she'd stood next to him in Philly while Eight played deadly games with all their lives. She'd felt this before, although not quite so strongly. She didn't take time to wonder about that.

Kione could *not* be their partner. But whom could she tell? Not Adam. He'd love it if she complained that she couldn't be around the unseelie prince without wanting to have sex. He'd think she was weak, afraid of a little temptation. But it wasn't fear, it was common sense. How could she help anyone while sexual need pounded at her every moment that Kione was around?

She'd have to confront the fae prince once they left here. For now, she tried to concentrate on Adam's answer.

"When I want a threat eliminated, I don't do it half-ass. I don't want even the memory of an enemy left when I'm finished." He took a second to stare at Utah.

Utah nodded. Message received.

Adam didn't do things half-ass even for a *perceived* threat. She thought of Jude. If he treated his other vampires the way he'd treated Jude, then he must have some powerful enemies.

"Ben here"—Adam nodded toward the leader of the Northwest vampires—"tells me that a competitor is luring a lot of our people away. No one knows who he is, but someone has to stop him. Permanently."

"A vampire?" Utah's interest looked sincere.

But then it would, since killing them was his

favorite pastime. Bitter? You bet. Lia pushed the thought aside. What Utah thought of her people didn't matter.

"Definitely." Adam smiled. And all kinds of cruel enjoyment lived in that smile. "We found one of our lost sheep and convinced him that dying quickly was a lot easier than drawing the whole tiresome process out. He confirmed that he'd switched his allegiance to another vampire. Unfortunately, I lost my temper and tore him apart before he could give a description." He shrugged. "I still have anger issues."

No kidding. She was surprised he'd held it together while he was with Fin. But then he was wary of Fin's power. Wouldn't want to lose it with someone who might be able to kick your ass.

Utah appeared surprised. Lia figured he'd thought the poacher was Seven.

"That still doesn't explain why you need both Utah and Kione. Seems like overkill to me." Lia shifted restlessly. She wanted out of here and away from Adam. And even with her back to Kione, she could feel his thrum of power vibrating low in her stomach, tempting her to clench around the pleasure. Her need to slip her hand under Utah's shirt and smooth her fingers across all that warm male flesh was too strong, too disturbing.

Adam glanced away. "I lost my temper with our lost sheep because he *couldn't* answer some of my questions."

She was puzzled. "You mean he didn't know the answers?"

"No. He knew the answers, but every time he opened his mouth to tell me, nothing came out. I have a bad feeling about this new bastard. He's strong enough to bend the minds of ordinary vampires, so I'm sending him something he might not be ready for." He nodded at Utah. "I know you're right for the job because I saw the results of your work here in Portland. I decided to throw in Kione for insurance."

Utah looked thoughtful. "Just wondering, but if you're the leader of the whole damn vampire nation, you must have a shitload of power. Why don't you eliminate this problem yourself?"

Uh-oh. Lia tensed. Utah looked relaxed as he asked his question, but he was tracking a little too close to major criticism. He was either very brave or very stupid. Adam had a short fuse coupled with his tons of power. And he'd use it on Utah in a second if he lost his temper.

But Adam was evidently in a good mood tonight. "Great question. I delegate. I have other things to do besides put myself on the front line for every little skirmish. It's how I've survived so long. I'm the vampires' last line of defense."

"Do you have any idea where this enemy might be?" Kione spoke for the first time.

Lia wanted to stick her fingers in her ears. His voice was a soft glide of sexual sensation across already raw nerves. She took a step away from

Utah. It didn't seem to lessen the compulsion of Kione's voice.

Adam looked impatient. "No. I've had my people scouring the city, but nothing so far."

"Guess we'd better start looking then." Utah's expression said he couldn't get out of here fast enough.

Adam nodded his permission for them to leave. "Take Jude's car."

He motioned at Jude, and the vampire handed Lia his keys. She didn't miss the frustrated anger in Jude's eyes. Adam was stripping away his pride, figuratively grounding him. Not a good thing to do if you wanted to keep one of your most powerful leaders loyal.

But then she shifted her gaze to Adam in time to catch a fleeting expression of satisfaction. Maybe he didn't want Jude's loyalty. If Jude rebelled, it would give Adam a legitimate reason to destroy him.

Lia turned to leave, but Utah held up his hand. "I'm a little surprised you didn't take more time to think about hiring me." Utah sounded only mildly interested.

"I have a useful skill. I can see the short-term future. I saw just far enough ahead to realize you'd be helpful." Adam looked smug.

"Interesting talent." Utah seemed impressed. "So I suppose I'm forgiven for all those vampires I made permanently dead?" His eyes had a wicked gleam.

"Of course not. Why would you think that? What would my people think if I didn't avenge those deaths? My reputation would suffer if I didn't kill you." Adam smiled a bad-boy smile that said, *Hey, what's a little death between friends?*

Lia had a fleeting thought. Adam was really a spectacular-looking man, but she'd never really noticed because he was such a jerk. Strange that Kione's nearness didn't make her want to put her hands on *him*.

Utah leaned against the tunnel wall and smiled back. A real smile. "See, that's what I like about you, vampire. You don't mess around with fake friendliness."

Adam nodded. "Don't worry, though. I won't do it until you're no longer an employee. Oh, and I never got a chance to explain company benefits: full health and paid funeral expenses. No retirement plan. You won't need it."

"I wouldn't count on that. I have a few years on you. I think I can make a couple of more decades."

Utah straightened and began to retrace his steps through the tunnel. Kione followed close behind. But Adam put his hand on her shoulder before she could leave.

"I have every reason to believe Utah will satisfactorily complete his job. And when he's finished, I'll have a special assignment for you."

She thought she knew what was coming.

"You'll kill him."

She didn't ask why he didn't do it himself. He'd

lay some lie on her like it would be easier if she did it because Utah wouldn't be expecting it. A bunch of crap. Adam was all about protecting himself. Given a choice, he'd always have someone else do the dirty work.

Sighing, Lia turned away and hurried to catch up with the others. When she reached Utah, she leaned close. "Be careful or you won't last long under Adam's rule. Tick him off and you'll end up like his wizards. He's into disposable parts as long as those parts don't belong to him."

"Thanks for the warning." His voice was a husky murmur that slid over her body and coiled low in her stomach. She dropped back a few feet, but the sensation didn't go away.

Once outside again, she drew in a deep breath of night air. Free. Sort of. Now to deal with the dark fairy. She turned to Kione. "We need to talk."

"Not here." Utah nodded to where Reed still lurked in the shadows beside the back door.

Without a word, they all climbed into the car. She drove for a block before stopping beside a small park. Even spending those few minutes closed in with Kione felt unbearable. She had an almost uncontrollable desire to reach over and slide her fingers between Utah's thighs to cup his obvious arousal. For the first time, she wondered how Kione's dark power was affecting Utah. She had visible proof it was doing something.

Lia couldn't get her door open fast enough. She climbed out and waited in the misty rain as the others joined her. Then she went on the attack. "Look, no offense, Kione, but I can't work with you." She didn't think she had to elaborate.

Utah spoke at the same time. "What the hell are you doing here? And don't give me any crap about Adam summoning you. I think this is where you want to be."

Kione's smile was an Arctic cold front. "You're right, I want to be here. I went to a lot of trouble to intercept the inbound demon and send him back to hell." He fixed his gaze on Lia. "You'll have to adjust because I'm not going away."

"Adjust to what?" Utah sounded a little too casual.

He was a lousy liar. Lia thought Utah knew exactly what Kione was talking about.

Real humor touched the fae prince's smile. "Everything about my power is amplified. Unfortunately for both of you, a large part of that power is sexual compulsion." He shrugged and for a moment looked almost human. "I can't make it go away, so you'll both have to cope."

"I didn't feel a thing."

Kione's smile widened. "There is no shame in telling the truth. You lusted after me, but you hungered for Lia even more."

Utah opened his mouth to refute Kione's claim and then closed it. He didn't look at Lia. And Kione conveniently forgot to explain why he was there.

Kione raised one dark brow. "Does anyone else have a complaint?"

"I do." Jude stepped out of the shadows.

Utah tensed. A dangerous predator. Jude hadn't bothered to rinse the blood from his hair or change his shirt. He breathed fury, his eyes narrowed, his stride a deliberate stalk. The beast in Utah responded to the threat. His soul stirred, licking its lips in anticipation.

Utah had focused his attention on Adam back in the tunnels—assessing his power, looking for weaknesses. Well, one of Adam's weaknesses was staring at him now. He'd seen Jude in action. Utah wondered if Adam understood the mistake he'd made tonight.

Jude stopped about ten feet away, his gaze fixed on Kione.

Utah's beast would love a fight, but not here. "Looks like you don't need your car to get around." He edged closer to Lia. If she thought he was being overprotective, tough shit. Jude's eyes had turned completely black, his fingers curved into claws. He wasn't here for a friendly chat.

The vampire shifted his gaze to Utah. "I don't *need* the freaking car, but it's *mine*, so no one else should be driving it."

Utah saw a flash of something unexpected in Jude's eyes. He had a sudden insight. Wow, didn't have many of those. Jude wasn't just pissed off about the car because of ownership issues. The car allowed him to fit into the human world. Maybe it made him *feel* more human. Hey, they were all trying to fit in, some harder than others. Utah could empathize.

Jude turned his attention back to Kione. "I didn't say anything in front of that shithead who calls himself our leader because this is personal. I want you gone from here."

Kione's expression didn't change. "No."

"They'll be here in a few hours."

"Good."

Jude curled his lip, exposing impressive fangs. "I won't try to stop them."

"I wouldn't expect it." Kione didn't seem even mildly concerned.

"Am I missing something?" Lia moved a little closer to Jude.

Utah hissed his disapproval, but she ignored him.

Jude glanced at her, and some of his coiled fury seemed to fade. "No. This is between Kione and me." He glanced at his car. "Put any scratches on it, and you'll pay in blood." Then he was gone.

"Do you want to explain what just happened?" Lia turned to stare at Kione.

"No." Kione walked back to the car and climbed in.

"Gee, thanks for keeping me in the loop. I feel like a valued member of Team Kione now." Lia followed him.

Utah stood alone for a few moments. It seemed like everyone had an agenda—Fin, Adam, Jude, Kione—that they didn't want to share. Lia? He didn't think so. She didn't want to be with him. She was pretty upfront about it. He could respect that. Finally, he joined the others in Jude's car.

"We need a plan to find this vampire-who-would-be-king." Utah didn't give a damn who ruled the bloodsuckers, but he was committed to the hunt.

Lia pulled away from the curb. She didn't say anything, but her body practically thrummed with anger. She took each corner as though if she whipped around it fast enough, she could toss both Kione and him into the gutter where they belonged. She was sexy when she was ticked. He didn't think he'd tell her that.

Kione stared out the window. "We search until we find a vampire. We ask some questions. If we don't get the right answers, we find another one. Does that sound like a plan to you?"

"Not a good one," Lia muttered.

Kione pulled his attention from the darkened streets. "You've been killing them, Utah. Where will we find good hunting?"

"Uh, did you miss the part where Adam said the vampire he questioned *couldn't* answer?" Lia was in sarcastic mode.

Utah figured frustration fueled her sarcasm.

She drove slowly now, glancing down every dark alley they passed.

Kione shrugged. "It doesn't matter. I can unlock minds."

"Head for West Burnside around Morrison. I've had luck there." Late-night crowds, booze, and dark places to hide. A vampire playground.

No one picked up the conversational ball. Utah thought about trying to pry info out of Kione about whatever was going on with Jude but decided against it. He had other things to worry about.

Whatever the unseelie prince was doing, it was messing with Utah's sex drive. His gas pedal was stuck, and he'd just burned out his emergency brake. He rubbed at a spot between his eyes as though he could rub away what he wanted to do with Lia. *Only* with Lia. Kione had been wrong about that.

Utah watched her through half-lowered lids. She was tense. Trying to fight what the fae prince was putting out there? Utah hoped so. Lust loved company. What did she want? He sure knew what he wanted. He longed to glide his hand up her inner thigh until he found the source of all her heat and desire. Then he wanted to put his mouth . . . He shook his head. Not what he should be thinking about right now.

But no matter how hard Utah tried to concentrate on ways he could help Fin find Seven while he was tied up with Adam the asshole, his thoughts kept returning to Lia. To the image of her bared body stretched out beneath him, to the soft warmth of her breasts as he cupped them, to the taste of her as he slid his tongue over her belly and between her legs. Jeez, she was right. How could he get anything done while they were cooped up with the prince of freaking sex?

After what seemed like a thousand miles of darkened streets and sexual fantasies, Lia pulled into a parking lot beside a bar and grill.

She didn't turn to look at them as she spoke. "This is it. We probably should take it on foot from here."

Utah exhaled deeply. Just in time. Another few minutes and he would've lost the battle with his beast, who thought that reaching over to drag her onto his lap without regard to screeching brakes and twisted metal was a great idea. He almost launched himself from the car. Kione got out more slowly, drawing that damn cloak around him. The bastard was smiling.

Fury fought free, and he turned on the fae prince. "Get your jollies from all this, Kione? Like to feel all those sexual emotions? Do they make you hard?"

"Hmm, and here I thought you were Mr. Stoic-and-Unmoved. Nice to know we're having a shared experience." Lia got out of the car and retrieved her sword.

Kione shrugged. "I feel no emotions, sexual or otherwise. They mean nothing to me."

Lia looked horrified. "No emotions? That's awful. Do any of the fae feel?" For the moment, she seemed to have forgotten her gripe with him.

"Some do. The younger ones. But emotions serve no purpose. They make you vulnerable. Humans are weaker because of them. I'm sure Utah will agree." He turned and started walking away.

Yeah, Utah got it. Rap's death had tied him into emotional knots, made him careless. In his past life, he would have remained coldly focused on what was important—the kill.

"The younger ones?" Lia caught up with Kione. "Guess looks are deceiving. You don't look old. Maybe late twenties. Do you die from old age? Are there any limits to how many years you can live?"

Her questions seemed to bother him. Utah had the feeling Kione wished he could bat them away.

But Lia refused to be ignored. "Why all the mystery? The more you refuse to answer my questions, the more I'll ask. Want to shut me up? Give me some answers."

Kione finally looked at her. "No, we don't die of old age. We live as long as we choose to live." He glanced away. "When we tire of our existence, we end it."

"Have *you* thought about ending it?" *How do you end it?* Utah would like to know in case the prince became more of a pain in the butt than he already was.

The pause was so long that Utah thought Kione might refuse to answer.

"Yes." And that was it.

Utah felt conflicted. If Kione died, then the wanting would end. But if Kione died, the wanting would end. See? Conflicted.

Time to cut the talk and get on with the hunt. "We can separate and go in different directions. If we find anything, we communicate through Kione." Utah had lost his cell phone in the car fire, and he didn't think Kione looked like a cell phone kind of guy. Thoughts were a lot quicker and quieter anyway.

Utah wanted to order Lia to stay near the car in case they needed it. He wanted to suggest she check out nearby bars. But he knew how she'd react. She'd think he was trying to keep her out of danger because he didn't think she could match up with a vampire. And she'd be right.

That bothered Utah. Once you started worrying about someone else's safety, you lost focus. She wanted to be a full partner in this hunt? Then let her take her chances. The thought wasn't as satisfying as he'd hoped.

"Can you handle this?" Kione studied him. "I've heard that you love killing vampires. Will you be able to control your bloodlust long enough to ask questions?"

"He has a point." She pulled her long coat more tightly around her so her sword didn't show. "I might forget we're partners if I show up to find you surrounded by the bodies of my people."

Annoyance warred with Utah's still powerful desire for her. How the hell far away from Kione did he have to get before the effect dissipated? "They're not *your* people. Humans are your people."

Lia moved closer to him, and he tried to ignore her. Couldn't do it. Warm woman and the night made a potent mixture.

"Vampires have always been *my* people. Warning: just don't go crazy and kill them."

He purposely ignored her as he answered Kione's question. "I'm a hunter. I was a hunter when you spelled the word with a capital H. A hunter knows how to wait." Utah knew his smile said predator loud and clear. "Just as long as I get the kill at the end."

Kione simply nodded before fading into the shadows.

Utah turned to Lia. "Maybe—"

"Don't say it. I'm an equal partner in this. I have my gun and sword. I grew up around vampires. I understand them. Don't worry, I'll do my part." Then she disappeared into a small stand of trees beside the bank.

He stared after her. Either she was very good, or he was lousy at guarding his expressions. But she'd assumed he thought she couldn't pull her weight. At least she hadn't guessed that he was worried about her. She'd hate that. *He* hated that.

Then Utah tried to give himself up to the hunt.

CHAPTER FOUR

He was worried about her. Lia watched from the cover of the trees as Utah disappeared into the darkness. It amazed her that he could hate vampires so completely and not hate her.

But she was still a human to him. He didn't see her as a serious contender for any kind of vampire leadership. He thought only power and strength mattered in the vampire world.

He didn't understand how she could lead because he hadn't known Katherine and how she changed the people around her. Growing up, Lia had fought to block the relentless parade of doubts her mind shoved her way—you won't be fast enough, strong enough, *good* enough. And every whispered putdown had her mother's voice attached. Well, she'd found a way to be *smart* enough, something Katherine never learned.

Lia didn't bother searching around the outside of the bank. She didn't sense any hunters here. Besides, why would any self-respecting vampire be out here in the cold and rain when the bar across the street held a full menu of drunken humans?

She crossed the street and went into the bar. The darkness inside cloaked her as she made her way to the ladies' room.

When she got the chance, Lia would explain things to Utah. She absently pulled her small zipped bag of makeup from her coat pocket—the one that didn't have her gun—and applied fresh lipstick, mascara, and some cheek color.

She'd tell him that her mother knew only one way to solve a problem—kill it. Katherine's sole strategy was to throw all her vampires at the enemy and hope to overwhelm them with numbers and pure ferocity. Sometimes it worked, but more often than not she lost a lot of her people. The vampire population in her territory had dwindled while other regional leaders like Jude gained people.

Her mother never tolerated differing opinions, so over the centuries she'd killed off her brightest people. The ones left were cowed, obedient, and . . . lacked creativity.

Lia pulled open her coat to assess her battle gear. Leather pants, calf-high boots, and a cute top. She changed cute to sexy with some strategic unbuttoning. Before slipping her makeup case back into her coat pocket, she took out a pair of dangly earrings and put them on. Then she checked her pants pocket to make sure she had enough money for some drinks. Finally, she ran her fingers through her hair and let her curls do their thing.

Too bad she couldn't take off her coat, but the sight of her sword would kill the party spirit and probably get her arrested.

Lia slipped out of the ladies' room and headed for the bar. She thought about what else she'd tell Utah. Maybe that she had the one thing her people needed desperately—the ability to find ways to protect the territory without depleting their numbers. She'd make sure Utah understood that a winning strategy didn't have to end with someone dying.

Lia chose a barstool that had no people on either side of her and ordered an Amaretto on the rocks. She loved sweet drinks. As she sipped it, she scanned the darkened room. Music blared and a few lethargic customers swayed on the dance floor. Her inspection stopped when she got to a man at the end of the bar. *Vampire.* Mid-twenties, pretty ordinary-looking, and probably hungry.

She went to work. Lia slipped out the straight pin she kept at the bottom of her gun pocket and pricked her finger. Then she squeezed until she had a pearl of blood.

Resting her open hand on the bar beside her drink, she waited.

Suddenly, the vampire's nostrils flared and he turned his head to stare at her.

Lia cocked her head to the side, exposing her neck. She hoped he just thought she was studying her bloody finger. Then she pasted a drunken smile on her face.

His gaze turned predatory.

When she was sure she had his complete attention, she lifted her finger to her mouth and slowly licked the blood from it.

He almost forgot to move like a human as he abandoned his stool and rushed to grab the empty one beside her.

Lia guessed he hadn't been vampire long. Jude or Adam would've been more cautious.

Ten minutes later, she'd cajoled him into admitting he was vampire—after all, who would believe the word of a drunken woman?—and they were headed out to his car.

She looped her arm through his and giggled. "That is so cool. I've never met a vampire before." Lia snuggled up to him. "Tell me everything about you."

He—jeez, they hadn't even exchanged names— was showing fang he was so anxious, but she knew he'd wait until there were no witnesses before he struck.

"I . . . can't." He shook his head. "I mean, I can't remember much stuff."

She stopped and widened her eyes. "Isn't that strange? I mean, can't you even remember the name of your head guy?" Lia shifted her expression to suspicious. "I don't know if I want to get into a car with a vampire who can't even remember his boss's name."

Lia waited for him to lie to her, to just make up a name. He didn't. He pressed the heel of his hand against his forehead in an effort to remember. There was something a little endearing about his need to tell her the truth. This was one who might be saved if he got out of Portland fast.

Finally, he blinked and smiled. "The name is Chris—" That's all he got out before pain dropped him to his knees. He clutched his head in agony.

Lia hated to add to his misery, but . . . She glanced around to make sure no one was looking before unsheathing her sword and plunging it into his back. Then she wiped the blade on a convenient patch of grass and returned it to its scabbard.

He was so shocked he didn't even scream, just rolled over to stare up at her.

"You're hurting, but you'll walk away from this. Let me give you some advice. Leave Portland as soon as you can stand up. Adam is out to kill any vampires who're joining up with the new flavor in town. And the new flavor is going down very soon. It's a lose-lose situation for you."

She would've added more to her lecture, but suddenly, Kione was in her head.

Utah has a hit. Meet me by the car.

The young vampire watched her walk away.

* * *

Utah ghosted from shadow to shadow, hugging walls and merging with the darkness beneath trees. Not too many humans stumbled by, but the ones who did would be easy pickings for any bloodsucker that wasn't too choosy about his food.

Even as the dark outline of the stadium came into view, he still felt the echo of his need for Lia. Yeah, so some of it had to do with how close his soul was to the surface. His beast didn't differentiate between hungers. One bled into the other. Then there was Kione. His reach must be longer than expected.

Utah almost missed the vampires. Two of them. Tucked up against the wall of the building next to the stadium. Trees and deep shadows protected them. The scent of blood told its own story.

Instinctively, he walled off his thoughts. He was supposed to contact Kione. Not an option anymore. His beast had edged too close to the surface. It didn't want to share a kill. Kione would probably show up, wiggle his eyebrows, and the two vampires would confess to everything. Where was the fun in that? Lia would remind him that this was about getting information, not slaughtering vampires. No blood. No death. The hell with that. His soul was in control. Utah welcomed it.

He glanced around. Good thing it was so late. Businesses closed. No stray humans wandering in the area. Only a few cars. The vampires had chosen a great spot to feed. Too bad they were due for a serious case of indigestion.

Utah crept closer and closer. Couldn't overrate the importance of surprise. Had to release his beast as near as possible, as far away from human eyes as possible. Don't give them a chance to run. His heart pounded, his breathing quickened. Yes, just a little nearer and . . .

He froze. Someone was stalking him. He could feel the presence of another even if he couldn't hear or see him. Utah remained still, not even breathing, as he assessed the new danger.

"Need help, brother? One for each of us."

Recognition hit him hard. Utah whirled to face Tor. Damn. "Where the hell did you come from?" His voice was a furious hiss.

Tor grinned at him and put a finger to his lips as he nodded toward their prey. The vampires were busy finishing up what looked like someone who'd waited too late for that last drink. They weren't paying attention. Too bad for them.

Utah's brother leaned close. "We're pack. Pack hunts together. I followed you."

"Does Fin know what you're doing?" Utah wanted to stay mad at Tor, but he couldn't. He'd missed him.

"You kidding? Fin knows everything. He didn't try to stop me, though."

Utah nodded. "We take both of them down, but don't kill them. We want enough left to question."

Once Tor and he had their fun, he'd open up the airwaves for Kione.

Okay, whispering done. Amazing that the vampires hadn't heard them. Most predators wouldn't let another hunter sneak up on them like this. Maybe the vampires had grown fat and lazy thinking they were the biggest badasses in town. Utah grinned. They were in for a surprise.

Tor left as soundlessly as he'd arrived. The old routine kicked in. God, it felt good. Utah knew his brother was working his way around the vampires, knew exactly how long it would take, knew the exact moment he stopped and prepared to free his soul. Utah crouched and did the same.

They leaped at the same time. Utah's soul caught him in mid-jump. Even though he knew anyone watching would see the shadow of his human form within his beast, he didn't *feel* human. He was twenty feet of focused death. Utahraptor. The familiar savage hunger and excitement for the kill filled him completely, overflowed in a frothing frenzy. You didn't get that kind of buzz from a take-out window.

As he leaped over the human's body to reach the vampire nearer him, Utah noticed that the man still lived. He stared up at Utah with wide glazed eyes. Not good.

Then Utah forgot everything as his soul screamed a silent challenge. He hit his chosen vampire before the bloodsucker even realized he was under attack. The force of his charge knocked the vampire down.

Utah held on to his prey with his bladelike claws while he attempted to disembowel the vampire with the foot-long curved talon on each of his back feet. He closed his jaws with their serrated flesh-cutting teeth on the vampire's arm. He would've preferred the bloodsucker's head, but he was holding on to his rapidly disappearing control. *Don't kill, don't kill, don't kill.*

A spray of blood from the vampire's torn stomach and the satisfying crack of a breaking bone drove him on. He didn't know what his pack mate was doing. Didn't care. Utah's soul was immersed in his battle—the hot coppery scent of it, the feel of flesh tearing, the contorted face of his victim.

It was a silent fight. Even seriously hurt, the vampire didn't want to call attention to himself. Besides, he was busy trying to play catch-up. He drove his fangs into Utah's jaw, the only body part he could reach, and ripped away.

Utah felt the hot flow of his own blood, and gloried in it. *Yes.* This was what he missed, the huge rush of knowing that another predator wanted to kill you unless you killed him first.

The vampire put all his power into trying to pry Utah's jaws open. Wasn't going to happen.

Suddenly, the vampire went limp. Utah dropped him. At the same moment, something flung Utah into the wall of the building with such force that he freaking bounced. He came off the wall with a furious scream.

"Be quiet. Sound carries. We don't want any late-night drop-ins."

Kione? The red haze of battle faded a little, enough for him to see the dark fairy standing there with Lia beside him. Tor had already returned to human form, and both vampires were down for the moment.

No. It hadn't lasted long enough. Adrenaline still spiked, zinging in nervous starts to every part of his body. Utah shook from the need to kill and kill some more.

"I can put you on the ground if that's what you choose. I'm not particularly happy with you right now, *partner.* Perhaps I misunderstood Adam, but I thought this was supposed to be a team effort." Kione stared at Tor. "And when did we gain another team member?"

Crap. Just what Utah needed, a bunch of snark from Kione. He shoved his soul back into its cave and returned to human form. "How did you know?"

For the first time, Kione laughed. Utah didn't like the way Lia's eyes widened as she watched the fae prince.

"You're easy, raptor. As soon as you tried to shut me out of your thoughts, I knew you'd found something."

"So you knocked down my wall and took what you wanted from my mind." Utah would've been a lot more pissed if what Kione said wasn't true. He *had* tried to block the unseelie bastard because he wanted the takedown all for himself.

"I didn't have to. I can find anyone or anything I've connected with. So once I knew you'd made a hit, I collected Lia and here we are." He didn't give Utah a chance to ask the obvious question. "I can't explain my powers any more than you can explain how you release your soul. Just know that no matter where you are, I'll be able to find you."

"Useful, but creepy as hell." Utah could imagine a few scenarios where Kione's talent would mess with his plans.

Lia's expression said she agreed with Utah. "We need to ask our questions and get out of here before anyone notices us standing around."

She obviously wasn't into the power struggle developing between Kione and him.

"I'll ask the questions." Kione was definite about that. "And I assume this is your brother. He looks exactly like you only more together."

Utah didn't care enough to challenge him for the right to ask the questions. He'd gotten what he wanted from the event. "Hey, knock yourself out. And yeah, this is Tor." He turned to his brother. "Meet Kione. He's the fae prince who helped save Lio and finish off Eight back in Philly. I don't know why he's here in Portland, but the vampires' big shit wants him to be our partner." He motioned to Lia. "You already met Lia."

Tor nodded at Kione, his expression neutral. Then he grinned at Lia. "Not only did I save your butt at the Museum of Art, but I was there when you challenged Jude."

Lia didn't return his grin. "How could I forget? You freed your beast and threatened all of my people."

Tor shrugged. "Vampires *aren't* people."

She looked as though she wanted to stomp Tor into the dirt over his aren't-people comment, but he didn't give her a chance. "Look, I've got things to do." He glanced at Utah. "Talk to you later." And then he was gone.

Kione didn't pay any attention to Tor's departure. He'd walked over to the vampire that Utah's brother had been battling. The guy was still flat on his back, and he didn't look like he'd be getting up anytime soon. "Look at me."

The vampire wasn't dumb. He didn't intend to make eye contact with Kione. He looked away.

"Look at me." This time Kione must've put some compulsion into his demand, because the vampire's head slowly turned toward him. He met Kione's stare, but he didn't look happy about it.

Kione's smile wasn't encouraging. "Good. Now tell me the name of the leader to whom you give your allegiance."

The vampire looked defiant. "Don't have to answer you, asshole."

"Oh, but you do." Kione's expression remained pleasant.

The vampire's didn't. His face twisted into an agonized mask. "Okay, okay, I'll tell you. Just stop that."

Stop what? Utah knew he'd have a lot to ask Kione when this was all over.

"I follow Ben. He's our regional leader. And we all answer to Adam." The vampire put his hands to the side of his head as though he were trying to hold his brain in.

"Stop it." Lia stepped toward Kione. "He gave his answer. He's not with Seven or Adam's rogue. Now let him go."

Utah figured it was too late for the vampire. The bloodsucker's eyes closed, and his body settled into that loose look that signaled his essence had left the house. Guess he'd decided to burn the house down after him because a thin trail of smoke drifted from his nose. Utah had heard the phrase "frying your brain," but he'd never expected to see the real deal.

Lia slowly lifted her gaze from the vampire's body to Kione. "You cold bastard."

Kione didn't blink. "When you go to war you have to expect some collateral damage. Don't worry, I'll take care of the body." As if on cue, the vampire disappeared.

Utah should've been solidly on Kione's side. The only thing he should have regretted was that *he* hadn't done the killing. Then where was the satisfaction at one less bloodsucker walking the Earth? Was he allowing Lia's distress to influence him?

He glanced at the remaining vampire. Young. About sixteen when he was turned. Panic filled the vampire's eyes. He was trying to roll over so he could crawl, but he was too badly injured. For the first time, Utah saw the human in the monster. He wondered if anyone would bother to see the human in *his* monster. Not that it mattered.

Kione walked over to the vampire. "Do you have anything more interesting to tell me than your friend did?"

Utah would never have believed he'd see a vampire frozen in fear. Well, now he had. The guy looked up at Kione with eyes wide and staring.

Kione sighed. "I suppose I'll have to heat up your brain as well."

"No." The vampire's gaze skittered from one to the other. "I follow Ben too. I've never heard of this Seven you're talking about. Please, I don't know what you want me to say."

Lia had already planted herself opposite Kione. She stared at him across the vampire's body. "Leave. Him. Alone."

Kione didn't lift his gaze from the vampire. "It seems you have a champion. Too bad that two of us here think you should join your partner in the final death."

Utah moved to Kione's side. "What's your name?" When had he started worrying about a bloodsucker's name?

"Dan." The vampire cast him a terrified glance.

"How long have you been vampire?" Why was that important to him?

"Six months." Dan's voice cracked.

A child. Utah was impressed. From what he knew of vampires, a six-month-old bloodsucker should be a single-minded, brainless feeding machine. Both vampires were probably young. That's why they'd been careless enough to be taken by surprise.

"I think he's telling the truth." Kione sounded impatient. "I can't get anything from his mind. There's too much fear." He looked at Utah. "Would you like to take care of this?"

Kione was extending an olive branch by offering him the kill. Funny thing, though. He didn't want to kill the kid. Kid? The *kid* had probably sucked more than a few Portland citizens dry.

"I won't let you." Lia drew her gun. "*Either* of you."

"Do you think you can stop us?" Kione's voice was deceptively soft.

"Scratch the 'us,' Kione." Utah couldn't believe he was coming down on the side of a vampire. "Let him go."

Lia looked at Utah, surprise and gratitude in her eyes. Her approval warmed him. Not a good sign. Maybe his reaction was just a residual effect of Kione's power. He'd rather believe that than admit . . . What? He didn't know and refused to speculate.

Kione turned his attention to Utah. Wicked anticipation lit his eyes. "And if I don't? Will you challenge me, raptor?"

Utah understood the hungry shine in Kione's

eyes, knew his own eyes must look the same. "Definitely."

The fae prince stilled. Utah tensed. He didn't fool himself. Kione would have him before he had a chance to free his beast. He wished he knew what the damn fairy was thinking.

The moment stretched on, the silent promise of death interrupted only by the vampire's terrified whimper.

Lia broke the silence. "Maybe you've forgotten why we're here. If you guys tear each other up, then I'll have to hunt down this rogue vampire by myself." She didn't look as casual as she sounded. She still held her gun ready. "I've already had to get his name for you."

"What?" Utah and Kione spoke in unison.

"His name is Chris."

She'd taken on a vampire and gotten a name from him? "How?" Utah knew his eyes were wide with shock.

"I met a vampire in the bar near where the car is parked. We talked. He told me."

Utah's stare promised he'd have the whole story later.

Kione took a deep breath, and the tension eased. "I don't understand all this passion over one vampire."

"I'm human now, but pretty soon I'll be like Dan here. That won't change the essential me, though." Lia lowered her gun a little.

"Are you sure?" Kione looked doubtful. "I've

seen what happens to the old ones. After a few hundred years, you won't remember your humanity. Humans will be merely a food source."

"Don't count on it." Lia sounded pretty definite about that. "I don't think Dan was a bad human, and I'd bet he's not a bad vampire either." Lia leaned forward, her expression intent. "Vampires are individuals—some bad, some good. Maybe you should find out which before killing any more."

Kione looked down at the vampire. "He's not worth drawing blood over. I'll wipe his memory and give him a new one. I'd rather not have Adam know I destroyed one of his people. It might damage his image of me as his helpless tool."

Kione went down on one knee beside Dan. "Look at me, vampire."

Dan didn't try to fight him.

"None of this happened. You split from your friend. You never saw him again. And you don't remember ever seeing any of us. You met with a strange vampire who attacked you. You managed to escape." He stood and turned his back on the vampire.

He walked over to the human who was still somehow conscious. "I suppose you want him saved too."

"Yes." Lia scanned the area. She slipped her gun back into her pocket. "Then let's get out of here before someone sees us."

Utah watched Dan roll over and crawl into the

shadows. It wouldn't take him long to heal enough to make it back to the tunnels.

Kione reached down and cupped his hand over the human's torn throat. The wound closed before disappearing. Then he placed his palm on the man's forehead. The man blinked and sat up.

"What the hell happened?" The guy got shakily to his feet. He stood swaying as he stared at them. "God, I feel dizzy." He glanced down. "Where'd all this blood come from?"

Kione locked gazes with the man. "I suppose you had too much to drink. I wouldn't know about the blood. Perhaps you'd better hope no dead bodies turn up around here. We were passing by and saw you lying here. Can you make it home on your own?" Kione couldn't quite twist his expression into something that resembled human caring.

"Yeah, I guess so." He braced himself against a tree. "Feel sort of funny. Uh, thanks for stopping." Then he pushed away from the tree and staggered toward the street.

"You have no idea how thankful you should be." Kione's whispered comment didn't reach the man.

"Wow, I'm impressed, prince. The healing, the mind wipe, all powerful stuff. I wonder what else you can do." Lia might be telling the truth about being impressed, but she didn't look friendly while she was saying it. "Too bad you enjoy killing so much."

Utah noticed that she'd put some distance between Kione and her. He could tell her it didn't matter. Kione's sexual compulsion had a long reach.

Kione's smile was a mere baring of his teeth. "It's 'too bad' that you don't understand the true nature of vampires. They deserve killing."

Well, what do you know. Someone who hated vampires as much as he did.

Lia interrupted Utah's thoughts. "Just got a mental bulletin from Adam. He wants us to report back to him. Now. Oh, and he wants you guys to drop your shields so he can reach you in an emergency."

Interesting. Utah couldn't keep Kione out of his head, but his wall must be working with Adam. Good to know.

Lia looked as though she was listening. "One more thing. Adam says to move your asses because it's almost dawn."

"Almost dawn? How time flies when you're spreading pain and destruction." Utah hated being ordered around.

"Do you think he's going to make us sleep in that tunnel?" Lia looked creeped out at the thought.

"I sleep where I choose." Kione started to walk back toward the car.

Utah glanced at Lia. Given a choice, he knew exactly where he'd "choose" to sleep.

CHAPTER FIVE

Lia worked on her impulse control as she drove back to the tunnels. She resisted the compulsion to slide her gaze across to where Utah sat in stoic silence. Was she the only one about to explode into a shower of erotically charged particles? Looked like it. Well, no way would Lia admit she was more susceptible to Kione than he was. And double no way would she allow Utah to know that her heat-seeking hormones had attached themselves to all the interesting places on his body.

She'd been strong all her life. Had to be if she'd survived as Katherine's daughter. Fine, so this wasn't like the other challenges she'd faced. This one came wrapped in the promise of pleasure. She'd identified the threat, and now she'd defeat it.

Kione gave what sounded like a fair approximation of a human sigh. "Your thoughts are no fun when all you think about is sex. And no, I won't stay out of your minds. I need *some* entertainment. But I do feel an obligation to explain something to both of you. What you're feeling has nothing to do with me. You have to be *looking* at me for it to happen."

Without thinking, Lia glanced at Kione in her mirror and almost took out an innocent garbage can sitting by the curb. She gripped the steering wheel, trying to stay on the road, trying not to abandon her driving in favor of flinging herself onto Utah and . . . She stole a quick sideways glance at him that dropped, and dropped, and dropped until it reached . . . Hmm. Lia allowed herself a purely self-indulgent smile. Mr. Stoic wasn't as detached as he looked. Body parts didn't lie.

She tore her gaze from Utah as the car wandered dangerously close to a streetlight. Then she took a few steadying breaths. "It must be hard for your friends not to be able to look at you." Lia tried to process what Kione had said. He couldn't be telling the truth.

"Then maybe it's lucky that I don't have any friends." There was no inflection in Kione's voice.

No friends? What good was immortality without someone to share it with? Lia tried to imagine a life with no family, no friends. She couldn't. Maybe she needed to cut Kione some slack. You didn't get much chance to practice your people skills when you were always alone.

"Must be tough." Utah kept his attention fixed straight ahead, but a strand of sympathy seemed to run through his comment.

It amazed Lia that Utah could feel any sympathy for someone else when he was so focused on avenging his brother. And he'd actually spared Dan's life. If she wasn't careful, she might even start to believe he had a few normal human emotions other than anger.

Kione's laughter was a harsh rejection of Utah's sympathy. "You think that no one ever looks at me? Think again, raptor. I have my own army of stalkers, beings that can only feel sexual excitement when they're looking at me. I'm not always the user." Bitterness laced his last sentence.

Lia didn't know what to say to that. Evidently, Utah didn't either, because no one spoke again as they drew near Adam's underground headquarters.

During those final moments, she puzzled over why she reacted so strongly to Utah when she *wasn't* looking at Kione. Sure, he was great-looking, but she'd been around beautiful men before, and her sex drive never drove *her*. Add to that the conflict-of-interest thing. Vampire lover versus vampire hater. Not a good mix.

It had to be the power of suggestion. She'd *expected* to feel lust when she was around Kione. So, she'd felt what she expected. No big deal. Now that she knew better, the unwelcome emotions would go away.

Lia parked Jude's car in its original spot and climbed out. She considered whether to bother bringing in her bag, but decided against it. She refused to sleep in that tunnel surrounded by Adam's vampires. Utah didn't retrieve his stuff either. Good. Kione didn't have anything.

"Kione, did you bring clothes with you?" Stupid question. No one appeared in the middle of a summoning circle trailing a rolling garment bag. She joined the men as Reed detached himself from the shadows beside the door.

"No. I'll find something tomorrow." Kione looked surprised that she'd asked.

Now, that was just sad. Not that he didn't have anything, but that he didn't expect anyone to care.

"I have a couple of changes of clothes if you need something to wear. Just take whatever fits you." Utah seemed to be trying for casual a little too hard.

The two of them were a lot more alike than they'd ever want to admit. Utah sounded uneasy with his own attempt at kindness. But then how much kindness had he experienced in his previous life? He must be struggling with all his shiny new human emotions. For maybe the first time, she stopped her headlong rush to be vampire long enough to appreciate being human.

Kione paused as though searching for a response he'd long ago forgotten. "Thanks."

Something about Utah's offer made Lia feel all warm and fuzzy inside. Uh-oh. It was hard enough to deny her sexual attraction to him without starting to like him as a person. She quickly dismissed the thought and turned her attention to Adam.

Lia decided Reed wasn't into exercising his vocal cords as he nodded and waved them into the building. They walked down the stairs and just like last time, someone opened the door to the tunnel before they could knock.

This time it was one of Adam's men. He simply stood aside for them to enter. Adam's guys were a talkative bunch.

She followed Utah until they reached Adam, and then she moved up to stand beside him. Kione stopped behind them. Adam still sat in the middle of the tunnel, but most of his people were missing. Probably out hunting. They'd be trickling back soon. Wouldn't want to be caught by the dawn.

"Any luck?" Adam didn't invite them to sit down.

Utah glanced at Lia.

"Chris. That's all I got." She shrugged.

Adam frowned. "Chris is a common name. No last name?"

"You were right about the mind control. The vampire who gave me the name couldn't get anything else out. He suffered for giving me that much."

Utah glanced around the area. "Where do you expect us to sleep?"

Adam shrugged. "There're plenty of cots. Choose one."

"It's too cold here." Lia shivered. "Call me wildly self-indulgent, but I want to sleep in a room with heat, a real bed, and a bathroom." Definitely a bathroom.

Adam didn't look impressed. "You sleep down here. And I want to know how you intend to find the damn vampire who's stealing my people."

"Since you didn't give us any clues about where to find this vampire, we'll just have to spend time canvassing the city until we come up with something that goes with Chris." Utah narrowed his gaze. "And no, we're not sleeping down here."

Whoa. Lia was impressed. Utah was challenging Adam. Brave but incredibly dumb. Could she love this guy any more? Fine, so sarcasm wouldn't help the situation.

She jumped in to soften Utah's declaration. "Think about it, Adam. You're vampire. You don't feel cold. But all of us do." She didn't know about Kione, but she included him anyway. "And I have to be near a bathroom."

Adam's expression said he didn't know why she couldn't just pee in a corner somewhere. "And if I insist?"

He sounded merely curious, but Lia suspected this was a defining moment in their relationship with Adam.

"Then that would make me mad." Utah didn't even try faking regret. "And when I lose my temper, my beast isn't too reasonable." He glanced around. "I'd pretty much fill up this space."

Adam still didn't look angry. "I'd be able to take you down before you could do anything."

Something in Utah seemed to grow and expand right in front of Lia's eyes. His threat was the complete silence of the forest right before the predator struck, the eyes shining from the darkness, the low rumbling growl that froze all who heard it. He was death, and thinking that thought didn't even seem over the top to Lia.

"Don't underestimate me or those who stand with me, vampire."

Utah's voice had changed in ways Lia couldn't pin down. Then she realized what it was. His voice had lost its humanity. She somehow knew she was listening to the voice of his beast. Not a comforting sound.

Kione moved to the front of the pack. "I side with Utah and Lia. This might be a safe vampire haven, but it really sucks in the comfort category. Don't try to make us stay. That would upset me. I do things when I'm upset. Like bringing the tunnels down around your head. No more hidey-hole, and the city won't be happy when a bunch of their buildings fall down."

Lia held her breath as a low grumbling worked its way from deep in the earth. The tunnel walls seemed to vibrate, and a few cracks appeared. Oh crap. And then everything stilled. For the moment.

Adam's mask was beginning to slip. He smiled, but his fangs ruined the effect. "Be careful, my fae friend. I summoned you, so you owe me your allegiance." He made sure he didn't look directly at the dark fairy.

Kione shook his head. "Adam, Adam, you really need to reread your unseelie handbook. We answer to no one. And we tend to be terribly disloyal. It's a weakness."

Adam dropped his mask completely. "I can send you back anytime I feel like it."

Lia was impressed. Adam in full fury was a scary sight. She wondered how many bridges she'd burned tonight over a bathroom. Would she regret her stand? Probably. Would she do it again? You bet.

"No. You. Can't." Kione lifted his own mask.

Ohmigod! Lia raised her hands to shield her eyes from the blaze of shimmering light that was Kione. Wind whipped around the transformed fairy, scattering loose papers and overturning chairs. Not ordinary wind, but moving air filled with immense power and a feeling of dread that had no reasonable explanation. The murmur of distant voices drifted on that wind, and Lia somehow knew the voices held death. She clamped her hands over her ears.

He wasn't facing her, but she could tell from the look of horror on Adam's face that Kione was definitely making his case.

Then suddenly, it was over. Kione was once

again the unseelie prince they all knew and sort of loved. Adam was making a real effort to look indifferent.

"This isn't worth making a big deal over." Adam shrugged. "Sleep wherever you want. Just make sure you keep looking for the vampire, and let me know as soon as you find anything." His expression said that they were dismissed.

No one spoke as they retraced their steps out of the tunnel. Back in Jude's car, Lia allowed herself to semi-relax. Taking a deep breath, she pulled out of the parking lot. She didn't ask Kione what had just happened. Utah didn't either. Once experienced, some things were better left alone.

"Adam is smarter than I gave him credit for." Utah actually looked at her. "He was pissed, but he held it all together. You should've stayed out of it, though. Once we find his rogue vampire for him, he'll be out for blood."

Lia was torn. How to react? His concern warmed her. No use trying to deny it. On the other hand, he was assuming she was the most vulnerable. Because she was human? Because she was a woman?

"Because you're under his leadership." Utah held up his hand. "No, I can't read your mind, but I *can* read your expression. Once this is over, he'll try to use his authority to remove you from power. Then he thinks he can kill you at his leisure."

"He's wrong. I'll make sure I'm vampire by then." She tried to ignore his disapproving stare.

More reason to resist any physical attraction. He'd hate her as vampire. "And I'll find allies. Jude isn't too happy with our glorious leader. If we all stick together, Adam won't be able to gather a large enough force to defeat us."

"Adam won't play fair. He's not the type." Kione sounded a little weary. "He'll hire assassins until one of them gets you. He'll never do the dirty work himself if he can find someone else to do it. Not admirable, but pretty pragmatic of him."

She'd had enough of discussing Adam. The only way she could function was to live in the moment and let the future take care of itself. "Where should we go to sleep? I think we should stick together and not go back to where we were staying. Just in case Adam decides before he goes to sleep that he wants to trade us in for more biddable minions. He has a bunch of efficient killers working for him. And not all of them sleep during the day."

Kione didn't look as though he cared one way or another. "Adam will have a tough time putting this genie back in the bottle."

"I vote for Fin's condo. At least we won't have to sleep with one eye open. Adam wouldn't try to take on Fin there." Utah gazed out the window. "Once we get a few hours' sleep, maybe we can think of a better way to find this rogue."

No one had anything to say about that all the way to Fin's parking garage and up to his penthouse suite. Strange, but just before she entered the garage, Lia thought she saw a man standing among the trees by the side of the building. Tall, blond hair. But when she looked again, he was gone. Probably her overactive imagination.

They didn't have a chance to ring the doorbell. The door was flung open and one of the Eleven stood there. Even though Fin had introduced them all last night, Lia couldn't put names with faces yet. It had all been too rushed.

She controlled her instinct to step back. Barely. Wow. He was almost as tall as Fin with a wild tangle of dark hair, eerie pale eyes, and a surprisingly sensual mouth that didn't do a thing to lower his scary index.

He dressed for impact. Sleeveless black T-shirt, torn jeans, and biker boots. Muscular and intimidating, he radiated bad attitude without saying a thing.

He glared at Utah. "I have better things to do than waiting around to jerk your ass out of the fire. I don't do babysitting."

"Go to hell." Utah started to walk past him, but paused. "No, wait. Don't go there. You'd like it too much." He glanced at Kione. "This is Gig. No one's ever seen him without his attitude."

Gig transferred his glare to Kione and her. Mostly to Kione. "What's he?"

Kione stepped forward. "*He* is a member of the unseelie court. And *he* doesn't have to turn into a freaking prehistoric monster to drill your ass through that wall. And *he* is in a rotten mood, so back off."

Lia glanced at Utah. He didn't look too concerned. He'd probably love it if they tried to kill each other. Well, she couldn't just stand here and do nothing.

Gig narrowed his eyes. He clenched his hands into fists. He took a step toward Kione.

She rushed into speech. "Gig's an unusual name. And it's short for . . . ?" Lia left the question hanging, hoping he'd pause to answer.

Gig looked as though he had to force his gaze from Kione. Lia figured he was getting hit by the dark fairy's sensual club.

"Giganotosaurus." He started to look away.

"Ohmigod." She wasn't faking her reaction. "I remember you. Back in Philly after I found out what the Eleven were I Googled dinosaurs. I was looking for the biggest and baddest. You were bigger than a T. rex. Fifty feet long." His size froze her blood. "For God's sake, don't lose your temper. Your soul would knock out walls, bring the building down." Okay, maybe not bring down the building. But eight tons of angry dinosaur would definitely get noticed by the neighbors.

Gig's smile was evil, crazy, and terrifying all at the same time. "I. Don't. Care." His insane smile widened. "And after my beast gets through bouncing him off whatever walls are still standing, I'll find out why he's making me want to screw everyone in this room."

Utah finally intervened. "Hold it, big guy. Kione's a guest of Fin's. You know what will happen if you attack a guest. Remember what happened to Al?"

Uncertainty touched Gig's pale eyes. "The room."

"Right. Think about it. Stuck in the containment room until Fin gets good and ready to release you. No stalking, no killing, *nothing*."

"No one ever told me about a containment room."

Utah answered Lia without taking his gaze from Gig. "A large reinforced room Fin has for any of the Eleven that lose themselves to their beasts. An in-house prison."

The no-killing part seemed to settle Gig down. He exhaled deeply and slowly unclenched his fists. Lia could almost see his soul receding. She was impressed. She'd have to remember to invoke the containment room the next time she met a ticked-off member of the Eleven.

"Fin said you'd be sleeping here." Gig still shot challenging glances Kione's way.

"He was in my damn head again. Just because I leave the connection open doesn't mean he has to use it." Utah seemed to gather his calm around him. It didn't look easy. "And I don't need you on call to save my butt. Where is Fin anyway?"

"Fin's busy giving Zero some mental static right now, so I'm supposed to show you to your rooms." Gig's expression said he'd rather be out somewhere killing and maiming. "Who's the woman? I know Fin introduced her, but he didn't give any details."

Utah didn't give Lia a chance to lay into Gig. "You know, you'd have a lot more friends if you didn't treat everyone like dirt. Hey, here's an original thought. Maybe you could even talk to a person when she's standing right in front of you."

Gig looked as though he was trying to decide if killing Utah was worth the effort. He finally turned to her. "Who're you besides Lia who knows a lot about vampires?"

She returned his glare. "I lead the Northeast vampires. I'm helping you guys find Seven." She left out her connection to Katherine.

"A *human* woman leads a bunch of vampires?" Translation: a dust bunny leads the monsters under the bed?

"A prehistoric pinhead thinks he can save the world?" Fine, so she had a raging case of juvenile one-upmanship.

"Hmmph." Gig started to turn away but then paused. He didn't quite look at Kione. "Impressive weapon you have there. I'd like to talk to you sometime. Maybe find out what else you can do." Then he walked off, leaving them to trail after him.

"Amazing." Utah sounded amused. "Feel honored, Kione. I've never heard Gig tell anyone he'd like to talk to them. He's mad at everyone 24/7, and he walks alone."

"He wants something. They all do."

His tone didn't leave much doubt in Lia's mind what he thought Gig wanted. She was horrified. How could he go through life thinking—?

Utah touched her arm. "You okay?" He sounded as though the words were being dragged from him.

She had been until he touched her. The sizzle and burn from that one touch seared a path straight through her confidence. She'd been so sure she could shut down any attraction to him. Uh-huh. That was working well. "Yeah. Fine."

She met his gaze. Concern? He was confusing her. She'd had him safely packed inside a box labeled "Murderous Ancient Predator," complete with a bloodred bow. Had she put him in the wrong box? She hoped not. She had to keep her prejudices strong. Because his one touch had raised a real problem.

She still thought he was hot. As in I-keep-forgetting-why-I-shouldn't-want-you hot. She had to fight those feelings. His blue eyes might promise clear skies and happy times for all, a summer picnic scenario, but they lied. Instead, they were the calm waters of a lake just before the monster rose to eat everyone. Picnic canceled. His tangled blond hair framed a face that hid dangerous shadows even on a bright sunny day. He was not your all-American guy. Utah had scary things going on inside him. And to want him was to dance in the fast lane at rush hour. That was a bad thing, right?

Not that what she thought really mattered, because he sure wouldn't want anything to do with someone who had "become vampire" penciled into her daily planner.

Lia watched his smooth stride as he followed Gig. She loved the way he moved, all coiled energy and fluid animal grace. Sexual. She didn't get a chance to inventory anything else about him before they reached her room.

She stayed in her room exactly five minutes. That's how long it took her to decide she didn't want to be alone with her own thoughts and doubts. Besides, now that her adrenaline had stopped spiking, Lia realized she was starving.

Pulling on a change of clothes, she headed toward the kitchen . . . where she found Utah rooting around in the fridge. She joined him. "Anything interesting?"

"Some roast beef. I'll make us a few sandwiches. Go relax. I'll bring the stuff to the living room." His words sounded normal, but tension thrummed beneath them.

Lia didn't argue with him. Rubbing shoulders as they'd peered into the fridge had triggered thoughts about creating friction with other body parts. She started to leave.

"Wait. You never told me how you got that name from the vampire." He held containers in both hands, so he shoved the door shut with his hip.

"I pricked my finger with a pin. He followed the blood scent. Then I played a drunk and stupid human who thought meeting a vampire was cool.

I wouldn't get into the car with him until he'd told me his leader's name. He was so lost to the hunger that he got it out before the pain hit him."

"Then?"

She shrugged. "I warned him to leave town and walked away."

He was silent for a heartbeat. "Is this a my-way-is-better-than-your-way thing?"

"No. It's about not having just one strategy to solve a problem." She took a deep breath. May as well say it. "I never knew Katherine. She rejected me right after I was born. Wasn't vampire enough. I think the idea that she'd given birth to a human horrified her. But I never gave up hoping I'd do something to make her proud, to make her *notice* me. So I worked twice as hard as everyone else. I learned to shoot and use a sword. But the most valuable thing I learned was to use my mind. I'd never be as powerful as her vampires, but I could be a lot smarter."

His gaze softened. "I'll admit it, I was worried about you tonight. But you saved my butt from Zero and got important info for us. I don't need any other proof. Your mother missed knowing an amazing daughter. Her loss."

Lia was mortified at the moisture gathering in her eyes. She blinked rapidly and turned away. By the time she reached the living room, she had her emotions under control.

Glancing around, she considered her options. Recliner? Safe. Couch? Unsafe. There was too much room. Dangerous possibilities had acres of space to explore, and a sensual powerhouse could sit down next to her at any moment. She chose the couch. Hey, she prided herself on being fearless. If she was afraid to sit on the same couch with him, what did that say about her bravery? But she did hedge her bets. She slid all the way to one end before turning on the TV.

She was flipping through the channels when he finally showed up with a tray of sandwiches and drinks. He put the tray down on the coffee table and sat down next to her. *Right* next to her.

"Anything special you want to watch?" She forced herself to meet his gaze. With all the craziness going on around them tonight, she hadn't had time to simply look at him. Oh, she'd recognized the pull he had on her, but now she remembered why.

"Nope." He got up and strode to the light switch. He turned off the lights. "Some of my beast's characteristics have bled into my human form. I'm sensitive to bright lights."

Lia decided not to mention that it had a dimmer switch. And dinosaurs with sensitive eyes? Sure. She watched as he walked back to the couch. He blended with the shadows too well. She glanced at the TV screen, now the only light in the room. Nothing of interest there. Everything that was interesting was seated next to her. Lia hit the mute button, picked up a sandwich, and waited for him to say something.

Lia tried to ride the silence, but it dragged on too long. She blinked first. "So what did you like doing in your previous life?" She figured she already knew, but a conversation had to start somewhere. Besides, she wanted to know more about him.

"Eating, killing, and mating."

Seemed to Lia that he'd had limited life experiences. "What do you like doing in this life?" She took a bite and tried to chew naturally, but when she swallowed, she knew everyone in the condo heard her gulp.

"Eating, killing, and . . ." He smiled before taking a bite of his sandwich.

His smile blew her away. No man had a right to look that delicious while still retaining his killer cred. His smile was dark with an undercurrent of just plain bad. She didn't think she'd ever be attracted to a sunny smile again.

While the room's shadows seemed to coalesce around him, and she filled the quiet with breathing that sounded way too loud, Lia searched for something else to say.

"What were you before you became a raptor?" Where had that question come from? Not from the part of her brain in charge of survival.

He stilled, his eyes narrowing. "What makes you think I was something else?"

Lia sensed that not only was she treading on thin ice, but some damn big cracks were opening right under her feet. "Common sense. Even if Fin was able to stuff your raptor soul into a human body, your beast wouldn't be able to function mentally as a human. You obviously have some higher-level skills. They had to come from somewhere."

"Maybe they're left over from my human donor."

There was something in his expression . . . Then it hit her. "You *know* you were something else."

He didn't answer for a long time. Then he exhaled deeply. "Every once in a while, I get these flashes of memory. Not from my raptor days. Fin is always in them, and he's not a friend. But as soon as I start remembering, I get a stabbing pain in my head and the memory goes away."

Lia leaned toward him. "Fin must be controlling your memories. He seems to be the only one powerful enough around here to do it." A few days ago, she would've said that was nonsense. But after meeting Fin? Anything was possible. "Have you talked to the others about this?"

"No. I don't even know if the memories are real."

"Have you talked to *Fin* about this?"

He glanced away from her. "Been thinking about it. Haven't had a chance so far with so much happening."

She could almost see him trying to reconcile what she was saying with his own experiences. Everything would've been fine if she hadn't taken that one step too far. "You're not really the raptor you think you are. You're something better."

Was that a flash of hurt in his eyes? It was hard to tell. Not much light.

"You're wrong, sweetheart. I'm exactly that raptor." He was fierce in defense of his soul.

Maybe she should try keeping her mouth shut occasionally. Lia felt the crack widen into a chasm, dumping her into icy water. About the same temperature as his voice right now.

He leaned closer, invading her space, daring her not to move away from him. "I might not remember some things, but I *do* remember the life I lived as a Utahraptor. With *this* soul. Everything else is just guessing. And if an animal soul offends your human sensibilities, too bad."

His beast was close to the surface. Excitement rippled through her. Excitement? Whoa, that was not the right response.

Utah reached out to skim his fingers along her jaw. Suddenly, the epicenter of all possible pleasure relocated to that small patch of skin. She gasped.

Lia gazed into his eyes, watched them flare with heat, and slowly slid her tongue across her bottom lip. Provocative? Tempting? Guilty. The woman reflected in his eyes wasn't anyone she recognized.

She watched his anger become something else. The "something else" caught at her throat and made her heart kick into a frantic drumroll.

"You know, I was ready to tear Kione's head off. I thought he was causing all those feelings. I owe him an apology." His voice was a husky murmur as he slid his hand behind her neck and pulled her to him.

Utah kissed her. Not a gentle first kiss. It was a kiss filled with tangled emotions he thought he'd need a lifetime to unravel—the savagery of his beast, the need built up over his short human lifetime, the anger at her rejection of his soul, and the desire to please her.

He wanted it to be only about his anger. His raptor wasn't good enough for her. But even as he dived into all the sensory pleasure enhanced by his animal nature, he knew it could never be about only one thing with her.

Tracing her lips with his tongue, he tasted her. He stored the essence of citrus and vanilla away to compare with the rest of her body. And Utah had no doubt he'd get the chance to do exactly that.

Because as he deepened the kiss, fighting his soul's demand that he abandon human behavior in favor of ripping her clothes from her luscious body right now, he felt something waken in her. It stretched, flexed its claws, and looked at him.

She wrapped her arms around him and met his ferocity with her own. Opening her mouth, she welcomed him in. He tangled his tongue with hers, explored her heat, and tasted her building excitement. And all the reasons in the world that he shouldn't be doing this went to hell. This was what *he* wanted, what his *beast* wanted. And neither one would be denied.

Lia pulled at his shirt, working her fingers underneath it, then splaying her hands across his back. Each point of contact was a searing promise of what was to come.

He kissed a path down her neck, losing himself in the warmth and smoothness of her skin. And as he lifted her top and pushed her bra out of the way so that he could reach her breasts, she transferred her hands from back to front.

Lia *touched* him. She pressed down on his arousal, gently massaging. He was so hard he thought he'd explode, and when she fumbled with his zipper, his beast roared to life. He leaned forward, sliding his tongue over her breast before drawing her nipple into his mouth. Her small moan drove him on.

But things were starting to spiral out of control. She'd managed to get his zipper down and was reaching for him. She didn't notice any change in him.

Utah abandoned her nipple to lay his head between her breasts. He breathed in deeply, trying to stop what was happening. *Slow down.* His beast ignored him. His control galloped farther down the rutted path leading to complete savagery. God, what would he do to her if his raptor slipped its leash? She thought just because he remained in human form that he'd act human. Not so. Mating for raptors was primitive, brutal, and usually ended with a complete loss of control. He'd hurt her.

Lia's hand stilled. She'd finally sensed the wrongness. "What's the matter?"

"Losing it." His voice was a tortured rasp. Need battered his defenses, knocking them down brick, by brick, by brick. Soon there'd be a hole big enough for his beast to crawl through. Damn. He'd been with women during the last few months. Control hadn't been an issue with them. Why now? "Want this too much. My beast doesn't understand gentleness, doesn't realize that humans can break. Might hurt you." His beast's frustration was a primal howl, beating at his mind, tightening his muscles into agonized knots.

Lia didn't freak out and pull away from him. *Thank you.* She remained silent for a moment before removing her hand from his cock. *No. Touch me. Now.* He forced the words back. She was doing the right thing even if the right thing killed him.

"I'll take your word for it." She slid her fingers through his hair, a calming gesture. "But I'm not exactly a delicate flower. I could hold my own."

Not against my beast. "Yeah. Better safe than sorry, though." He leaned away from her. What the hell had just happened?

His body screamed its fury. *Hunger denied. Deal with it.*

She bit her lower lip before releasing it. He riveted on its damp fullness—a reminder of lost pleasure—even as he tried to force his beast back into its cave. Finally, it went, growling and clawing every inch of the way.

He watched her pull down her top with fingers that still trembled. She took a deep breath. Then she smiled. "We'll have to practice. Sort of work up to it slowly. Practice can be fun too." Her smile faded. "I'm selfish. I want it all now."

Time for hard truths. "No matter how human I look, I'm still raptor here." He tapped his heart. "When my brain shuts down, and my senses take over, the beast runs free. Oh, I might not change forms, but he's still in control. He doesn't understand words like 'gentle' and 'foreplay.' He goes for the kill every time." As explanations went, that was an epic fail. Sounded like he had zero control.

She didn't look disgusted, but he was glad he couldn't read her mind right now. Let him keep his illusions.

"Has this happened before when you were . . . ?" The rest of the sentence faded into the obvious.

"No."

"Well, hey, that's something at least." For whatever reason, she almost looked pleased. Go figure.

Suddenly, he froze. What the hell? Someone was in his head. No one he recognized. He pushed against the presence. It didn't budge.

"I tried to wait until the main event was over, but since it's been canceled, I decided now was an okay time to connect. We need to talk. Now. I'll meet you in the lobby. Bring Lia with you."

Utah sent an automatic denial. *Not. Now.* Who was this?

"Forgot to introduce myself. Seir, the bad seed. Hurry. Fin's not paying attention right now. Don't know how long that will last. Have to strike while the iron is hot and all that crap."

"What's wrong?" Lia frowned. Her lips were slightly parted, swollen from his kisses.

"Son of a bitch." He heaved himself from the couch. "We have company down in the lobby."

She raked fingers that still shook through her hair, leaving it tousled and beautiful. "Who?"

"Fin's brother."

CHAPTER SIX

F in's *brother*?" Lia was still trying to catch her breath after what almost happened, an "almost" that had torn her down to her most basic components. Those basic components had nothing to do with protecting herself or staying safe.

And now Utah had hit her with Fin's *brother*. "Who is he? *What* is he? Why didn't I know about him?" She fumbled with her bra, pulling it back into place and smoothing her top down.

"His name is Seir."

"Just Seir? Does he have a last name? Do any of you guys have a last name?" God, she'd almost made love with him, and she didn't even know his last name. The scariest part? She didn't care.

Lia tried to ignore how sensual he looked all

mussed and rumpled. Had she missed the part where he pulled up his zipper? Lots of symbolism there, all along the lines of the gates of paradise clanging shut.

"I don't know about Seir, but my last name is Endeka. All of us are Endekas. Fin's creation. It means eleven. Everything comes down to numbers with him."

Figured. "So tell me about this Seir?"

"Let's go. I'll tell you what I know on the way down."

"Wait." Lia left him standing there as she raced back to her room. She threw on her coat. Not because she intended to go outside but because she needed to hide her gun and sword. Utah had a prehistoric killer on call. She didn't.

He was pacing impatiently when she returned. She kept up with him as he strode toward the door.

"Some of the other guys have met Seir. I haven't. Not sure what he is, and Fin isn't talking. Seir has helped us a few times. He made a cameo appearance during the dustup with Eight in Philly. Helped Jenna stay alive. Guess you missed him there. No one seems to know where his true loyalty lies. We only know two things for sure: Fin won't make contact with him, and Seir waits outside Fin's condo in every city we visit. Sort of creepy if you ask me."

Memory flash. A tall, blond man standing among the trees. "Is it safe to meet him alone?"

Her mind was racing. She thought she'd identified all the variables. Evidently not.

Utah shrugged. "He's never attacked any of the Eleven. Besides, if we tell anyone about this, they might feel obligated to tell Fin. And he might try to stop us."

Lia kept quiet on the elevator. She agreed with him. And she was curious. The mysterious Fin had a brother. Who would've thought?

The elevator opened to an empty lobby. Not surprising given the early hour of the morning. Lia did a quick scan. No one at the night guard's desk. That *was* surprising. She reached into her coat pocket, wrapping her fingers around her gun. Then she followed Utah out of the car.

Leashed power raised the hair on the back of her neck even before she spotted the figure half hidden in a shadowed corner of the room.

A man sat cross-legged on the floor, his head tilted down, his long blond hair falling around his face. A face she couldn't see.

Beside her, Utah tensed. Lia could swear she sensed his soul creeping closer to the surface. Was that normal? She'd never felt this attuned to anyone before. Wasn't sure she wanted it now.

"Seir?" Utah stopped and waited.

The man lifted his head. His face delivered the same emotional punch as Fin's. Both had an unearthly beauty. But Seir's hair framed that incredible face in a tangled glory shading from intense to pale gold. His eyes were an icy blue.

Then he smiled, and his resemblance to Fin faded a little. There was real warmth along with wicked humor in that smile. Lia thought Fin could take some lessons from his brother. That didn't mean Seir wasn't dangerous. Eight had done a lot of smiling too, and he'd been a freaking psychopath.

"Lia and Utah. You're alone, so I assume you left my brother sleeping peacefully. Good. He was always the wet blanket at every party."

Seir rose to his feet in one fluid motion. Lia figured he was over six feet but not as tall as Fin. He reached them in a few easy strides. She had only a fleeting impression of his clothes—black leather jacket over a T-shirt deifying Jim Morrison, jeans, and boots. But no one would ever notice his clothes unless he hid his face.

She dared a quick glance at Utah. In a world suddenly populated by beautiful immortal men, she still preferred Utah's savage beauty. It was honest. His eyes promised nothing, gave nothing away. But she knew when he walked with her, the night shadows would never claim her. Did she forget anything? Oh, and he was the most sensual creature she'd ever met. Kione might be a lust-inducing machine, but it was all fake. Utah was hot nights, tangled sheets, and screaming orgasms.

"What do you want?" Utah met Seir's gaze.

He was too direct. Lia wanted to ask a few questions leading up to why he'd called for this meeting. "What are you? Why do you wait outside the condo? What's between you and Fin?"

Seir looked at her. He was still smiling, but for a moment, she saw something cold and assessing in his eyes. Then the moment passed.

"I'm whatever you want me to be." He shrugged. "And I wait outside the condo because I know if I stand out there long enough my ass of a brother will come out just to try to get rid of me." Unholy glee moved in his eyes. "Then the fun begins."

"One answer out of three. Guess I have to be satisfied with that." Lia didn't try to hide her irritation.

"Guess you do." Seir's attention returned to Utah. "I have info that you and Lia can use. And yes, I know you're hunting for a rogue vampire that's siphoning off Adam's people." His smile widened. "I know because I followed you. See, I don't spend all my time watching Fin's windows."

Cold washed over her. How had he followed them? She'd kept her eyes open. The roads were empty in the early hours of the morning. She would've made a tail. But then Tor had found them too. The thought made her uneasy.

"Why do you care what we're doing?" Utah narrowed his eyes. He radiated distrust.

Lia didn't blame him. Seir made her nervous. Sort of like when someone you think you know takes off his Halloween mask and a total stranger is staring at you. Who hid behind that beautiful smiling face?

"Bored. I get tired trying to outwait Fin. Be-sides, this whole 2012 thing fascinates me. And whenever I help one of you guys, it always leads to a fight. You entertain me."

Lia might've taken him at face value if she hadn't forced her attention away from his in-credible smile long enough to spot the mockery in his eyes. He was playing them. She'd bet he was getting a lot more than entertainment from the Eleven. What? It all had to come back to Fin somehow.

"Say what you have to say." Utah glanced beyond Seir.

Lia followed his gaze, and for just a moment thought she saw a pair of gold eyes gleaming from outside the lobby's wall of windows. She shuddered.

"You'll find what you're looking for under the Burnside Bridge. The homeless make easy pick-ings. Adam's rogue hunts there."

"How do you know all this?" Lia strained her eyes to see outside the window. The eyes still stared back at her, gleaming and unblinking. Not human. "Who's outside the window?"

Seir turned to look. "A friend. He's just making sure I get out of here in one piece."

Lia didn't believe that for a minute. If Seir had even half the power she sensed in his brother, he could flatten this condo without breaking a sweat.

"I know all this because I listen." Seir broke eye contact to glance down at a ring he wore.

That was no answer at all, but Lia didn't care about that. Now that he'd called attention to his ring . . . What was that symbol? It looked like a triple spiral. Connected. Significant to Seir or just a random design? Jeez, she was looking for hidden meanings in everything.

"Well, thanks for listening. What do you want in return?" Utah the cynical.

Seir laughed. "Hey, I'm just doing this out of the goodness of my heart. But if you really want to repay me for this and future gifts, get my hard-headed brother to meet with me."

Utah shook his head. "Don't think it's going to happen. But I'll mention it to him. Best I can do."

Seir simply nodded before turning and walking away. A few seconds after he left the building, the golden eyes winked out. And a confused-sounding voice rose from behind the guard's desk, followed shortly after by the groggy guard himself.

"Damn. Must've dozed off." He cast a wary glance their way. "This never happened before. Hope you won't tell anyone."

"Nothing happened while you were out." Utah glanced at her. "Ready to head back up?"

She did a lot of thinking on the way up in the elevator. "Something about Seir is off."

"Yeah, I felt it too. But then, he's Fin's brother." He shrugged as if that explained everything.

They didn't say anything else until they were once again standing in the living room. The TV was still on mute, and the sandwiches still lay un-eaten on the tray.

Tension wrapped Lia's head in tight bands of pain. Great. The perfect end to a crappy night. She thought about those moments on the couch. Okay, maybe not all crappy. She glanced at Utah. Even with a headache pounding away she'd be willing to . . .

No, she wouldn't. He'd withdrawn. She could feel it. Did he regret almost sleeping with the enemy, or at least future enemy? Or was he just thinking about what Seir had said?

She sighed. "I'm going to my room. I have a headache."

He raised one brow.

"No, really."

"You haven't eaten for a long time. Hunger feeds a headache. Sit down." He dropped onto the couch.

Lia sat down, but she kept some space be-tween the two of them. She reached for a sand-wich. If she was chewing, he wouldn't expect her to make small talk. They ate in silence for a few minutes.

But she couldn't keep quiet for too long. "So what do you want to do when all this is over?"

He stared at her blankly.

"Oh, come on. You must've thought about it. Ten months and it'll all be over. What then?"

He put down the sandwich he'd been eating. A line formed between his eyes. "Never thought about it. There's no guarantee that I'll make it to 2013, so why get ahead of myself?"

She could only gape at him. "Everyone makes plans for the future."

"Not me. If I have a future, I'll worry about it when I get there."

He sounded flip, but his eyes looked somber. Or was she just reading what she wanted into him? Maybe not somber, just tired.

"Ty and Al got married. They're counting on having a future."

His eyes darkened. "So did my brother. Rap wanted to be a paleontologist after everything was over. Who better to study dinosaurs? He had it all planned out. He figured that Fin would loan him the money to go to school. Then he walked into a restaurant in South Philly and it all ended. I come from a time when you didn't count on your next meal until you'd killed it. Seems like that attitude works now too."

His cynicism horrified her. "I can't believe you think that way. I mean, you take all kinds of chances every day. Why not take a chance on your future?"

"I take chances because I'm not afraid to die. That has nothing to do with what you're talking about."

She'd had enough of this conversation. His attitude shouldn't bother her, but it did. They could decide what to do with Seir's information later.

Lia took a last bite from her sandwich and

stood. "I'll see you in the morning." She reached for the tray.

"I'll take care of it."

"Thanks."

His silence followed her out the door.

Back in her room, she took time to do two more things before taking a shower and climbing into bed with only her frustrated sexual fantasies for company. She called Phil, her second in command in Philly, to make sure everything was okay. Then she opened her laptop and hunted for the symbol she'd seen on Seir's ring.

And when sleep once again eluded her, she took a break from her sexual fantasies for a reality check.

She liked him too much, *wanted* him too much.

He loved Rap. Lia didn't want to think of him as a loving brother, or a loving anything. They might be forced to work together for a while, but she had to keep the word "enemy" front and center in her mind. Because she was going to have to kill him when this brief truce was over. And she didn't doubt for a minute that he'd kill her with no regrets if she became vampire.

She'd believed all that enemy stuff at the beginning. Did she still believe it? God, she didn't know.

When she finally fell asleep, Lia dreamed of her mother.

"Did you pass on the information to Fin?"

"Yeah." Seir watched him pace the rooftop, his

gleaming red hair swinging in time to each long stride. "Why the hell do we always end up on freaking roofs? You know how much I hate high places."

He stopped pacing long enough to flash Seir a grin. "I like roofs. There's nothing between me and the stars. Besides, I enjoy making you nervous." His grin widened as he moved to the roof's edge and peered over. "Sure you don't want to come over here? The view's magnificent."

Seir swallowed hard. "I'll take your word for it." He looked away and met the stare of the black jaguar crouched in the shadows. It watched him from shining golden eyes. "Don't you get sick of him, Balan?"

"I ignore what annoys me. You would be wise to do likewise. He finds it too easy to . . . push your buttons."

Balan's voice in his head irritated the crap out of Seir. The damn cat always sounded so superior. "Push my buttons? Learning the vernacular quickly, aren't you?"

"I do what I must to blend in."

"Right. Blend in." Seir turned away from the big cat. "I noticed that Balan isn't the only one mellowing a little. You're calling him Fin, the name he chose for himself in this time. Does that mean I get to use the name he chose for you—Zero?"

"Fin and his damn obsession with numbers. Who would name themselves Fin meaning infinity?"

"I guess he figures he's a forever kind of guy."

Zero shrugged. "I can be Zero for the short time we're here . . . and he can be Fin. Names change nothing between us." He glanced at Seir, his expression neutral. "Since you did what I asked, does that mean you're on my side this time?"

"I'm not on anyone's side. I please myself."

One second Zero stood at the edge of the roof, the next he appeared beside Seir. Seir sucked in his breath. "Don't do that. It bothers me."

"I live to bother you." Zero's laughter echoed in the night. "Do you think they'll take the bait?"

"Don't ask me. Jump into their minds to find out."

"Fin protects his own while they're under his roof. Their minds are closed to me."

For whatever reason, that made Seir happy. "I think they will. I wonder if they'll tell Fin."

"He already knows. The bastard doesn't miss anything." Zero shrugged. "We'll just have to see what happens."

This seemed as good a time as any for Seir to ask the question nagging at him. "Why are you doing it this way? You don't need to go through all this crap of raising a nonhuman army to destroy humanity. You did it with an asteroid last time. Why not do the same thing now?"

Zero grew thoughtful. "A challenge? He's grown more powerful over the eons. Perhaps I want to prove I can defeat him on *this* playing field." He shrugged. "Besides, the whole purpose of all this is the rise of the new and the death of the old. Nonhumans should have to work for ownership of this planet. And if they fail, I can always take care of things as I did before."

"If he lets you."

"I'm still the stronger." He cast Seir a sharp glance. "As long as it remains a one-on-one fight."

Seir refused to rise to the bait. "Why do you hate him so much?"

Zero looked honestly shocked. "It was never hate. *Never.*"

When Lia entered the dining room late in the afternoon, Fin sat at the head of the table. He was the only one there. He wore a short silver metallic jacket with a black T-shirt underneath. With his silver hair and eyes, he was almost too shiny to look at.

He smiled. It was beautiful and cold.

At least there was food on the table. Her gaze slipped past the toast, eggs, bacon, and fruit. Coffee. Yes! If she had to talk to Fin, she'd need caffeine.

Lia sat two seats away from him. Close enough so he didn't feel insulted but far enough away to avoid being sucked into his personal vortex. She poured some coffee and took her time adding the cream. He waited patiently.

Finally, he spoke. "I'm glad we're alone. I have things to discuss with you."

Way to ruin a perfectly good day. She gulped

her coffee. The steaming liquid burning a hole in her esophagus kept things real. "Talk."

"Utah and Kione will be here soon, so I'll keep this as brief as possible."

He leaned toward her, and she resisted the impulse to lean away.

"You understand what's at stake, Lia."

"Remind me." She needed time to wall up her defenses against him. Strange how she instinctively knew she'd need them. Fin wasn't a person you relaxed around.

"Zero and his men are raising an army of nonhumans. They go to a city, train recruits, and then send their students to other places to repeat the process. On December 21 their armies will slaughter humanity."

"There're only ten of you guys. How do you expect to stop an army?"

He leaned back, and she breathed a little easier.

"We won't have to stop an army if we cut off the heads of the hydra before December 21. Eight and Nine have already bought their one-way tickets back out into the cosmos, and once there they can't return until the end of the next cycle."

"Why bother with an army? Why not destroy everyone themselves? A natural disaster erased the dinosaurs."

"They're forbidden to kill humans directly, hence their need for minions. A natural disaster isn't any fun. No challenge. And only Zero has the power to call forth that kind of apocalyptic event. He resorted to the asteroid to destroy the dinosaurs because he didn't have any intelligent life forms to mobilize."

Now there was something she hadn't known. "Seems there're a lot of cans and can'ts attached to all of this."

Fin shrugged. "Those are the rules of the game."

Rules of the game? A shiver worked its way down Lia's spine. Could Fin sound any more cold, more disconnected from humanity? And Lia wondered what kind of unfeeling monster would think of mass murder as a game. Maybe she didn't want to meet the cosmic rule maker.

"Now for your part in all of this."

Here comes the bad part. Lia could feel the sucking sensation as the tide rushed out on her personal tsunami. Any second the giant wave would appear on the horizon.

"Millions of years ago, I had a series of nine visions. They detailed where and when each of Zero's immortals could be defeated. The visions also showed me the nine human women necessary to do it."

"Women?" She knew what was coming, but she couldn't stop it.

"Kelly and Jenna took out both Nine and Eight. Not a coincidence." His gaze grew intense. "We need you."

In times of crisis, she thought silly thoughts.

She was picturing the old recruiting posters that said Uncle Sam wants you. And the giant finger of fate was pointing directly at her.

"I was in one of the visions."

He nodded.

The wave towered over her, then crashed on the beach, sweeping her off her feet.

"I saw you reaching out. You had something in your hand. I didn't see Seven, and I didn't see what you were holding. But I knew that its touch would banish Seven from Earth. I saw lots of trees and what looked like a column of smoke in the background. Then the vision ended."

She fought to the surface as the wave dragged her out to sea. "You're a powerful guy. Why don't you just find Zero and whip his ass? You don't need me."

Emotion too brief to identify moved in Fin's eyes and was gone. "My visions didn't include me 'whipping his ass.' Too bad."

"Can't you ignore the visions? Free will and all that stuff?" She was desperate.

Fin just stared at her.

"Right. No cheating." Her gaze skipped around the room, searching for an escape. "At least did your vision show me making a triumphant exit from all this?" *With Utah's arms wrapped around me.* Oh damn, she hadn't meant that last thought. Had she?

"I don't see outcomes."

Then what good were his damn visions? Anything could go wrong. "What if I decide to walk away now?"

"You won't. The visions don't lie. It *will* happen. The tough part will be finding whatever you were holding in your hand." He shrugged. "Sorry. I don't have any more information. But once we follow up on the tip Seir gave you last night, I want—"

"Wait. You know about that?"

He smiled. This time it was genuine. Lia decided that any woman could ride to glory on his smile. Well, except for her. She preferred Utah's hard-edged smile.

"I never sleep deeply. I sensed the moment he entered the building. Shen is handy with electronics. I'm hooked up to the building's security cameras. I saw you meet him."

She nodded. "And you heard us through Utah's mind."

"No. Actually, it was your mind. Utah was busy trying to block me just in case I was awake. I could've blasted through his block, but he would've known I was there." His smile faded. "I've already spoken to him."

"Let me guess. He was ticked."

"A little."

"You could've just kept an eye on the cameras and not listened in if you were worried about our safety."

Fin didn't bother shrugging. "You think I

should've trusted him to tell me what happened? I didn't notice him contacting me as soon as Seir called to him. Did I miss that part?"

"No need for sarcasm." Okay, so Fin was right about that.

He leaned forward, but his gaze didn't seem focused on her. "Listen to me, young one. Trust is usually misplaced. Trust no one, and live a long life."

Something about his voice had changed, taken on a cadence that didn't sound natural. He was creeping her out. She could've asked the same questions of him that she'd asked of Seir. *Who are you? What are you?*

"You're not like the rest of the Eleven, are you? You were never a dinosaur romping across the prehistoric landscape." That revelation wasn't a shocker. It was a no-brainer. Anyone could see that Fin was different. "If I can see it so clearly, your men should too. But they don't, do they?" She narrowed her eyes. "Because you've messed with their minds. What don't you want them to know about you?"

Lia regretted the questions the moment they left her lips. She swallowed hard and gripped the arms of her chair as his eyes bled purple.

"Be careful."

He didn't sound angry, but his eyes shone with emotion. She wished she could ID it.

"I do what I think is best for all of us."

For all of us. Well, Lia recognized a god complex when she saw it.

"Now, since I'm already . . . upset, do you have anything else to ask?"

Purple still pushed out the silver in his eyes, but any hint of emotion was gone.

A sudden thought gave her the courage to ask one more thing. He couldn't eliminate her. She was in his vision. If he wanted to get Seven, he needed her. *Unless he tears you apart in an uncontrolled rage.* She pushed that possibility aside. Fin might get angry, but she couldn't imagine him losing control.

"Why won't you at least meet with your brother? That's all he wants, just to talk to you. I feel kind of sorry for him. After all, he's still family."

For some reason, her comment amused him. He leaned back in his chair, and his eyes shone silver again. "Sometimes family is the most poisonous of all."

Katherine. He was right. Lia was the wrong person to lecture him on family.

"Okay, so now I know you can bend minds into pretzels. Are you going to take away my memory of asking you these questions?" She had to know even if she forgot immediately afterward.

"No." For a moment he sounded almost weary. "Regardless of how powerful you seem to think I am, I can't manipulate the minds of thousands. I'll have to trust that you're smart enough to remember what's at stake. The survival of your species is more important than any minor concerns."

Warping men's minds wasn't minor. But she

kept that thought to herself. She concentrated instead on breaking her toast into small bits and sipping her coffee.

Thankfully, Utah and Kione showed up a few minutes later. Utah looked fierce and gorgeous and she wanted him more than . . . How had this happened so fast? A few days ago, she might've been crouched in an alley aiming at his head. Now her aim was a lot lower and didn't involve a gun. She contemplated her toast, but it had no answer for her.

Utah sat next to her. The soft fabric of his sweater slid over her arm. She shifted so that the contact remained. Talk about static cling.

Kione sat down a few chairs away from everyone. He still had his cloak wrapped around him. Strange. It was warm in here. Hadn't Utah offered to loan him something to wear?

"Now that everyone's here, we can talk about tonight." Fin included all of them, but he was watching Kione.

"Can't we at least eat in peace?" Utah loaded up his plate with eggs and bacon.

She started to mention the fat content of that plate but then shut her mouth. His cholesterol count wouldn't kill him.

"You can eat in peace on December 22." Fin's gaze never strayed from Kione.

Lia glanced at the fae prince to make sure she hadn't missed anything the first time she took a quick peek at him. Nope, looked the same. But then she realized he was sitting by himself. Lia didn't know why, but his aloneness bothered her. Sighing, she beckoned to him. "Move over."

Kione didn't respond for a moment, but finally, he moved to the chair next to hers. He made sure not to make eye contact. She appreciated the gesture.

Fin smiled at Lia. "I spoke with your father. I assured him you hadn't asked the first vampire you met to change you."

Lia was *not* amused. "Dad needs to stop checking on me." Every time her father did something like that it reminded her of the insecure little girl who wasn't brave enough or strong enough to make her mother love her. She hated the feeling.

"He loves you." Fin said it as though the power to love was a strange human disease he didn't understand and definitely didn't want to catch.

If they'd been alone, Lia would have asked him if he'd ever loved anyone. Then she remembered his trust issues. Nah.

Fin turned his attention back to the silent Kione. "Welcome, Kione. I've wanted to meet you. I'm sorry I missed you in Philadelphia."

Kione's nod was strangely formal. "You were busy at the time."

Utah followed the conversation while making sure he didn't look at Kione and trying not to think about Lia. He'd liked it a lot better when he'd believed the dark fairy's power was driving his interest in her beautiful little bottom and full breasts. Now? He'd have to work harder to focus on his work. Last night had been a revelation. No one to blame but himself for the emotions he'd unleashed on her unsuspecting head and other body parts.

"What brought you to Portland, Kione?" Fin glanced away from the fae prince as Greer pushed open the kitchen door. Fin motioned at him, and the chef disappeared back into the kitchen.

Kione countered with a question of his own. "What are you? And don't tell me you're just one of the Eleven. Your power is . . . extraordinary." He seemed unsettled by the knowledge.

Utah thought that not much managed to unsettle the prince.

Fin shrugged. "I am what I am. I don't think it's relevant to this discussion."

"Perhaps I don't feel it necessary for you to know why I'm here." Kione leaned back in his chair.

Fin smiled, the smile Utah knew meant he wouldn't rip your head off right now, but he was keeping future options open.

"You want me to play a guessing game?" Fin raised one brow. "I suppose I can do that."

Greer emerged from the kitchen carrying a tray. He unloaded a pot of fresh coffee and a plate of pastries onto the table.

"This is Greer." Fin didn't seem to have any trouble meeting Kione's gaze.

But then Utah couldn't imagine Fin feeling any

kind of sexual compulsion. He was too controlled, too cold, too . . . Utah abandoned that line of thought. What his leader felt wasn't Utah's business.

Greer offered each of them a tight nod and a piercing stare. Greer might look small and harmless, but Utah knew what lived in him. He'd bet on Greer in most fights.

"Greer is Otherkin. His soul is tiger, but it's trapped forever in his human body." Fin watched Greer return to the kitchen before turning back to Kione. "But most of us are trapped in some way, aren't we?"

For just a moment, Utah had the feeling Fin was talking about himself. Crazy.

Fin studied Kione. "I know Adam doesn't have the power to command your obedience, so you're here for some other reason." He looked thoughtful. "It has something to do with Jude. He said 'they'd' be here in a few hours."

Kione's gaze sharpened. "You were there?"

Fin looked at Utah. "He was there. I heard through his mind."

The fae prince sent Utah a contemptuous glance. "You allow him to use you like that, raptor?"

Utah didn't give Fin a chance to answer. "'Allow' is the operative word. He's my leader. There are things he needs to know." The incident with Zero was still fresh in his mind.

Fin leaned forward. "What did Jude mean by 'they'?"

"His five vampires." Lia jumped into the conversation. "Their clan was attacked centuries ago. They were the only survivors. The clan was so feared that no one would claim them. If Jude hadn't taken them in, the rest of the vampire world would've destroyed them."

Fin looked back at Kione. "What's between you and these vampires?"

For a moment, Utah thought Kione would refuse to answer. Finally, he exhaled deeply.

"The fae forces of the unseelie court fought and destroyed their clan. I led those forces."

Kione calmly poured his coffee and then added so much sugar and cream that Utah figured it couldn't possibly taste like coffee anymore.

"And how did the vampires repay you?" Fin's eyes gleamed with fascinated interest.

Kione put his cup down. "Why do you want to know?"

"You helped us back in Philadelphia. You could help us here. I take care of those who line up on our side."

"I don't line up on anyone's side unless it suits me." Kione didn't reach for his coffee again.

Fin nodded. "I understand." He waited a heartbeat. "Al told me about his meeting with you in Philadelphia. And about your . . . problem. Show me."

Utah looked at Lia. She shrugged.

"Al talks too much."

Utah thought it would end there. So Kione

surprised him when he pushed back his chair and stood. And without saying another word, he opened his cloak to expose his bare chest.

What the hell? Every inch of Kione's chest was covered with angry red welts. The damn things almost looked like they were pulsing, as though they had a life of their own.

"What happened to you?" Lia's voice was soft with sympathy, her eyes wide in horror.

Kione pulled his cloak around him and sat back down. Everything about him, from his stiff back to his thinned lips, said, *I don't want your sympathy. Leave me alone.*

Kione kept his gaze averted from Lia. "The five surviving vampires cursed me for my part in the slaughter. I've carried the marks ever since."

"And now?" Fin looked thoughtful.

"Jude will tell them I'm here. They'll come for me." Kione's smile was the coldest thing Utah had ever seen. "And I'll destroy them. Once they've all met their final death, the curse will be broken."

"Why didn't you destroy them before this?" Fin never broke eye contact with Kione.

How was he doing that? Just thinking about meeting the fae prince's gaze made Utah want to do wildly erotic things to Lia's body.

"I didn't know where they were. I finally found them in Philadelphia with Jude, but I wasn't in any condition to fight. When I went searching for them again, they'd scattered and dropped off my radar. I knew Jude was the key. If I kept following him, he'd eventually call them to him. Now it's happened."

Utah wanted to know why Kione had helped destroy the vampire clan, but he decided now wasn't the time to ask. He let Fin do the questioning.

"Why do you wear the cloak without a shirt?" Fin took a sip of his coffee.

"The pain was . . . bad, but I finally found a wizard who sold the cloak to me. He'd woven a powerful spell into it. The cloak eases the pain a little, but it has to be touching my skin."

Fin stood. "If I take away the pain, will you agree to help us find Seven?"

Lia looked as startled as Utah felt. Could Fin do that? A familiar unease poked at him. None of the Eleven knew the extent of Fin's power. At first, they'd thought he was like them, a man with the soul of a prehistoric predator. Well, they'd seen enough to know now that he wasn't. Then what was he? And why was he with *them*?

Something flashed in Utah's mind. An amorphous memory, half formed, of a time before he hunted as a raptor. A time when Fin was . . . Suddenly, pain stabbed at his head and the memory faded, leaving nothing but a feeling of horror. His heart pounded and his breath felt frozen in his chest. What the hell . . . ? Hadn't this happened before? And each time he thought he'd snag the memory, it slipped his line.

Lia touched his arm. "Are you okay?" Her soft question calmed him.

"Yeah. I'm fine." He took a deep breath.

Someone was watching him. Utah glanced up. Fin met his gaze. His eyes shone purple. Then Kione broke the connection.

"I can't be bought." Kione's voice was tight, his words filled with a meaning that seemed to go beyond Fin's offer.

Fin shrugged. "I'm not trying to buy you. I'm simply offering a temporary partnership. We're trading favors."

Utah almost snorted. Right. Fin was trying to buy him.

Surprisingly, Kione didn't reject him outright. "I have healing skills, but I couldn't take away my own pain."

"I'm outside the realm of experience for those who cursed you. They won't have fashioned their curse with me in mind." Fin motioned for the unseelie prince to come stand in front of him. Kione hesitated, but then walked to the head of the table.

"Remove the cloak."

"First tell me what you're going to do."

Fin looked impatient. "I'm going to take away the pain. I can't do anything about the welts, and I probably can't take the pain away permanently. But you'll be pain-free for a few weeks."

Kione looked as though he wanted to ask more questions, but the promise of no pain even for a short time must've kept him quiet. He dropped his cloak from his shoulders.

Then Fin reached out and placed his palm flat against Kione's chest. The dark fairy shuddered, but held still. From what he'd seen of Kione so far, Utah guessed that not many people had ever touched him. He had his keep-away vibe dialed to high at all times.

Fin tensed. His face lost all color, skin stretched tight over jaw and cheekbones, every plane thrown into stark relief. He didn't say anything. He didn't ask for help. His eyes shaded from deep purple to almost black.

Fin was in pain. Agonizing pain. Utah's beast sensed it even if Fin said nothing. And the instinct to protect a pack mate kicked in. If Fin was hurting, that must mean he was drawing Kione's pain into himself.

Utah moved to his leader's side. How many times had Fin saved the butts of different members of the Eleven? He never asked for thanks, and no one had ever stepped up to help him. Utah wasn't sure what he could do, but maybe he could siphon off some of Fin's pain. It was worth a try.

Utah clasped Fin's free hand. Pain hit him like the slap of an icy wave on a winter's day. He gasped and fought the urge to drop Fin's hand. God, how had Kione lived with this? Cramps doubled him over, tearing his breath from his body and almost bringing tears to his eyes. The pain sliced through his veins like a jagged knife and stabbed at his head. He fought down the need to scream. Fin was taking the worst hit, and he still stood strong.

Suddenly, when he thought he couldn't take it for one more second, he felt someone clasp his hand. Through the black wall of pain crushing him, he recognized her. He took strength from the warmth of her skin pressed against his, the sense of comfort it brought, and the gradual easing of the agony.

And when he felt her clench against the pain flowing into her, he squeezed her hand, hoping he was giving back some of the comfort along with the hurt.

After what seemed like years, Utah could finally think past the torture. He was sweating. Everyone dropped hands, and he sat down next to Lia. He still shook from reaction as he automatically put his arm across her shoulders. "Thank you" seemed inadequate, so he said nothing to her. "How the hell did you live with that, Kione?"

"I retreated into madness until I found the one who sold me the cloak." He stared at Fin. "The bargain is struck." Then he looked at Lia and Utah, careful not to make eye contact. "I owe you."

"Tor is waiting in the hall. He'll find a shirt and jacket for you." Fin's color was returning.

"I'll accept the shirt, but the cloak stays with me." He picked it up. "I can't take the chance of losing it." A pause. "I'll need it again once Seven is gone."

He didn't smile as he turned to leave the room. "I'll wait for you outside. I need to be alone for a while. I don't even remember the last time I didn't feel pain, and I want to see what the world looks like without it."

Utah fought to maintain cold detachment. He couldn't do it. And that scared him. All these emotions—desire for Lia, sympathy for Kione, worry for Fin—were messing with his main agenda. He didn't want *anything* to dilute his hatred for all things vampire.

Utah didn't watch Kione leave. He studied Fin. "Are you okay?"

Fin nodded. "Thanks to both of you for pitching in. The pain was more than I expected."

Lia shuddered, and Utah tightened his grip on her shoulders. He felt the exact moment when she gathered herself together, when she didn't need him anymore. He dropped his arm, and found he regretted the loss.

"Well, that was an experience. Never want to repeat it." She brushed a few strands of hair away from her face. "I have a few things to do in my room. Give a shout when you need me."

How about now? Utah bit his bottom lip and concentrated on the pain. Sex wasn't on the afternoon's agenda.

Fin nodded.

She didn't glance at Utah as she left the room. He watched the sway of her hips with unblinking intensity. His beast also watched. For once they were on the same page.

When he finally forced his thoughts away from Lia and into the moment, Utah realized Fin was watching him.

"I don't give a damn about Adam's rogue, but you have to keep him happy. So I think we can combine the search for the vampire with the one for Seven."

"You're going to follow up on Seir's tip?"

"Yes."

"You trust Seir?"

"No. But that doesn't mean I can afford to ignore any leads, even from him." Fin wrapped his fingers around his coffee cup. "The heat feels good. Pain is too damn cold."

"I'm listening."

"I looked up Burnside Bridge online. It's right in the geographical center of Portland. A good jumping-off spot for any place in the city. Seven would be smart to headquarter near there. We know that Seven is recruiting nonhumans. I'd be willing to bet that a lot of the missing vampires are going to Seven and not to Adam's rogue." He turned to stare out the window, his reflection forming a silver halo framed by darkness.

Utah wasn't into symbolism, but the reflection seemed somehow fitting. "So let's hear your idea."

Fin motioned him over to an open laptop sitting on a side table. "I pulled up records showing where the biggest recent spike in homicides has been. It's probably a lot more than the police know because most of the bodies haven't been found." He pointed to a spot on the Google Map filling the screen. "There. Burnside Bridge. We'll do a sweep and see how many vampires we catch in our net. And if we bag a few other entities, that's fine too. Seven isn't just recruiting vampires. And if we find Adam's Chris, it's icing on the cake. But information about Seven is our priority."

"And how do we catch a lot at one time?"

Fin shut down the computer. "We provide bait."

Utah raised one brow. "Bait?"

Fin's smile flashed as he turned away. "Us."

CHAPTER SEVEN

Lia couldn't remember when she fell down the rabbit hole, but it must've been back at the condo when Utah said they were personally baiting the trap to catch some vampires.

All because Fin's brother gave them a tip. The brother he didn't trust because Fin didn't trust anyone. It made perfect sense.

Now here she was, wedged into Fin's SUV with Kione, Utah, Fin, Tor, Q, and Lio.

Were they crazy? She tapped Fin on the shoulder. "Do you really think any vampires will be stupid enough to attack you guys?"

"Yes." Fin never took his eyes off the road. "I never underestimate the stupidity of others."

She wasn't sure if that was an insult to the intelligence of all vampires or just Fin being overconfident. "Adam won't be too happy if you start messing with his guys."

"I called Adam before we left the condo. I told him to keep the people he trusted away from the Burnside Bridge tonight."

"And he went for your idea?"

Fin's strange silver eyes gleamed at her in the mirror. "Adam is arrogant and vicious, but he's not stupid. He saw the advantage of letting us take all the risks."

Lia sat back in her seat. She watched the shapes of darkened buildings whiz by in the night. And thought about Utah. She might not be looking at him, but every sensitized inch of her body was aware of him seated next to her. When she turned her head, he was staring at her.

"I think you should stay in the SUV." Utah's expression said he was ready for her hit.

In the seat behind him, Tor chuckled. "Man, you have some kind of death wish."

She took a deep calming breath. "I have my sword, my gun, and a lifetime spent studying how to fight vampires. I've survived other battles. I can handle this."

"This won't be about brains. It'll be about speed and brute strength." Utah looked frustrated. "I don't think—"

"I don't care what you think. I want to be part of this." *Need to be part of it.* Just one more proving ground. For a moment, she wondered why she had to keep showing Katherine that she was worthy. Her dead mother didn't care. *But I care. Will always care.* And in a flash of insight, she recognized her obsession for what it was. Bet she'd blow someone's mind if she ever took this to a shrink.

Utah touched her arm, and she almost jumped out of her seat.

"A little nervous?" His grin was a flash of hotness that took her mind off her neuroses. "Just want you to know that I'll be close by if you need me."

Lia wanted to show him a hard, kickass face, but her lips kept quirking up. He'd walked into this one. "I'll remember that. I mean, if I *need* you. For *anything.*" She looked at him from under her lashes.

His expression changed. Those blue eyes heated and he gripped his bottom lip between his teeth. Then he released it. She stared unblinking at the full wet sheen of it, imagined its taste as she slid the tip of her tongue across it. She raised her gaze to his.

He smiled. It was a slow, sensual peeling back of layer after layer of reasons that she should back off this man, leaving the bare truth exposed. She wanted him in her bed, in his bed, or on the floor, if that's what kick-started him. She wanted him naked, stretched the length of her body, touching every inch of her with his bared flesh. And if they went up in flames, so be it. Extreme pleasure had its price.

"This is it." Fin pulled into a darkened side street.

Thank you, God. Lia wouldn't have lasted another city block.

She climbed out to find Utah by her side. They listened to Fin.

"We'll spread out. But stay near the bridge. Try to look down and out, nonthreatening. We don't want anyone sensing what we are until it's too late for them to run. And remember, this is all about capturing not killing." He glanced around him. "There's a skateboarding park under the bridge, but no one should be there now. I'll make sure no homeless are sleeping close by."

Everyone had on dark clothes, even Fin. He wore a hoodie and had pulled the hood as far forward as he could. No one would notice his silver hair unless they got real close. And if they got that close, it was too late for them anyway. Lia shoved her hands in her coat pockets to warm them. The solid feel of her gun calmed her.

Kione hadn't said a thing since leaving the condo. He'd put on a shirt, but still wore his cloak. "I don't know how to look 'nonthreatening.' I choose not to pretend to be prey." He faded into the night.

Fin didn't seem upset by his departure.

Q glanced at the sky. He appeared eager to be gone. "Why did you decide to tag along tonight? We could've handled a bunch of vampires."

Lia wasn't sure of that. No matter how powerful they were in predator form, they were vulnerable as humans.

Fin scanned the darkness. "I'm here to keep humans away from the area. That means stopping bridge traffic. We don't need witnesses." He paused. "Besides, there's always the chance that Seven will show."

Lia spoke up. "But your vision—"

"My vision showed a possible solution. It wasn't proof that Seven wouldn't kick all your asses along the way. I don't want to be ticking off names on my active roster."

"Got it." She shifted her feet, anxious to be moving. It had started raining again.

They ghosted toward the bridge. How could large men move so silently? Lia had always thought she was quiet, but she was a rhino tap-dancing on a tin roof compared with these guys.

Somewhere along the way, Q freed his Quetzalcoatlus soul. He took to the sky on giant wings. The biggest flying animal that ever existed—she'd done her research—his shadow would have blocked out the moon if there'd been one.

When they reached the Willamette River, Lio disappeared. Liopleurodon. Even looking at an artist's representation of the eighty-foot-long sea predator gave her chills.

That left Fin, Tor, Utah, and her. Fin took a moment to switch off all the lights in the area. Great. She loved the challenge of fighting blind.

Finally, Fin left too.

They were in the shadow of the bridge by now. No one spoke as they separated. Utah threw her a hard look that promised he'd be near and dared her to make a big deal out of it. She almost found his protectiveness endearing. Was she really that into him? Uh, yeah.

Lia settled down with her back to the wall of the skateboarding park. She rested her sword by her side and had her gun hidden in her lap. Then she tried to look nonthreatening.

It seemed like she'd waited forever. Again and again, she'd forced her mind away from thoughts of Utah. Distractions got you dead.

And just when she'd decided the night was a loss, they came. They glided out of the darkness, black on black, moving like shadows but so fast the human eye could barely follow their paths. Silent. Deadly.

But Lia had lived her life among them. She maintained her I-am-clueless-prey body language while reaching for her sword. She pointed it upward, ready to skewer the first vampire who saw her as a juicy treat. She moved her gun from her lap to her side. The safety was already off. Finally, she eased a syringe from her other pocket. The only time she needed it was when death wasn't the desired outcome.

Lia had done this enough times to feel pretty confident. Vampires never expected their victims to fight back.

She didn't worry overmuch about striking a

killing blow, just one that would take her attacker down long enough for her to pump the industrial strength tranquilizer into his or her neck. Then let the questioning begin.

The vampires moved too fast for her to get an accurate count. Maybe a dozen. *Too many.* There'd have to be a freaking seventy-percent-off-all-humans sale to draw this kind of vampire interest.

A double-cross by Adam? No, he had nothing to gain. Who else would . . . ? Seir. Could be. There didn't seem to be lots of brotherly love happening between Fin and him.

Lia gathered herself. She watched the vampires pause before reaching their supposed victims. They *knew.*

But the knowing didn't help them. They thought they were a safe distance away. They weren't. Utah and Tor exploded from their crouched positions, changing in mid-leap.

The vampires had numbers on their side, but they didn't have the pure savagery and pack skills that Utah and Tor had. And no one must have told them that the Eleven in their animal forms were just about indestructible.

Lia searched for Utah, but she couldn't tell which one was he in the darkness. She edged closer, always making sure her back was to a solid surface.

Death was dressed in basic black tonight, but it couldn't have been any more gruesome if it were in high definition and living color.

The raptor nearer her leaped onto a vampire. Gripping his victim with razor-sharp teeth, he held the vampire in place with hooked claws. Then he shredded the vampire with his sicklelike toe claws. Quick, efficient, bloody.

The coppery scent wrapped around Lia at the same time as blood splattered her exposed hands and face. She wiped her face with the arm of her coat and kept creeping closer. This wasn't the first time she'd been within splashing distance of death. It came with her life as Katherine's daughter.

She did draw the line at watching the raptor rip the head from what remained of the vampire. Lia turned away . . . in time to see that at least one of the vampires had come armed with something other than his arrogance.

He'd pulled out a gun and was aiming it at the raptor. He wouldn't score a kill, but he'd slow down his target. Lia didn't hesitate. She raised her gun and fired. A head shot. The vampire's scream was cut short as the second raptor removed said head from his shoulders.

The raptors drew the vampires from under the bridge to where Q could reach them. His screams echoed eerily over the water. The vampires weren't prepared for an aerial assault.

One of the vampires evidently didn't like how the battle was shaking out. He decided to swim home. The monster that rose from the river to take him sucked the breath from Lia's body. It was one thing to read about Lio's ferocity and eight-inch-long teeth, but it was something else entirely to see what he could do with one bite.

She cursed the darkness. Lia figured the raptor that stayed closer to her was Utah. She needed to see his human form within the predator to remind herself that this was really Utah, not a bad take from *Jurassic Park*.

Lia shifted her gaze long enough to wonder why none of the vampires had come for her. *Hey, easy kill over here.* And as if conjured from her thoughts, a dark shape raced toward her.

He never reached her. A raptor took him down right in front of Lia. She frowned. There was something she needed to remember. She did a quick scan of the area. Torn and decapitated vampires everywhere. These weren't the powerful of the vampire world. Adam or Jude wouldn't have gone down so easily. And now Utah or Tor was about to kill one of the last. Oh crap. Fin would be ticked if they didn't keep at least one of these guys alive.

Raising her syringe, she leaped at the vampire. The raptor lowered its head and shoved her away. She sat down hard and rolled to avoid the bodies.

Still clutching the syringe, she watched the battle in unblinking horror. The vampire had managed to crawl onto the raptor's back. He sank his fangs into Utah's neck. And yes, she was sure after his head bump that it was Utah. Tor would probably have just mowed her down.

The vampire was hurting Utah. Now wasn't the time for self-analysis, but she couldn't stop her thoughts. Why didn't she feel any kinship with the vampire? He was putting up a hell of a fight. He could be any one of her people from back in Philly. But his blood-smeared face and dripping fangs froze her inside. Was she looking at her future?

Lia switched her attention to Utah. He swung his head and gripped the vampire's leg between those deadly teeth. She winced at the snap of breaking bone. The vampire screamed.

She knew what to expect once he dragged the vampire off his back. Lia had seen him do it with the last vampire. He'd claw out the vampire's stomach, then rip his head off.

Glancing past Utah, she saw Tor methodically tearing apart the last vampire standing. The two raptors, Q, and Lio hadn't accounted for all the carnage. Kione must be doing his part too.

She scooted back to avoid the spreading pool of blood. Damn. Everyone had gotten carried away. This would be a waste if they ended up with no one to question.

Lia forced herself to focus on Utah, the way he was now, with his soul in complete control. She'd bet even if the light was better she wouldn't be able to see his human form within his beast. There was no human left in him, in any of them.

Take a good look. If she wanted the man, then she also had to accept this part of him. Could she?

More to the point, should she want someone she'd have to walk away from in a short time?

Utah had finally dislodged the vampire. *The last one.* Clutching her syringe, she ran at the raptor again. There was only one way to do this. And she hoped to God that Utah was alive and aware inside the monster.

She waved her hand in the raptor's face. Then without giving herself time to worry about whether he'd rip her apart to get to his victim, she leaned down and emptied the syringe into the dazed vampire's neck.

Lia felt the raptor's hot breath on her neck and shuddered. She straightened and stared into the beast's eyes. So *much* bloodlust. "Back the hell off, Utah. We need at least one of them alive to question."

Since she wasn't suicidal, she crept slowly backward, keeping her eyes fixed on the raptor.

So she didn't see the woman who appeared beside her.

"You wanted to know why none of the vampires attacked you. Okay, one did, but he paid for not obeying instructions. I told everyone to ignore any humans and concentrate on the Eleven."

"What?" Lia spun to face her.

"This was a costly raiding party. I arrived too late to save any of my people. But that's an acceptable trade, because I'll have you as well as one of the Eleven to take home."

Lia had an impression of long dark hair and a pale face before she felt a light touch on her cheek, and then everything went black.

Utah's beast forgot about the vampire at his feet. A woman was standing beside Lia. The woman touched her, and Lia just disappeared. He leaped for the bitch. She met his gaze and suddenly, he was flung back into human form. That didn't slow him down, though.

But even Utah's rage couldn't keep Fin out of his head. *"Back off. I'm coming."*

The hell with that. Nothing mattered but getting to the woman and making her return Lia.

"Utah. No!" Fin appeared about twenty feet away from him.

Utah didn't listen. He reached the woman and grabbed for her. Instead of doing the expected and either running from him or attacking, she simply touched his hand.

Fin was the last thing Utah saw. His hood had fallen off and his silver hair whipped around his face. But his eyes weren't fixed on Utah. He stared at the woman.

Utah carried the image of Fin's shocked recognition into the darkness.

"Such a fierce and beautiful animal."

The soft croon was accompanied by the cool slide of fingers along Utah's jaw. Female. Unfamiliar. He lay still, absorbing the feel of his surroundings, the woman next to him. What the hell had happened? He reached for Fin with his mind. Nothing.

The memories came—the vampires, a woman beside Lia, Fin's face, and then blackness.

Lia. She'd disappeared. Utah opened his eyes.

The woman leaning over him smiled. "So aggressive. So *alive.*"

As opposed to dead like her? Utah controlled his instinct to attack. That hadn't worked well the first time he'd tried it.

He held completely still, not even breathing, as she trailed one finger down his throat. She paused where his pulse beat so hard she had to hear it.

Where was Lia? He didn't dare take his eyes from the woman to look around.

"I have a lust for living things, my gorgeous one. I just drink them up."

"Then they're dead." Way to go, Captain Obvious.

The woman's eyes widened for a second and then she laughed—husky and warm. He could see her fangs.

"I keep my favorites alive. I sip from them and savor their unique flavors." She leaned down and trailed her tongue over his pounding pulse. "It would be a sin to gulp someone as wonderful as you."

So he wouldn't die right now. That was something. He tried to move his arms. Restrained. Figured.

"What happened to the woman you took?" He had to know.

"Lia?" She leaned back to study him. "She's quite an exciting acquisition. A human leader of vampires. I think I'll keep her too. But of course I've attached a few conditions in her case."

What conditions? At least she was still alive. Time to find out something about his captor. "Who're you?"

She looked delighted that he'd asked. "I'm Christine. Which one of the Eleven are you?"

"Utah." He narrowed his gaze. This must be Lia's Chris. Her vampire hadn't gotten the whole name out. If Christine weren't a vampire bitch, he'd have to admit she was beautiful. There was nothing subtle about her. Long black hair, pale skin, almost black eyes, and full red lips. "How do you know about the Eleven?"

"Seir." Amusement touched her eyes. "He explained all about 2012 and the immortals you're hunting." She shrugged. "I really don't understand why you're trying to protect humans. What have they really done for this planet? It's time for another species to have a chance."

"Did he mention why he was helping you?" Utah took stock of his surroundings. He was resting on some kind of cot. He tried to rock it. No luck. Must be bolted down. The room was tiny and bare except for one chair. Not large enough for his raptor.

"I got the impression he didn't like your leader."

She pushed her hair away from her face. "Do you mind if I just take a little taste?"

Her smile promised he'd enjoy every sip she took. And if not for Rap, he probably would have.

"I can't stop you." But he was tempted to try. He clamped down on the impulse. Better to wait until he had space to free his beast.

Her laughter sounded wickedly delighted and as sexy as hell. He wasn't tempted.

"You're right, but I like to give those I treasure a feeling of empowerment."

"Just do it." He ground his teeth against his need to fight, to shout and curse at her. Memories of Rap's death rolled over him. Still raw, still agonizing.

Christine didn't need a second invite. With a small purr of pleasure, she grabbed his hair and tilted his head back, baring his throat.

And when he felt the sharp prick of her fangs, he tensed; refusing to give in to the pleasure her feeding offered him, focusing only on the pain, on his hate, on *Lia*.

When she finally released him and leaned back, he watched her. She licked his blood from her lips. His beast didn't find that revolting. In fact, his beast thought he should return the favor by breaking his bindings and tearing out her throat. His beast was into primitive payback, no higher-level thinking skills needed.

That's why he needed to keep his soul safely tucked in its cave. Teeth and claws alone wouldn't get Lia and him out of here. He'd bet Christine had lots more like her on the other side of that door. He'd choose his moment. "Why not free my hands and feet? I'm not going anywhere."

She raised one brow.

Utah swallowed his fury and said what needed saying. He couldn't jeopardize Lia's safety by indulging his temper. "Oh, come on. My raptor wouldn't fit in here, so I won't be turning my beast loose on you. And I can feel your power. I don't think I'll be much danger to you in my human form." The truth. Her power almost suffocated him in this small space. If she was Adam's competition, then he might as well pack his bags and leave town.

She thought about that for a moment and then released him. "Perhaps when we get to know each other a little better, you might see the advantage of working for me instead of Fin."

"Could happen." Utah forced thoughts of admiration, awe, and good old-fashioned fear to the forefront of his mind. With her power, he didn't doubt for a moment that she was rooting around in his brain. He didn't try to keep her out. That would just make her more suspicious and more determined to crack his code.

"What about Lia?" He didn't want to sound like he was begging, but . . . he was begging.

Christine's smile returned. "She's fine. I'm not a complete barbarian. I'll have her brought here after she's had a chance to clean up." Her smile widened. "Perhaps I'll help you clean up"—she slid her gaze the length of his body—"after I've taken care of a few things."

Utah watched her rise and move to the door. He locked his muscles to keep from leaping at her while he thought nonthreatening thoughts.

As soon as she left, he tested the door. Throwing himself at it and kicking had no effect. And since she hadn't left a crowbar lying around, he was forced to give up the effort, at least for now.

A short time later, someone opened the door, pushed Lia inside, and relocked it. She just stood there staring at him.

Utah controlled his impulse to rush over and wrap his arms around her, to hold her close and absorb the warm realness of her. *Safe.* He wanted to promise that she'd always be safe with him. But he didn't know if he could keep that promise, didn't know if she'd appreciate his insinuation that she couldn't keep herself safe.

He didn't move. Something about the way she looked stopped him. She seemed brittle, as though even a touch might shatter her. Not fear. Something else.

What had Christine done to her? Her coat and weapons were gone. "Come over and sit down." He patted the seat beside him on the cot.

She seemed to shudder, but then she walked over and sat next to him. "You're okay. I was afraid . . ." Her voice trailed off as she ran her finger over his throat. "She bit you."

"Yeah. It's nothing. The vampire bitch thinks I'm pretty awesome, so she decided to keep me in working order by just taking a few sips." He was trying to make light of it, to show Lia it was no big deal, nothing for her to get upset about.

She didn't react the way he'd expected. "Vampire bitch? Is that one word or two?"

Her tone warned him to tread carefully. There was something here he didn't understand. He shrugged. "Do you want me to call her something else?"

"Christine. You can call her Christine." She lowered her head and knuckled her eyes. "Oh hell. Call her vampire bitch if you want. It doesn't matter."

"What happened?" Utah couldn't keep his hands from her. He put his arms around her and pulled her close. She'd shed her coat somewhere, and he could feel her shoulders tighten. She was so slight next to his bulk. But she fought big, so he tended to forget her size. He tried to ignore his surge of protectiveness.

For a moment, she remained stiff in his embrace, but then she relaxed against him with a sigh.

They sat that way for a while. Utah smoothed his fingers over her hair. The damp Portland air had turned it into a riot of curls. He waited. She'd tell him when she was ready.

While he waited, he thought. He hadn't wanted to like her, and he sure as hell hadn't wanted to admire her. Those kinds of feelings made things tougher in the end, because he'd bet anything that Adam had tagged her to kill him when his usefulness was over. It made sense. She'd be the one with the best chance of catching him off guard, and Utah figured Adam was the kind of guy who went with the odds. When she made her move, he'd have to . . .

Utah wouldn't have hesitated over that word a week ago. Now? He'd have to find an alternative, because he couldn't kill her.

Lia sighed, and his attention snapped back to her.

"She took me to another room something like this. Seemed like a storeroom of some kind with a bunch of gardening tools." Lia didn't look at him as she spoke. "Christine explained that she didn't have any use for humans in her grand scheme of things, but that I fascinated her. A human leader of vampires. I was unique, and she liked unique. So she offered me a deal."

Utah tightened his grip on her. He'd hate this deal, whatever it was.

"Christine has big plans. Portland won't be able to hold her. She definitely wants Adam's job. So she'll need strong regional leaders she can count on."

"She offered you a job?" That wasn't bad. All they had to do was play along until Fin found them. And he *would* find them. Utah didn't doubt that.

"Sort of." Lia ran her hand absently along his thigh.

Utah sucked in his breath. Nothing like the danger of imminent death to trigger all kinds of appetites.

Lia stilled. She moved her hand from his thigh. He knew she sensed the need building in him. Was she afraid her touch would release his beast? Did she expect him to pounce on her? He smiled. Could happen. At least the pouncing part. She was safe from his soul, though. He'd bound it in chains forged from his will. At least the physical manifestation of his beast.

Utah felt his smile fade. She didn't trust his control. Smart woman. Because his control was a tenuous thing at its best. At its worst? He thought back to the vampires he'd just destroyed. Not once had he considered letting them live until Lia got in his face.

He met her gaze. She didn't look away.

"Make love to me, Utah."

CHAPTER EIGHT

Lia watched him, searching for a clue to his thoughts. His expression didn't change, but his eyes swam with conflicting emotions: shock, desire, suspicion.

"Now? Here?" Utah's voice gave away nothing of what he felt.

"Yes." She wasn't about to try to explain, because that would lead to a lie. Lia hoped he wouldn't muddy things up with lots of talk.

"Why?" He got up to pace, back and forth from the door to her in two quick strides, each step almost crackling with suppressed energy.

Now things got tricky. "Maybe the last few hours reminded me of my mortality. Maybe I don't want to pass over to the other side with unfinished business."

"That would be me?" He looked puzzled.

If that crease between his incredible eyes wasn't so cute, she'd probably plant her fist right there. How could he not realize what she was trying to say?

"Maybe I want to go out with a smile on my face." No smiling going on now, just a you-big-doofus glare.

He glanced at the door.

"No one will pop in anytime soon." Christine would take a while locating her guy and then convincing him to pay a visit.

When Utah looked back at her, something hot and hungry glowed in his eyes.

Lia shivered. It was a good shiver, the kind you got right before opening the present you'd waited forever for. "And before you ask, yes, you're the only one who can put that smile on my face." She stood to emphasize her point.

There was one chair in the room. Without comment, he picked it up and wedged it under the doorknob.

She had time for only a startled squeak before he reached her and backed her against the wall.

He leaned in close, his breath warm on her neck, his words hot and impatient. "We both want you, but I don't think we'll all fit on that little cot."

Lia surrendered to her need. She reached up to run her fingers through his hair, concentrating on the silky flow of it, storing the memory away. "Who's going to have time to lie down?"

His soft laughter nestled close to her heart. It was a thing to be nurtured because it was so rare.

He shrugged out of his jacket and let it fall to the floor.

"It's amazing how the threat of death brings everything into focus, makes it all more intense, more urgent." She glided her hands up his arms and across his broad shoulders. His muscles bunched beneath her fingers.

"Not for me, sweetheart."

He kissed the sensitive skin right behind her ear, and she made a small sound of pleasure. Lia abandoned his shoulders to sneak her hands under his shirt and massage a path down his back. Smooth. Sexy. Lia figured she'd die of pheromone fever if she kept touching him. But hey, everyone had to die sometime.

"I've felt this way since . . ." He paused to suck in his breath as she worked her fingers down the back of his jeans to cup his ass.

"Hmm? Since when?" She dug her fingers into his flesh, craving the realness, not caring if she left her desire imprinted on him. Lia smiled. He wouldn't be showing his luscious butt to any of the Eleven with her fingerprints branding him.

"Since the first time I saw you." Utah seemed surprised by his words.

Her fierce joy surprised Lia.

"You're a dangerous woman." He nipped gently at her earlobe and then kissed a path down the side of her neck. "I like that. A woman with a gun and sword makes me hard."

She muffled her laughter against his chest. Her amusement faded as she felt the pounding of his heart. There was nothing calm or contained about it. The heart didn't lie.

And while she was contemplating his heartbeat, he was busy doing other things. Utah tugged at the bottom of her shirt, and she reluctantly abandoned his gorgeous butt to raise her arms. He slipped it off in one swift movement along with her bra. Then he stripped off his own shirt.

"Wait. Not getting equal access here." She laid claim to his belt.

"Then you'd better move fast." He flicked his tongue across one nipple at the same time he somehow removed her pants.

Her panties were gone before she even had his jeans peeled down to mid-thigh. But Lia didn't complain because she was enjoying the thrill of discovery too much. "No underwear?"

"Underwear isn't natural." He emphasized his point by nudging her panties out of the way with his toe while running his hands over her stomach and hips.

"Neither are jeans." She finally was able to slide them down his legs. When had he gotten rid of his boots?

He stepped out of his jeans. "Yeah, but sitting

in a jail cell doesn't feel natural either. So I'll put up with them."

Lia lost track of the jeans discussion as he braced his hands against the wall on either side of her and leaned in. He took her mouth in a long, drugging kiss.

She wanted to savor the sensations, but there were too damn many of them. The texture of his tongue against hers, aggressively male. His taste. Nothing as dull as toothpaste. He tasted of the elemental and dangerous, of something that beckoned to the wild child in her.

He moved closer until they touched, fused from chest to thigh, forming a searing path of want that dried her mouth and turned the rest of her into a pliable conduit for anything he chose to do.

And as she concentrated on the pleasure-pain of her supersensitive nipples scraping across his skin, he whispered in her ear.

"You scare me." He didn't sound happy about the admission.

His warm breath touched nerve endings that raced the length of her body to trigger responses in other places. The lights flicked on in all her secret spots. She clenched her thighs, trying to maximize the sensation.

"How?" She was only half concentrating on his answer because she'd managed to work her hand between their bodies and was tracing a line with her fingers over his hard stomach down, down, down.

"You make me . . ."

He simply stopped breathing as she reached her destination. Lia smoothed her fingers along the long, hard length of him. Utah shuddered against her. She cupped each sac, lightly tracing small circles of invitation with her fingernail before going on to the next.

"I make you what?" She was having some breathing problems of her own.

"Feel." He breathed the word out on a long exhalation.

Lia muffled her laughter against his muscular chest. "Hate to break it to you, but I think it'd be pretty tough not to feel, considering." She gently squeezed his sacs.

"Don't mock me, woman." He emphasized his fake ferocity by putting enough space between them so that he could reach his target.

He traced a path of hot anticipation around one breast with the tip of his finger before lowering his head. She couldn't stop a small moan of joy as he closed his lips over her nipple and showed her the cost of that mockery. *Please, please keep going while I think up more mockery.*

Her world narrowed to one tiny point on her body. He scraped his teeth lightly across the sensitized nub before sliding his tongue back and forth, back and forth until she wanted to scream. She bit her lip to stop anything from escaping. The sound of too much enjoyment might annoy Christine's minions.

But when he closed his lips tightly over the nipple and showed her the true meaning of "tease," she had to *do* something or else explode messily all over him.

Tangling her fingers in his hair, she guided him to her other nipple. "You supersize *my* feelings, raptor." She'd meant it to come out light and playful, but she recognized the desperation beneath the words. Lia was feeling too much right now, but she couldn't stem the rising tide. She was in danger of drowning.

"Have. To. Explain." Between each word, he worked his way down her body, kissing and nibbling an erratic path that threatened to wander off course a few times.

She lost her grip on his hair, so she simply anchored herself by grabbing his shoulders.

"In my other life . . ." He dropped to his knees in front of her.

Lia spread her legs. Wanting. Needing. And God help him if he disappointed her.

". . . sex was the flash of a camera. It lit one scene, one *moment*. Then it was done. No thoughts attached. Sensations limited to that one flash." He broke off his explanation to lick a warm path up the inside of her thigh.

And everything inside her ran molten, burning new pathways for her senses to follow. Her legs trembled, and she couldn't stop them.

"Now, I *feel*. Not just with all my senses, but up here." He tapped the side of his head.

He *didn't* tap his chest. Lia's heart gave a sad, dejected thump. Dumb heart. Expecting things that weren't going to happen. Didn't *want* them to happen. Her heart would just complicate things.

And as he raised his gaze to meet hers, she memorized the exact shade of his eyes and how his long lashes were so much darker than his hair. Just in case . . . She refused to finish that thought.

"What're you thinking?"

His voice was soft, husky, and so erotic she almost forgot what he'd asked.

"I'm thinking that years from now they'll find my remains, just a pathetic little cinder cone, all that'll be left of Mount Saint Lia."

"Your words are expanding my feeling field. They've gotten all the way to here." He reached between his thighs and wrapped his fingers around his cock.

Lia felt his touch between her own thighs. And as he slid his fingers over his erection, her body responded. She was damp, her yearning so deep she almost reached down to stroke herself to ease the pressure building and building. Who knew? She'd heard of a meeting of minds, but this was . . . insane.

Then she forgot about everything as he leaned forward and *touched* her with his tongue.

Her knees buckled, and the only thing that kept her from collapsing in a boneless heap was his firm grasp of her hips.

He teased the swollen nub that was the center of

her being right now. And each flick of his tongue set off a mini eruption. Her personal magma flow rose closer and closer to the surface. Any minute now she'd blow the top off her mountain.

Lia signaled the imminent explosion in a fevered whisper. "Now, now, *now*."

Utah rose in one lithe motion. Then he nudged her legs farther apart with his knee. "Sure you're ready?" Pressing tightly against her ready switch, he rubbed his knee back and forth to make sure.

Bastard. She rode his knee as she raked her nails down his hard, sweat-sheened chest. "I'll. Kill. You." As awesome as his knee was, it wasn't a substitute for—

Without warning, he clasped her bottom and lifted her. She braced her back against the wall and grabbed his shoulders to steady herself. Then she wrapped her legs around his hips.

He slowly lowered her onto his cock.

Lia closed her eyes and *felt*—the stretching, the filling, the friction, the . . .

Her eyes popped open. He'd been right. Her mind wanted in on the action. Because without her mind, every feeling simply had a "the" in front of it. She needed *him* in every one of those thoughts.

His hair clung damply to his face, framing all his savage beauty. He stared at her, his eyes so dilated they almost looked black. She could see herself reflected in them—hair wildly tousled, eyes heavy-lidded, and lips parted.

She smiled. "Let's dance, raptor."

Utah returned her smile, only his was a lot more erotically charged. "Hang on." His words promised a lot of hot, sweaty action. She tightened her grip on him.

She'd thought he'd filled her completely. Lia was wrong. With a powerful upward thrust, he buried himself in her. She gasped as she wiggled her bottom around to get optimum stimulus. Now it was his turn to gasp.

He lifted her slowly off his shaft. She clenched around him, resisting, resisting. His muscles flexed with his effort. Finally, he lowered her again, and she felt as though she was coming home.

He picked up the rhythm—lift, lower, lift, lower. Each time he lowered her, he thrust. And each thrust dragged a moan from her. She wouldn't survive all the delicious friction.

The pressure built in her belly, heat and heaviness pressing down, gathering itself, waiting for the moment when she couldn't contain it one more second.

What if this is the only time?

No, no, no. Now wasn't the time for her mind to betray her. She pushed the thought aside and dived back into the rhythm of sex.

His thrusts were coming faster and faster. She'd wrapped her arms around him, and everything was a blur of sensation. The feel of him inside her touched, touched . . . A lot more places than she could describe. The touching drove her into a frenzy, made her claw his back and clamp her teeth into his shoulder to anchor herself to Earth.

What if this is the only time?

Oh damn. Not that again. She'd just have to work past it. Lia didn't wait for him to thrust. She rose off his cock and then slammed back down. Again, and again, and again.

Now, now, now! She stopped breathing as her orgasm took her and shook her like a giant castanet. Oh. My. God. The spasms went on and on even as she sensed Utah shuddering in the throes of his own climax. *This.* This was worth dying for.

And as she clung to his body, the waves of intense pleasure fading in ever-widening circles, she realized she was crying.

What if this is the only time?

The hell with Utah's theory about feeling with your thoughts. She wasn't inviting her mind to her next party.

When Utah finally lowered her to her feet, she had to hang on to him for a minute. She was that weak. Neither of them said anything as they quickly dressed.

Lia kept her head down, even when he guided her to the cot and pulled her down beside him. She wouldn't let him see her tears. Tears she didn't understand.

But she should've known she couldn't keep anything from him. He tilted her face up and just looked at her. Then he wiped the tears from under her eyes with his finger.

"What do you fear, Lia?"

Lia had believed she feared nothing. Well, she'd revisited that belief. "You." *What if this is the only time?*

He wrapped his arms around her, holding her close against the demons haunting her tonight, and filled the silence with his chaotic thoughts. They had to get out of here. He had to protect her. What the hell did all these emotions mean? And how had he allowed this woman to push ahead of Rap in his mind, his *heart*? No, not his heart. Not yet. But it was getting close. Too close. He couldn't let that happen, and if he thought about it long enough, he'd remember why.

But he steered clear of what he really wanted to know. Why did she fear *him*? He'd expected her to say she feared Christine. Understandable. Was it all about his beast? He didn't think so.

He didn't get a chance to give in to temptation and ask why because someone tried to open the door.

"Damn." Utah leaped from the cot and reached the door in one stride. "Who is it?"

"Christine. I assume you're trying to keep me out. It won't work."

"Didn't think it would." May as well let the bitch in. He moved the chair from the door and backed away.

But it wasn't Christine who came through the door first. As the door was pushed open, someone shoved Jude into the room. Christine stood outside with several of her people.

Utah stared at them. Not vampire. What were they?

Christine smiled and waved at him. "They're werewolves. Strong and able to run errands during the day. Very useful."

Utah would've commented on the strangeness of that if Adam wasn't using Kione and him. Evidently, vampires were equal opportunity employers.

"I'll leave you three here for a nice cozy chat while I get things ready for the big event." Christine winked at Lia. "I hope you're worth it, Lia. Jude took a lot of persuading."

Jude glared at her. Utah could see new blood on the vampire's clothes. The wounds must've already healed.

No one said anything until Christine closed the door. Then Jude flung himself at the door, but it didn't budge.

"Already tried that." Utah returned to his seat on the cot beside Lia. She rested her hand on his thigh. She'd grown pale. This was a tough night for everyone. "Why are you here, Jude?"

Jude took a moment to examine a tear in his jacket, but Utah suspected he was taking time to think about what he wanted to say.

Finally, he switched his attention from his jacket to Lia. "You didn't tell him?"

Utah didn't like the sound of that. He stared at Lia. She wouldn't meet his gaze.

"I told you that Christine wants me to work for her." Exhaustion seemed to pull apart each word. Lia leaned back against the wall.

Utah nodded.

"Just not as a human."

It took a moment for the implication to sink in. "Explain."

"If I become vampire, she'll hire me."

"And if not?" His beast sensed his anger and inched toward the cave entrance.

Lia shrugged. "I die."

The silence pounded at Utah. He wanted to drive it away with his roar of fury. *Control. Calm.* "How much time did she give you to think about it?"

"Until she could get Jude here. I told her I wanted him to be my maker." She cast Jude an accusing stare. "Thought you'd put up more of a fight."

"Did my best, babe." But Jude wasn't looking at Lia. He was watching Utah.

Utah figured the vampire knew where the real danger lay.

Lia didn't seem to realize she was digging her nails into his thigh, but Utah welcomed the pain. It provided a distraction. He needed that right now. His soul wanted out, and it didn't care that the room wasn't big enough, or that he'd crush Lia and Jude in the process. All it wanted was a shot at Christine.

"We'll figure this out. It won't come to that." Utah's mind skittered down dozens of corridors, all dead ends.

She finally looked at him. No emotion showed in her eyes. "Don't do anything that'll get you killed. Fin needs you alive."

What about you? Do you need me alive?

"I was going to become vampire anyway. This is just moving the schedule up a little." She might as well have been discussing a change in her dentist appointment for all the feeling in her voice.

Utah knew this had to be her way of coping with what Christine was forcing on her, and everyone coped in different ways. His way was to go out and kill something. But God, he'd like to hear a little more horror in her voice.

Utah turned to Jude, who'd planted himself in the chair and looked about as dangerous as a vampire could look. "Can you fake turning her?" Yeah, he was grasping at straws.

Jude smiled, but it didn't reach his eyes. "Not a chance. It's pretty tough to fake draining someone and then giving her your blood. I think Christine would catch on."

Utah was starting to feel desperate. He'd always been a top-of-the-food-chain guy. He wasn't used to this feeling of helplessness. He turned back to

Lia. "Tell Christine you want me there when it happens. She said she was getting things ready, so it won't happen in this room." Maybe the space would be bigger. His beast would find a way to stop it. Hell, even if it wasn't bigger, he'd fight in human form. Whatever it took.

Lia didn't say anything to him. Instead, she spoke to Jude. "I'm sorry about dragging you into this. I didn't think she'd be able to find you. And even if she did, I thought you might beat her. She must have crazy power even for a vampire."

Jude looked puzzled. "You don't know?"

Utah didn't give Lia a chance to answer. "Know what?"

Lia took her hand from his thigh as he leaned forward.

"Christine isn't a vampire."

CHAPTER NINE

Utah snorted his disbelief. "She had her fangs in my neck. She took my freaking blood. If it looks like a vampire, bites like a vampire, then it's—"

"Still not a vampire." Jude sounded weary of the whole thing.

Lia thought her head would explode. Too many life-altering events crammed together. She couldn't get a handle on the bam, bam, bam effect. Sort of like a giant pileup on the interstate during a fog. "How do you know she's not vampire? I didn't sense anything."

Jude closed his eyes and leaned back in his chair. "No offense, but you're still human. I'm vampire. I know my own. She's a fake." He thought about that for a moment. "Okay, a really powerful fake."

The silence dragged on too long for Lia's strung-out nerves. Finally, Utah said what they all must be thinking.

"Seven." Utah sounded disgusted. "Has to be. She had enough power to knock me out of my raptor form. And right before she took me, I saw Fin's face. He knew her. She played everyone. There never was any rogue vampire stealing Adam's people. And we all assumed Seven was a guy. Seir set us up. He's working for her."

"Doesn't add up." Jude finally showed some life. "He helped out a few times in Houston and Philly. What made him switch sides?"

"Don't know. Don't care. I'm going to kill him." Utah's eyes were coldly determined.

"What is Seir? I mean besides Fin's brother." Lia was trying hard to concentrate while keeping her thoughts from creeping back to Utah. The only good thing about so much happening at once was that he hadn't had time to think. How long before he started questioning her reason for making love with him? She hoped he didn't think about it for a long time.

Utah shrugged. "Demon? Who knows?" His expression said it didn't matter. Seir was dead.

Lia watched Utah take a deep breath and visibly try to ratchet down his bloodlust.

"So here's where we are." Utah raked his fingers through his hair. "She's blocked my line to Fin, so we can't count on help from him in time to stop this."

Lia winced. He'd injected a mega shot of loathing into the word "this."

"We won't be able to match her power, at least not in a straight-up fight. If she takes us to a larger room, I can free my beast, but that didn't help much back at the bridge. If we can catch her by surprise, we might have a chance."

"A few too many ifs." Lia had to make one thing clear. "I want you to let me become vampire. It's what I've always wanted, just not this way. It'll give us more time to plan an escape that has a chance of succeeding."

"No." Utah's rejection was harsh and didn't allow for compromise.

Lia glanced around the tiny room. No listening devices that she could see and not many places to hide one. Just to make sure, she slipped off the cot and knelt to look under it. Nothing. She talked softly, hoping her voice wouldn't carry to a sharp-eared guard on the other side of the door.

"Fin had a vision of me. At some point, I'll be in a position to touch Christine with something symbolic of her number. Fin didn't see the where or what of it. He did see that I'd be someplace outside with smoke rising behind me." She took a moment to curse the vagueness of his stupid vision.

"When that moment comes, I'll send her back out into the cosmos." If everything worked according to Fin's damn vision. She wasn't counting on that happening. "Wherever we are right now doesn't match the vision, and I don't have a clue what the symbolic thingy is. So I'd say that now isn't the time to engage Christine."

Utah maintained a stony silence.

She sighed and forged onward. "It'll take me a few days to rise as vampire. I don't think Christine will kill you guys while that's happening. You're trophies, and I think she'll try to convince you to work for her." At least that's what Lia hoped. The uncertainty would kill her even if Christine didn't. What if she woke to find they were dead? Her heart squeezed into a tight little ball of dread.

"What do you want us to do?" Utah still didn't look receptive.

"Go along with her. I mean, this is what Fin wanted. We've found Seven, and now we have a chance to work from the inside to stop her." She didn't look beyond that. They'd find a way to either escape or get rid of her.

Jude was more open to her suggestion. "Look, Utah, we have to face facts. It's not just Christine out there. I'll be the first one to attack once I think we have a chance of surviving."

"Even if that chance comes too late?" Utah glared at Jude.

"Too late?" Jude glared right back. "Hey, talking to a vampire here. The vampire life has lots of perks. It's a hell of a lot cooler than lugging a freaking dinosaur around inside you."

Not for Utah. She saw the rejection of all things vampire in his eyes. *He'll die before watching me become vampire.* He hated them that much. Something small and hopeful withered inside Lia.

She made her decision. Utah would despise her once she became vampire anyway, so she might as well tick him off in a major way. She'd do whatever it took to keep him alive.

Lia had only one more thing to say and then she'd shut up. "I think it'd be best if Christine thinks she still has us fooled. Telling her we know she's Seven won't gain us anything."

The two men nodded, and conversation died as each concentrated on his own thoughts. They didn't have long to wait. When the door finally swung open, Lia was ready.

Christine stood in the doorway along with a bunch of nonhumans. She'd changed into a long black dress. Lia tried to look casual as she stepped between Utah and Christine.

"Utah's not thinking too straight right now, Christine. He's not a huge fan of vampires, so he sort of resents what Jude is about to do. You might want to restrain him so he doesn't do anything to get himself hurt." Lia didn't turn to look at Utah, didn't want to see his expression of betrayal.

Christine clapped her hands in a strangely girlish gesture. Okay, it was creepy.

"I knew I made the right decision with you, Lia. You're already making yourself useful." She waved Lia aside so she could see Utah. "I understand your feelings completely, my beautiful raptor. But we can't have you interfering with Lia's big moment."

Lia finally worked up the courage to look at Utah. He was staring at Christine, a look of horror on his face.

"What did you do to him?" Lia clenched her fists so tightly her nails dug into her palms. She welcomed the pain.

Christine waved her concern away. "He's fine. I just limited what he could do. He'll walk and talk when I want him to, but other than that, he'll be a silent witness. I'll release him once everything is over."

Lia flashed back to Philly. Eight had done the same thing to Kione, frozen him in place. *I'm so sorry, Utah.* Somehow, she didn't think he'd be in a forgiving mood.

Jude looked grim as Christine led them from their small room down a hallway to . . . Lia blinked. A garden center? They were in the store part, surrounded by gardening tools, pots, and other stuff. All the windows were boarded up except for two glass panels at one end of the large room that allowed them a view into the greenhouse. Lia didn't visit many greenhouses, but the plants she could see looked a little too healthy. It was a jungle in there.

But that wasn't the disturbing part. Nonhumans five-deep lined the walls. They watched with avid curiosity, and some with obvious hunger. She glanced at Christine. "These aren't all vampires."

Christine looked excited as she scanned the room. "I'm an inclusive leader. I believe the future is in bringing together many different beings under one umbrella." She swept her arm to include all of her people. "Vampires, demons, shifters, I accept them all."

They stopped in the center of the room where Christine had erected an elaborate altar. Red silk was the decorating fabric of choice. She'd clustered plants around the altar. Lia controlled her need to roll her eyes. She'd hoped to become vampire in an intimate setting involving only her maker and her. Now she was part of a Hollywood production.

Christine handed her a long white silk robe. "Put this on. It'll keep your clothes from getting more blood on them, and it looks really spectacular against the red."

Lia slipped into the robe. Great, now she was playing the virgin sacrifice. Could this get any worse? She glanced at Utah. He watched her from burning eyes, the only part of him that could move. She sighed. Nope, he'd never forgive her.

Christine looked giddy with the thrill of it all. She clapped her hands and a line of humans paced into the room. They looked like sleepwalkers. Silently, they formed a ring around the makeshift altar.

Lia swallowed hard. She had a bad feeling about this. *Keep talking.* "So what's with the greenhouse?"

"I'm obsessed with the magnificence of life."

Lia looked at the humans. Maybe she was wrong, but she had a feeling good old Christine was pretty fond of death too. "What are the humans for?"

"They'll help my people celebrate your great moment." She waved vaguely. "Isn't there some kind of saying about an army marching on its stomach?"

Lia couldn't save these people, she couldn't help Utah or Jude, and she sure as hell couldn't help herself. This was Philly all over again. She hadn't been in control there either. Fury washed over her. Once she was vampire, someone would pay for this. And if anything happened to Utah . . . No, she wouldn't go down that path.

Keep talking before you turn into a chittering idiot. And yes, she was scared. See how far she'd evolved? She was admitting to so much terror that she wanted to curl up in a fetal position on the floor.

"How long have you had the greenhouse? Where exactly is this anyway?" She didn't give a damn about the greenhouse, and she didn't for a moment think Christine would give her its location.

"I took it over three weeks ago. The first thing I did was drink to the former owner." She put her fingers over her mouth and giggled. "Oh, wait. I meant that I drank the former owner."

This was so bizarre. Immortal destroyers of

humanity shouldn't giggle. Even Eight, a raving psychopath, had displayed a certain whacked-out dignity.

"You don't need to know anything else." She glanced at the altar. "It's time."

Oh crap. "It's awful hot in here." For the first time, Lia realized she was sweating.

Christine shrugged off her complaint. "I hate cold. I love lots and lots of wonderful heat. Life thrives in heat." She closed her eyes, almost a look of ecstasy on her face. "I love my blood hot."

Okay, more info than Lia wanted.

"It's too cold outside. But that's fine"—a sly look crept across her face—"because I'm going to heat things up in this town."

"Maybe you should've settled in Florida." Lia resigned herself to what would come next. She'd run out of meaningless conversation.

Christine opened her eyes. She smiled. "I'll go there next."

Not if we can help it. Lia looked at Utah. He watched her with unblinking intensity. She turned away from what burned in his eyes.

Christine glided over to the altar, her long black dress rippling behind her like some evil night wave. "Lie down here." She looked at Jude. "Don't block my view when you drain her. I don't want to miss a single drop. You don't get this on HBO."

Now that the moment had come, Lia's heart pounded out its last desperate beats, her breathing quickened; frantic gasps for air she would soon not need.

Too soon, too soon. Of course, it wasn't too soon. She'd been looking forward to this moment her whole life. Besides, once she rose, she'd be able to kick some serious ass. Dad would be disappointed, but her change wasn't unexpected. She forced calming thoughts to take the place of the chaos building in her soul.

One more thing to do. Lia began to withdraw the tentative strands of attachment she'd sent Utah's way. He'd really meant nothing to her. Sure, they'd made love, but she had to initiate the whole thing. What could a vampire and a man with the soul of a prehistoric predator have in common anyway? They could still work together, but that would be where it ended. In fact, once she became vampire, she wouldn't be any help to him. He needed a human to keep him off Seven's radar. So once she told Adam that there was no vampire raiding his territory, she'd fly back to Philly, back to her old life.

And if she didn't completely believe everything she'd just thought? Well, she would. Eventually. She went over to the altar and lay down.

Jude followed her. He leaned over her, his dark hair falling forward and shielding them for a moment. "Are you sure, Lia?"

"Choice is not something either of us has. Yes, I'm sure."

"There won't be any pain." He brushed her hair away from her face.

"Pain wouldn't be a bad thing." It would keep her from thinking.

Against her better judgment, she turned her head so she could see Utah one more time through human eyes. He was bathed in sweat, every muscle tensed against the invisible restraint Christine had wrapped him in. Agony shone from his eyes. Lia couldn't meet his gaze, she just couldn't.

She looked back at Jude in time to see a flash of rage in his eyes. He was being forced into this because of her. Time to bring down the curtain on a light note.

Lia forced a smile and hoped it didn't look as ghastly as she thought it did. "Will I have to call you Daddy now?"

Jude's lips tipped up in recognition of her effort. "Call me anything you want. Hey, once you rise you might even be able to whip my ass." And then he lowered his mouth to her neck.

Just as he'd promised, Lia felt the sting of his fangs and then nothing else. A languorous sense of pleasure and well-being washed over her. She couldn't seem to think anymore. Jude was doing that. And as darkness swallowed her, she was grateful.

Utah forced himself to watch, even when he wanted to close his eyes against the horror. The bitch had at least left him that option.

His beast screamed its rage, trapped two times over. It couldn't escape its cave, and he couldn't escape whatever mental shit Seven had thrown at him.

He refused to ever again call her anything but Seven in his mind. The name Christine humanized her, and he never wanted to make the mistake of thinking she had any human qualities.

He'd met Lia's gaze right before Jude sank his fangs into her neck. In that one moment, he hoped she saw everything in his eyes. The question. Why had she helped Seven bind him? He could have at least tried to stop this. *She didn't want you to stop it, dumbass. This is what she wanted.*

Utah had no way of expressing his sorrow and fury, no way of doing anything except choke back all emotion. Once again, he was in that restaurant in Philly, crouching over his brother's body, knowing he'd failed to save him. He was batting zero when it came to saving the ones he . . . What? Loved? No, he didn't love Lia. But he sure as hell cared a lot about what was happening to her right now. And someone would pay for this.

"The transformation is a beautiful thing. Lia will emerge a magnificent butterfly." Seven sounded almost awed. All her people murmured their agreement. They sounded hungry.

A butterfly with fangs. Utah didn't see anything beautiful about that.

And then he poured himself into Lia's dying. He heard her heartbeat slow and then falter. His heart pumped harder as though he could compensate for hers. Instinctively, he took deeper and deeper breaths to help her live. *Please live.*

But his will alone couldn't keep her alive. And when her heart took one weak final beat before falling still, he silently raged against his helplessness. Where was Fin? Where were his brother and the rest of the Eleven? Where was the almighty fae prince? What good was all their power if it couldn't save one small human woman?

Utah finally closed his eyes. He didn't want to watch how Jude intended to force his blood down her throat. He *hadn't* loved her. Then why did this hurt so much? He swallowed hard. She wasn't the same woman anymore. She was vampire. Knowing that, he'd stop caring pretty fast.

The only way he knew it was finally over was when Seven released him. Too late, too late. It was a mantra that could only be silenced by Seven's death. Problem. She couldn't die, so he'd have to be satisfied by something less but just as permanent.

"Open your eyes, my beautiful raptor. Jude has taken her to her resting place. You're such a silly child. You should be celebrating her change." She laughed at him.

Hate blossomed in him. He kept his gaze averted as he opened his eyes. If he looked into her eyes, Utah wouldn't be able to control his need to tear her apart. Then she'd kill him, and Lia's sacrifice would've been for nothing.

Unfortunately, he turned to glance one last time at the altar. And forgot all about control.

The vampires had watched the show and now were descending on the free buffet. They ripped into the strangely unresponsive humans, tearing out throats, gulping down blood, ignoring the smears and spatters coating them from head to foot. They made no noise, and their victims died silently, without trying to defend themselves.

This was too much. Seven had turned to talk with someone. She wasn't watching him for the moment. Utah crouched, ready to spring. Even if he could take out a few of them before . . .

Someone touched his arm. "Not a good idea, raptor."

A man stepped in front of him.

Seir. The need to kill was a compulsion that curled Utah's fingers into claws and brought his soul screaming from its cave.

Fin's brother shook his head. "Back up and dust your brain off. My brother would go ballistic if you forced Christine to kill you. Then he'd have to call you guys the Nine. I don't think nine is his favorite number." He grinned. "Besides, I have a gun. This close, I could kill you before you had a chance to change."

Utah glanced down at the gun pointed at his chest. "I'm going to kill you." Utah wanted to make that perfectly clear.

"Uh-huh. Got that. We'll discuss it later." He scanned the crowd. "Christine wants me to take you back to your room. Now might be a good time."

A quick glance showed that it was too late to save any of the humans. Utah took a deep breath and stepped away from the precipice. He couldn't help Lia if he was dead. Seir was right about that. He nodded, and Seir led him back to the small room with the big memories.

Lia's scent still clung to the room. Her *human* scent. That thought tore a hole in Utah that promptly filled with ice.

Seir stayed in the room with him. He even closed the door and locked it so they'd have privacy. Then he dropped the gun to his side. Utah figured there was a catch. He wasn't a favorite of the gods, so no one would offer up his enemy to him this easily.

"Want to explain why I shouldn't kill you right now?" Utah sat on the cot and tried not to imagine Lia seated next to him, her hand on his thigh, her warmth enveloping him.

Seir remained standing by the door. "Because I'm the only one who can get you out of here. Oh, and I'm Fin's brother. I have his power. I don't need a gun to stop you, but people always respond better when I have a prop."

"And why would you help us get out of here?" Utah could reach him in one leap, before Seir could bring up his gun. His raptor wouldn't fit in the small space, but Utah was angry enough to do lots of damage in his human form.

Seir shrugged. "I miscalculated. Everything went to hell back at the bridge. You weren't supposed to be taken. So now we wait for Jude."

What game was Seir playing? "You want me to believe you're on our side?"

Seir stifled a bark of laughter. "Hell no. I'm on my own side."

Whatever else he might have said remained a mystery because someone unlocked the door and flung it open. Seir slipped behind the door, his gun ready. Utah stood, ready to launch himself at whoever came through the door. But whoever opened the door didn't step inside. He just shoved Jude into the room, slammed the door shut, and locked it behind him.

Jude turned his back on Utah to face Seir. He didn't get a chance to ask anything, because suddenly Seir moved. One second, he was by the door, and in the next instant, he stood between Utah and Seir. Stretching out his arms, he touched both of them at the same time.

Blackness and then . . . Utah blinked. He was outdoors. There were trees and . . . He looked up. Fin's condo. He was outside Fin's freaking condo. What the hell? Beside him, he heard Jude's low curse.

Utah looked around. It was just Jude and him. Seir was gone. No explanation. Nothing. "No. This wasn't the way it was supposed to happen." He grabbed Jude's arm. "Where the hell is Lia?"

Jude scanned the area. "Christine made me take

her down to a small room under the back of the building. There're a bunch of them down there. Guess that's where the vampires spend their days. Lia should rise in two or three nights."

"Do you know where this garden center is?"

Jude shook his head. "After Christine beat the crap out of me when I didn't jump at the chance to visit with her, she did her teleport thing. I landed inside the building. Guess that was the same way she got you and Lia there."

Utah nodded. "I wonder why she didn't just freeze you like she did me? She didn't have to fight you."

"I made her chase me all over the city. Guess she was in a shitty mood."

So Seir was the only one who could tell him where the damn garden center was.

Jude stood beside him in silence.

Utah wondered if Jude sensed how close to death he was. Frustration hammered at Utah. Bloodlust flooded him, urged him to kill everyone, starting with the vampire he'd watched drain Lia. He could almost taste the blood, feel the adrenaline rush as he tore through flesh and bone.

Civil war raged within him. The human part of him fought to be heard above the roar of his beast. He had to use his brain. Find Fin. Tell him what had happened. Get the rest of the Eleven out on the streets searching for Lia. *Don't lose control.*

His beast only knew one word. *Kill.* Utah took deep breaths, trying to drown out the drone of that one word repeated over and over and over in his head. He wanted to clap his hands over his ears, but he knew that wouldn't help.

And as suddenly as that, Utah knew. This moment, in this spot, would define what he was. He could become raptor and drown his fury, his failure, his fear in blood. Or he could think like the human Fin wanted him to be.

"So have you decided?" Jude sounded a little too casual.

"What?"

"Are you going to take a shot at destroying me?"

Utah turned to look at him. "Not tonight, vampire. I have to talk to Fin." He didn't look back as he strode toward the condo entrance.

He thought about Lia all the way up in the elevator. She was safe for the next few days. But he had to find her before she rose as vampire. She'd be confused, hungry, maybe disoriented. What if she attacked Seven?

So what do you care? She's vampire now. Not your concern. But Utah knew she was very much his concern. He just wasn't sure why.

Utah didn't get a chance to bang on the condo door because Fin flung it open first.

Fin's quick scan seemed to satisfy him that Utah was in one piece. "Everyone's in the dining room." He turned and walked away.

Utah followed him to where the rest of the Eleven along with Kelly and Jenna sat around the large table. They watched silently as Utah took a seat beside his brother. Fin sat at his usual spot, the head of the table.

Tor leaned close. "Was worried about you, bro."

Something inside Utah uncurled a little. He was with pack again.

"Tell us." Fin didn't waste words.

Utah managed to hold his rage in check as he ran through the night's events. He watched Fin's face when he told everyone that Seven had taken them and that Seir had set them up. Fin's expression never changed.

Utah was tempted to brand Fin as a cold bastard—he'd done it a lot before Rap died—but he remembered that even as Fin had sent the soul of his brother to its resting place somewhere in Arizona, he'd mourned. The memory of Fin's sorrow redeemed him in Utah's mind. Barely.

When Utah was finished, everyone turned to Fin.

"We haven't had any luck finding where you were kept. Knowing that it's a garden center will help. But once Seven discovers that you and Jude have escaped, she'll move her operation elsewhere." Fin tapped his finger on the table, his expression thoughtful.

Utah had to find out. "Do you know Seven? I got the feeling you did."

Fin stared at Utah. Utah tried to meet his gaze, but it was like looking into the heart of chaos—terrifying and overwhelming. Utah had to look away, and he hated himself for his weakness.

"Yes." Fin's voice had no inflection, no warmth, no *humanity*.

Utah had opened his mouth to delve deeper when his thoughts disappeared into that familiar fog. Pain stabbed at his head. He rubbed at his temple while he tried to recapture his line of questioning. He couldn't remember.

"It looks as though there's only one person who can give us the information we need." Fin stood. He walked to the wall of glass to stare out over the city and river.

No one said anything until Tor turned to Utah. "Did I miss something? Seems like half the conversation is missing."

Utah shrugged.

Fin finally turned back to them. "My brother is getting what he's wanted for millions of years. He's forced me to talk to him. Seir will be here in a few minutes. I'd like all of you to stay."

CHAPTER TEN

"Y ou and Seir would be a lot more comfortable if we weren't here."

Al's wife wasn't speaking for the rest of them. Utah felt the excitement building around the table.

"Shush, Jenna." Kelly jabbed her sister in the side with her elbow. "We all want to hear." Ty's wife still had her tabloid reporter instincts.

"I'd rather you stay. Some of you have met Seir. Those who haven't, I want you to know him. He's capable of many things. He's—"

"Here." Seir emerged from the room's shadows. He hadn't been there a moment ago.

With all those crazy shades of gold in his hair and his icy eyes, Seir would look right at home on any branch of Fin's family tree. Seir might smile more than Fin, but Utah would bet he could be as cold as his brother.

Seir dropped onto the chair at the opposite end of the table from Fin. "I guess I arrived just in time. Were you getting ready to tell them what a disappointment I was to you, brother?" He grinned, but it didn't reach his eyes.

"I was getting ready to tell them you were powerful, manipulative, self-serving, and a lot more fun to be around than I ever was. Did I miss anything?"

"I think you left out the loving brother part."

Utah would've missed it if he hadn't been watching Seir. For just a moment, he saw real hurt in Seir's eyes. Interesting. What had happened between these two?

"I don't have time for a touching reunion. You set us up." Purple flooded Fin's silver eyes.

Seir looked relaxed. He seemed to be enjoying Fin's anger. "Umm, maybe I got it wrong, but I could've sworn the only dead bodies around that bridge belonged to the vampires."

"Utah and Lia were taken." Fin's voice vibrated with power. The table shook.

Now Utah was getting concerned. He wasn't alone. The rest of the Eleven leaned forward.

"Yes, well, that wasn't supposed to happen. If you hadn't spent so much damn time trying to keep me away from the bridge instead of being there with your men, no one would've taken them." Seir's good humor seemed to be fading.

"So now you're blaming me?" Fin's eyes were completely purple. "You haven't changed. Still trying to shift the blame. Still playing both ends against the middle."

"You stubborn bastard." Seir's eyes freaking glowed. Pale blue ice backlit by cold fury. "This isn't right. It's never been right."

Utah had reached his limit. He slid back his chair and stood. "Could we put a hold on the family feud for a second while I ask a question?"

The silence was complete as everyone turned to stare at him. And within the silence, Utah heard it. *A heartbeat.* Not his own. What the . . . ? There was something wrong with this heartbeat, though. It had a hitch in it. *Thump-hitch-thump, thump-hitch-thump.* Almost as though it was two different beats trying to be one but separated by the strange hitch. Didn't make any sense, so he dismissed it.

"Where's the garden center?"

Reluctantly, Seir shifted his attention from his brother. "It's on Burnside Street just down from the bridge. But Christine moved everyone out as soon as she discovered you and Jude had escaped. I went back to check after I dropped you and the vampire off here." He shrugged. "I don't know where she has Lia now."

Fin nodded at Spin and Q. "Go check. See if you can get a sense of where they went." He didn't watch the two men leave as he turned his gaze back to Seir. "Was this whole thing Zero's idea?"

Fin's question caught Utah by surprise. He'd assumed that Seir had been working with Seven. He hadn't thought it went any higher up the chain.

For the first time, Seir seemed to avoid Fin's gaze. "Yeah, maybe. It's tough keeping everyone happy."

If Utah wasn't so mad at Seir, he might think that was a weird thing to say. He growled low in his throat. He should've tried to tear the bastard apart when he had the chance.

Fin actually smiled. "And so you make no one happy."

Seir didn't answer.

"I think you know more about Seven than you're telling us, brother."

"Not half as much as you know, *brother*."

Utah was busy trying to put it all together. What secret messages were Fin and Seir sending each other? It was definitely in code, because Utah didn't have a clue what they were talking about.

Ty stepped into the conversation. "What's going on? I was there when Seir helped us in Houston and Philly, so now you're saying he's working for Zero? How can he be connected to both of you?"

Utah felt the collective intake of breath. *Connected?* He barely had a moment to consider the thought when the fog and pain rolled in. But for the first time, Utah fought it. And when the pain finally ebbed, he retained one thought. Fin was hiding something important from them. Utah had no proof. He couldn't even remember what Fin and Seir had said a few seconds ago. But he *knew*. A quick glance around told him he was the only one. The rest of the faces around him showed no shock, no confusion, only ordinary interest.

When Utah's gaze reached Seir, he found that Fin's brother was watching him with narrow-eyed intensity.

"Perhaps you should've made our talk private, Fin. You missed one. Careless, careless." Then he smiled at Utah, a smile that promised he'd be Utah's best bud forever.

Utah knew that smile lied. Something was going on he didn't understand, and he hated the feeling.

Fin glanced at Utah before transferring his attention to the rest of the Eleven. "I wanted you to meet my brother because he's going to be here for a while."

"No." Seir straightened in his seat.

"Yes." Fin smiled. An honest smile. "You'll be my guest, and we can have long brotherly talks. You might remember things about Seven that could help us find her." He shrugged. "And you won't be able to get into any trouble here."

"I wouldn't count on that." Seir looked outraged. "You can't keep me here."

Fin raised one brow. "Oh, but I can. I'm still your older brother."

Utah saw the moment when Seir decided to test his limits. He locked gazes with his brother.

The condo shook. Books flew off shelves, paintings fell from the walls, and the power filling the room made Utah feel as though a giant hand was pressing him down, and down, and down until he couldn't breathe. Smoke detectors went off, and in the distance he could hear the sound of breaking glass.

Then it was over, and Seir slumped in his chair. He glared at Fin. "Jerk. Where's my room?"

Fin looked more self-satisfied than Utah had ever seen him look. He glanced at Utah. "Take him to one of the guest rooms. Oh, and it's almost dawn, so you won't need to report back to Adam until evening. I'll call him and explain what happened."

Utah nodded. The rest of the Eleven got up to leave. Tor lingered.

"You okay?" Utah's brother looked concerned.

"Yeah." No. He had to find Lia. It was a compulsion, and he didn't trust compulsions. But he wouldn't involve his brother.

Tor nodded, but he didn't look like he believed Utah. "If you decide you need me, call. I'll be ready."

Utah clapped him on the shoulder. No words were necessary. This was what having a brother should mean. A small part of him pitied Fin and Seir.

"You're supposed to show me to my prison cell." Seir stopped beside Utah. "Will you chain me to my bed?" A wicked little smile worked at the corners of his mouth. "The kink calls to me. Maybe you . . . or your brother could entertain me there."

Crap. Tor broke all kinds of speed limits getting away from them. Utah turned on Seir. "Follow me. And no entertainment packages come with your room. Shit, I'm surprised Fin didn't kill you years ago."

"If he had, there'd be a hole in his heart he could never fill." Seir poked at his chest. "Seriously. A real hole."

If Utah didn't distrust everything Seir said, he'd almost believe Fin's brother meant it. "Where do you think Seven will take Lia?" That's all he cared about, not Fin's and Seir's family drama.

They stopped outside one of the guest rooms.

"Somewhere warm. Seven's totally into the heat and life thing. She drove me crazy with it—the plants, the blood, the bullshit. She kept saying she was going to heat up the city. I'd believe her."

Utah watched Seir open the door and step into the room. "Is Fin really keeping you here?"

Seir looked frustrated. "Believe it. I'll always be his little brother. Just when I think I might catch up to his power, he has a growth spurt."

Utah had one last question. "You said Lia and I weren't supposed to be taken. What *was* supposed to happen?" Not that he'd believe what Seir said.

Seir shrugged and turned away. "Doesn't matter. It didn't happen."

Then he shut the door, leaving Utah trying to

work through the riddle that was Seir. Finally, Utah turned away from the room . . . and almost bumped into Fin.

Fin motioned him to follow and led Utah to his office. Utah sat across the desk from Fin and waited.

Fin swung his chair so he was facing the bank of windows behind his desk. Dawn was just beginning to lighten the sky. "All of the Eleven are scouring the city for Seven. I've assigned them different areas. You and Kione can search wherever you want. He has extraordinary skills, so give him his head."

Utah laughed. "You think I could stop him?"

Fin's smile didn't have any real humor attached to it. "I'll be staying here to keep an eye on my brother and to mentally mess with Zero. I have to keep him out of the equation while you search for Seven. I don't have a human to put with you, so we'll just have to hope Kione's skills are up to the challenge."

"When you and Zero play your mental games, do you ever talk to each other?" Utah was curious about Zero. He'd be lying if he said he wasn't.

"Our 'mental games' consist of giving and receiving pain. No communication involved. The migraine is my best friend and most feared enemy. I try to cause him so much pain that he can't concentrate on the rest of you guys. But the pain runs both ways."

Utah nodded and started to rise.

"Oh, and Jude's five vampires will be hunting tonight. They're supposed to help find Seven and protect Jude from Adam's bullying, but they know Kione is here. They'll be looking for him." Fin swung his chair around to face Utah. "He's your partner and our ally until Seven is found. If the vampires show up, call me."

"Do you have any idea why Kione destroyed their clan?"

Fin shook his head. "But I do know we don't need this kind of distraction now."

For once, Utah agreed with him. And as he headed out of the condo to meet Kione, he just hoped Lia could hold on until he found her, because he *was* going to find her. Not Seven or even the almighty Zero would stop him.

Utah was in the elevator when he remembered what Kione could do.

Lia dreamed in dying color, coated herself in it, sank into it, became something else in its hot embrace. And when she finally opened her eyes, her need for it bound her with bands of searing agony. *Blood.* She'd never imagined she'd wake to this craving, the kind that made her want to claw out her stomach. Right now, insanity would be a relief.

She woke to darkness, and a presence. The darkness was dense, filled with power, and hopefully some freaking blood. Her reasoning couldn't reach beyond that point.

The presence drew near. "What a beautiful little vampire, all new and hungry."

Someone stroked her hair, and she tried to bite his hand.

He—the voice definitely belonged to a he—laughed softly.

"I'm sure you would rather have risen to find Jude at your side, ready to introduce you to your new life. Unfortunately, he's not available. But I should be able to supply what you need."

The man's voice was low, with a mesmerizing quality that managed to calm her a little. He'd get blood for her, lots of blood. Hopefully, not from an unwilling source. But right now, she didn't care. She needed blood, blood, and more blood flowing down her throat and putting out the fire that raged through her body.

Beside her bed—yes, she was definitely on a bed—the man moved. And then the scent of blood washed all logical thought from her mind. She sat up, reaching, clawing for the source of that scent. She barely recognized the man's wrist when he pressed it to her lips. All she knew was that blood welled from the cut in his flesh. Lia fastened her mouth tightly around the wound and sucked.

Random thoughts and emotions turned liquid and formed a whirlpool that circled around only one thought—she had to please this man.

She closed her eyes. His blood, oh my God, his *blood*. Like a living thing, it slid into her, searching, searching . . . And when it found the right spot, it felt as though it curled up, waiting. Warm and powerful, it seemed right, it *belonged*.

After what seemed a way too short time, he pulled his arm away from her. She opened her eyes. While she sat trying to decide whether it was worth pursuing him for more blood, he got up and turned on a light.

Oh wow. Lia flung her hands over her eyes. She hadn't been prepared for the enhanced vision thing. Everything was so bright and sharp it actually hurt her eyes. Gradually, she took her hands away, and immediately squinted against the light.

"It will get better."

The man's voice was the same—deep and filled with a subtle compulsion. Now that she'd emerged from her first bloodlust, she recognized its pull on her. Lia turned her head to look at him.

Not human. He was too beautiful. Long red hair in a dark shade she'd never seen before. She couldn't drag her eyes away from it. No human ever had hair that glittered and gleamed like that. It reminded her of . . . The thought floated away on the euphoria filling her. She'd think about his hair later. Wow, would you look at that face. Pale, smooth skin stretched over incredible bone structure. Large eyes that seemed to swirl for a second before they settled into a brilliant blue green. And sensual lips that most women wouldn't be able to resist.

But she could resist, because . . . She tried to latch on to the reason. There was someone else who had more sensual lips, a someone else whom she *couldn't* resist.

A question popped into her head. "Where am I?"

The man returned to his seat beside her bed. "You're at my place. I rescued you from Christine. You'll stay here until Fin claims you."

Her mind searched its database and finally located Fin. Leader of the Eleven and major pain in the ass. He wasn't the one with the irresistible lips.

"I'll have to lock you in when I'm not here, Lia. Can't have you out draining random Portland citizens. But I'm sure you won't be here long."

Lia felt she should argue with the locking-up part, but she couldn't work up the will. She did have to know one more thing, though. "What's your name?"

"Frost." He sounded distracted.

Lia rolled the name around in her mind. "Unusual."

"Fitting." He sounded amused.

She began to feel the pull of sleep. "Is it close to dawn?" There were no windows to give her a clue.

"Yes." He leaned close to her.

His scent went with his name—ice and wind-driven snow. "Good. Maybe when I wake things won't be so jumbled in my mind." She blinked and tried to focus. *His hand.* There was something about his hand . . .

"Sleep deeply and remember . . ."

Lia flipped off her awake switch before he finished his sentence. But somewhere during her
dreamless day sleep, he came to her. She didn't
see him, but she heard everything he said.

"Your thirst will be unbearable when you're
alone with Utah. You won't be able to control it.
And you won't stop feeding until he's dead. You
will also refuse to hunt Seven."

His compulsion slipped through the cracks in
her consciousness and took root.

"This is important, Lia. You won't remember
who told you these things, but you'll know them
to be true. Believe me. Trust me."

She believed. She trusted. All faded into deeper
sleep.

CHAPTER ELEVEN

U tah and Kione stood in the empty parking lot of the fast-food restaurant. Heartburn hell. Utah had gone from a diet of fresh meat to eating rubbery, overcooked beef patties and soggy fries. They'd been the last customers. Someone flipped off the outside lights.

"Tell me again why you can't find her." Utah pulled his coat tighter against the Portland chill.

"I've already explained. Maybe you should've listened the first ten times I told you." Kione was not a patient person.

"I didn't understand the first ten. Maybe I'll get it this time."

Kione stared at him.

Utah looked away. He didn't need a raging case of lust on top of all the other emotions boiling over inside him.

"One more time, raptor. I can find someone once I've made a connection with them. I made a connection with Lia. But the Lia we knew no longer exists. She's vampire now. Therefore. I. Can't. Find. Her."

"She'll still be the same person inside the same body." And if he kept repeating this, he might eventually believe it.

"There're certain events in our lives that change us forever." Kione's voice softened. "And we're never the same."

Utah barely noticed. "We've searched every damn corner of this city." Frustration beat at him. Three days and nights with no sign of Lia or Seven. "Maybe they've moved out of the city."

Kione looked doubtful. "Christine needs lots of new recruits and a plentiful food supply for them. She won't get either out in the country."

"Yeah." Utah scanned the area. Darkened buildings. A few streetlights. No foot traffic and almost no cars passing. "The big jump in homicides and disappearances has been all over the local news. She's not reining in her newbies."

"Why should she? That's what she's selling—a free-for-all killing spree."

Utah noticed that Kione was constantly watching the shadows. He didn't blame the guy. With Jude's heavy hitters in town and hunting for him, Kione had to stay alert. Utah almost wished the five bloodsuckers would find them. He'd put his money on Kione. Besides, it would give Utah's beast an excuse to vent its pent-up rage.

Suddenly, Kione froze.

At the same time, Utah caught a scent. Whatever was here crouched just beyond a nearby streetlight's circle of light. He couldn't see it, but the smell was familiar. Feline. Not a house cat, and not anything he recognized.

Kione relaxed a little. "I sense no aggression."

Utah wasn't so sure. A large predator might kill just for the hell of it. Besides, a big cat prowling the city streets was way outside of normal. He decided to take the initiative. "If you're a shifter, come out and talk." *And if you're not? Better run because the animal control people will be on your tail.*

The shadows rippled and moved. Darkness coalesced into a huge black cat. It stalked them, golden eyes glowing. Jaguar. All the human stuff Fin had downloaded into his brain when he first rose was coming in handy.

"Who are you?" Kione didn't move.

Utah took a step forward. His philosophy was that prey stood still or turned and ran. A predator always advanced, because a timid hunter never lived a long life. He wouldn't show weakness in the presence of this animal.

The male voice in his head was unfamiliar.

"I am Balan, the messenger for those you call by numbers. I am honored to meet another God of the Night and a mighty fae prince."

God of the Night? Utah almost snorted, but decided it might not be wise to piss off someone with a connection to Seven. "I'd say it was an honor to meet you too, but since Seven has taken one of ours and is busy trying to kill us, I guess I have to put you in the enemy camp."

Balan circled them, moving with a powerful grace, his unblinking golden stare shining in the darkness. *"I am not the enemy. I am simply a messenger. I observe and report, nothing more."*

Utah wasn't so sure of the simply-a-messenger part. He felt a power in the cat he couldn't identify.

Kione finally spoke up. "I assume you have a message for us." The edge of his cloak lifted as the wind suddenly kicked up.

"Your power stirs the heavens, prince. An impressive display, but I have a cat's aversion to getting wet. Please control it until I have gone." Balan turned his attention to Utah. *"Seven is only responding to your aggression. If the Eleven would leave us in peace, no one else need suffer."*

"Leave you to destroy humanity? Not likely." Utah watched the jaguar pause in the shadows.

"It will happen whether you wish it or not." Balan seemed to sink farther into the darkness until only his golden eyes were visible.

Utah rushed into speech, afraid the cat would leave. "Where has Seven taken Lia? Is she okay?" Not that he expected Balan to answer his questions, but he had to try.

"Lia is well, but Seven no longer has her. She now resides with my master."

"Who is . . . ?" God, Utah wanted to shake the information out of the cryptic bastard.

"The one you name Zero."

Utah felt the name as a punch to the gut. Fear for Lia clenched his stomach into a tight knot. This was what it meant to be human, this terror for another. He didn't know if he'd survive his humanity.

"Your message?" Kione prompted Balan.

"My master wishes to make an exchange. He will trade Lia for Seir. He wishes you to take this message to Fin."

Utah pounced on the important part of Balan's message. They could get Lia back. "Why doesn't he contact Fin himself?" All they had to do was to release Seir. *Get it done, Fin.*

Balan made a coughing noise that sounded strangely like laughter. *"Fin has never been reasonable where Zero is concerned. My master feels that because you have an interest in Lia, you will present his message in a way that may convince Fin to accept. Besides, you had no human with you and so were easy to track."*

"Hate to tell you, kitty, but Fin probably already knows about it. My mind is open to him." Utah didn't know why he felt the need to irritate Balan. Maybe because the cat oozed superiority.

"You are rude. But that is to be expected from one

who is only a few months removed from his primitive state." He offered a good imitation of an offended sniff. *"And Zero is keeping Fin occupied at the moment. Your leader is not aware of my presence."*

Utah couldn't get past Balan's comment about his rudeness. "Maybe I wouldn't be so *rude* if you and your master weren't being assholes by holding Lia hostage." He wasn't acting too smart. He shouldn't be antagonizing the cat, but he couldn't help it. The memory of Rap's death was still raw and bleeding. It made him afraid for Lia. And when he was afraid, he struck out. A newly discovered character trait he'd have to control.

"How many times must I tell you that I merely—"

"I know, I know. You only observe and report. Got it." Utah glanced at Kione. He didn't trust himself to say anything more.

"And if Fin agrees, where will the exchange take place?" Kione seemed to be keeping the wind in check, but a few drops of rain were beginning to fall.

"Tell Fin of this meeting. If he agrees, meet me outside of his condo. We can make arrangements then." Balan was backing away, fading into the darkness.

Suddenly, the sky opened, dropping buckets of icy rain on them. The jaguar squalled and hissed his outrage as he disappeared.

Kione's laughter followed the cat into the night.

Amazed, Utah turned to him. "I can't believe it. The man has a sense of humor after all. It's almost worth standing in a cold rain to experience the wonder of it." He pulled his coat shut. "Let's get out of here." Putting his head down, he ran to the car.

Even as they climbed into the car, the rain lightened. Utah drove toward Fin's condo while thoughts of what he'd say to Lia when he saw her again filled his mind. "Hi," seemed a little inadequate.

"You care for Lia." Kione made it a statement.

"Sure. She's my partner." Utah hoped he'd drop the subject.

"I'm your partner too, but I don't think you'd have the same feelings if Zero took *me*."

Utah shrugged. "You can take care of yourself a little better than Lia." He thought about it. "Yeah, you're my partner. And sure, my feelings for you aren't the same as my feelings for her. But if Zero had you, I'd come for you. It's what partners do." It's what *pack* does. *Then why couldn't you help Rap?* He shoved the guilt aside and thought about Kione. "You know, when I first met you I thought you were this cold, strange guy. Hey, you're still this cold, strange guy, but now you're pack." Utah was surprised that he meant it.

Kione's silence made Utah uneasy. Finally, the dark fairy spoke. "Thank you."

For someone who claimed to have no emotions, Utah heard a lot of feeling in those two words.

"In honor of my official pack status, I have a few words of wisdom to offer. Don't deny feelings that make you happy. Appreciate what you have when you have it. And never assume your power makes you invulnerable." Bitterness laced Kione's every word.

Utah sensed Kione had a ton of personal experience to back up that advice, but he also sensed that now wasn't the time to dig.

"Will you still care for her now that she's vampire?"

See, Kione *had* to ask that question. "I don't know." In the beginning, he thought hating her as vampire would be easy. Now? He didn't think it would be easy at all. As he drove the rest of the way to Fin's condo, he tried to figure out why she'd become so important to him.

Shen opened the door and pointed them toward Fin's room with a warning that it might be wise not to disturb him now.

The hell with that. Utah wasn't going to wait another minute to tell him about Lia. Kione trailed behind him. Even in what he had to know was a safe environment, Kione never looked relaxed. He always seemed to be expecting an attack.

When Utah reached Fin's door, he knocked politely. When that got no response, he pounded away. There was a time before Lia when he would've given his leader the space he needed. Not now. Lia's freedom came first.

Fin finally flung open his door. "What?" His question was an angry growl.

For a moment, Utah could only stare. This

wasn't the Fin he knew. This man was pale, his silver hair a tangle around his face, his eyes filled with a manic gleam.

"I hope this is important, Utah, because Zero just finished frying my brain, and I'd really like to kill someone."

"Kione and I had a visit from Balan. You know him."

"Yes. He goes where Zero goes." Fin closed his eyes and rubbed his temples.

"He gave us a message to pass on to you from Zero. It's about Lia. Can we come in?" Asking for permission to come in was only a formality. Utah didn't intend to leave until he'd talked this out.

Fin ran his fingers through his hair before stepping aside. Utah and Kione walked into the room and waited while Fin closed the door.

A quick glance showed a completely sterile room. Nothing but the basic furniture. No artwork, nothing lying around. Impersonal. Utah had pictures of his brothers on the nightstand by his bed, and no one would ever accuse him of being neat. Well, at least when it came time to move on to the next city, Fin wouldn't have much packing to do.

"Sit down." Fin waved them to the couch while he dropped into a chair. "So you met Balan."

Utah decided to get right to the point. "Zero has Lia. He'll trade her for Seir."

Fin leaned back in his chair. "I suppose Zero

wanted you to know first because he didn't trust me not to turn down the trade without asking the opinions of the rest of the Eleven."

"Yeah, something like that." It was sort of scary how Fin could always read people's motivations.

"Logically, I *should* turn down the trade. Seir is the bigger threat of the two. He could tip the balance if he chose to throw in with Zero permanently."

Utah opened his mouth to reject Fin's reasoning, but Fin raised his hand to stop him.

"Of course, Zero doesn't know about my visions. He doesn't realize how important Lia really is. So it looks as though my loving brother and I won't get to reminisce about the old days after all." Fin sounded like he didn't give a damn, but his eyes bled faint purple, a sure sign he was feeling some emotion. "I assume Balan wants you to pass my decision on to him. Tell him yes. Then find out how Zero wants to handle the trade."

Relief washed over Utah. If Fin had nixed the trade, he would've had to figure out a way to rescue Lia on his own. And while Utah thought about possible trade scenarios, Fin talked to Kione.

"Since Adam considers Lia one of his, I'll have to tell him about the trade. He'll want to have a representative there. Jude will probably volunteer." Fin waited for Kione to come to the logical conclusion.

Kione nodded. "Jude will bring his five vampires with him."

"I can ask Jude to keep them away, but I can't demand it."

"Do you wish me to stay away?" Kione's expression remained neutral.

"Do you want to stay away?"

"No." The one word was a savage declaration of what he *did* want.

"I'll trust that you won't turn this into a killing event." Fin managed to look threatening without moving a muscle. "At least until the trade is made."

"I'll try to control myself." Kione almost smiled.

Fin turned his attention back to Utah. "Balan's probably waiting outside for my decision. After you pass the information on to him, go tell my brother."

The telling-Seir part surprised Utah. "I thought you'd want to give him the good news."

"Then you thought wrong. Zero put a lot of effort into his mind games tonight. Only politeness is keeping me from pounding my head against the wall. After a few minutes with Seir, I'd be trying to kill him."

"Then?" Utah was starting to feel like a freaking errand boy.

"You and Kione can sleep here." Fin yawned. "Oh, and you don't have to fill me in after you speak with Balan. I'll be in your head at the meeting. Make sure to leave the door open."

There was nothing more to say, so Utah and Kione left.

Balan waited for them in the darkness. They saw the golden gleam of his eyes before they saw the rest of him.

Utah was tired. He didn't waste time on the niceties. "Fin's okay with the trade. Where do we meet and what are the rules?"

"I'm pleasantly surprised. I did not think he'd agree so easily." Balan cast a baleful glance Kione's way. *"I do not find you amusing, my unseelie friend. Dump water on me again and you'll see what powers I own."*

Kione wore his fake puzzled frown. "But I thought you only observed and reported. You'd resort to violence?"

"I could make an exception for you." He shifted his attention back to Utah. *"Each side will be allowed ten representatives plus their leader. We will meet with you at two A.M. tomorrow at the International Rose Test Garden in Washington Park."*

"A rose garden?" Utah glanced at Kione, who shrugged. "How do we get there?"

"I would suggest Google Maps."

"Sure. Where else?" Balan and Google Maps. An unexpected combination. "Why'd you choose a rose garden for the meeting?" Utah would've picked an indoor arena somewhere.

"Christine will be making the exchange for us, so she chose the site. She has an obsession with living things, and the garden's plant life is quite spectacular." Balan's cat eyes grew sly. *"Rosebushes have thorns. Perhaps she hopes blood will be shed. It is another of her obsessions."*

"Any other rules?" Utah noticed that Kione's attention had wandered. Once again, he was searching the darkness.

"There will be no violence."

Utah nodded, and Balan disappeared into the night.

Kione had nothing to say as they reentered the condo. Utah finally couldn't stand it anymore.

"When they make their move, you know I'll have your back."

Kione stopped in front of one of the guest rooms and turned to him. "No one has stood with me for a very long time, raptor. I'll remember this." He went into the room and closed the door before Utah could say anything.

It seemed like everyone's job was done except for his. Utah had to visit Seir before he could head for his own room. He wasn't looking forward to this. Seir was like a man wearing layers of masks. It didn't matter how many masks you yanked off, you'd never be sure if what was underneath was the real person. Maybe Utah didn't want to see the real person. Maybe there *wasn't* a real person.

When he reached Seir's door, he knocked with more force than necessary. Utah hoped he was sleeping. Like *he* should be doing right now.

Seir must've been awake because he opened the door too quickly. He didn't say anything as he motioned Utah in.

Utah looked around. Hey, he had something in common with Seir. They were both slobs. Seir had flung a shirt over a chair, dropped his pants on the floor, and kicked his shoes off. He wore clean clothes, so Fin must've loaned him some of his. A half-finished drink sat on the coffee table.

Seir flopped onto the couch. He didn't say anything, just picked up his drink.

Utah opted to remain standing. He'd make this quick. "Zero has Lia, but he's willing to trade her for you. Fin agreed. The exchange is set for two tomorrow morning at some rose garden."

"Why didn't my brother come to tell me this?" Seir didn't sound particularly interested. He stared into his drink.

"Zero gave him a hard time tonight. Guess he has a headache. And you irritate the hell out of him. He figured he'd end up trying to kill you if he came himself."

Seir grinned. "He likes to play the cool and together guy, but Earth wouldn't survive if he ever really lost his temper. Makes me proud to call him brother."

Now was as good a time as any to ask Seir a question. "What did you mean when you said Lia and I weren't supposed to be taken?"

Seir shrugged. "I figured Fin couldn't resist coming, and I knew Christine would make an appearance. When she showed up, Fin would toss her butt back out into the cosmos. Then he could move on to another city. Didn't shake out that way. I was hanging around because, well, it was my show. But big brother was so worried about what I would do that he missed his chance."

"Truth?"

Seir finally looked at him. "Maybe, maybe not. It's whatever you want it to be."

"Yeah, figured that. Well, at least you know Zero values you. He's giving up Lia to get you back." Utah didn't know why he bothered to say anything nice to the jerk.

"No one values *me*, raptor. They value my power. I haven't mattered for a long time. I'm just a tool." He smiled. "Like you."

Utah's patience was fading fast. He turned to leave.

"One more thing." Seir was back to staring at his drink. "Zero and Fin will probably give each other a wide berth at the exchange. But if you ever see the three of us together, I mean *touching* close, run like hell." He paused.

Come on. Utah wanted out of here.

"Doomsday stuff happens when we're together." He didn't smile as he said it.

The cold, clammy hand of premonition rested on Utah's shoulders all the way back to his room. But as he closed his door, he purposely shut out all thoughts of Seir. He had other things to think about.

A short time later, Utah lay in bed. He couldn't stop his personal Rolodex of reasons he hated vampires from flipping over and over and over.

They were cold-blooded killers. They were freaking parasites. They couldn't be trusted. The reasons went on and on. Yeah, some of them were just hearsay, but he was willing to believe any vampires-are-the-devil claims he heard because . . . He wanted to. And if some of those claims also fit him, well, he chose to ignore them.

What about Lia? How would he feel about her? For the first time he actually tried to decide why he even cared. Fine, so he thought she was as sexy as hell. But that was only part of it. She was smart and brave and . . . flawed. Flawed like him. He felt a kinship. Most of all? Lia treated him like a person. And as much as he thought that vampires weren't people, he *knew* that he wasn't.

He fell asleep with all his questions unanswered.

This was just weird. Utah couldn't believe they were doing this in a damn rose garden. There was something strange about the place. It was February, cold, and rosebushes shouldn't have leaves or flowers. These did. And it wasn't cold *here*. In fact, he'd taken off his coat.

"Christine is doing this. She always brings the heat. She's a life freak. She'd try to grow stuff in the middle of Times Square and water it with tourists' blood." Seir's mockery was back. "She's bought completely into Zero's out-of-death-comes-life crap. Kill the human polluters, and Earth will bloom again."

Utah was keeping Fin's brother close. It would sort of ruin the trade if one of the major players disappeared. He looked around. As far as he knew, Fin and Zero were patrolling the perimeter to make sure no humans noticed what was happening. The good guys were on one side of the field with rows and rows of rosebushes separating them from the bad guys.

Only the good guys weren't all good. There were good guys Kione, Ty, Spin, and him. Then there were Adam and Jude's five vampires. Not so good. Too bad Jude wasn't here to help control his men. Utah saw Adam's hand in that. He hoped Jude was okay.

And considering the black looks passing between the vampires and Kione, he hoped they'd hold it together until after he got Lia back.

Across the rows of rosebushes stood the bad guys. Utah recognized only one of them—Seven. She had Lia with her. But he hadn't gotten a good look at Lia because the rest of Seven's legion of darkness had clustered around her.

"Christine's brought an interesting mix with her." Seir wasn't about to shut up. "Some vamps, a few demons, werewolves—"

Adam appeared beside them. "It's time to make the trade. Seir has to come with me."

The vampire looked so smug that Utah wanted to rip his head off. Of course, that's what he felt like doing to every vampire. Lia was *his* partner, so he should've been the one going into the middle to do the exchanging. But Adam had pulled rank. Jerk. Adam didn't care about Lia, he just wanted to be seen as the big freaking cheese of the vampire nation. Utah wouldn't be surprised if one of Adam's people whipped out a camera and turned this into a photo op for the son of a bitch.

Wait, something else occurred to Utah. Where was Adam's rage? Why wasn't he royally pissed at Seven for siphoning off a bunch of his vampires? Utah narrowed his eyes as he watched Adam and Seir stepping over rosebushes on their way to the middle of the field. The vampire wore a strange expression as he watched Seven come forward with Lia.

Utah's heart pounded, his breathing quickened. Had Zero treated her okay? She looked the same. He took a deep breath to relax the tightness in his chest. What would she say? What would *he* say?

No words were exchanged as Lia followed Adam back to their side of the field and Seir walked away with Seven. Then Seven's people faded into the darkness and were gone.

Utah's rush to meet Lia came to a sudden halt as someone spoke.

"The time has come for you to die, fae bastard."

Aw, shit. Utah turned to look at the five vampires. They'd formed a semicircle around Kione. The unseelie prince was standing his ground, though.

"Your curse wasn't enough punishment? No one can say that you don't know how to hold a grudge, bloodsuckers." Kione smiled, and a distant rumble of thunder disturbed the silence. "But then so can I."

Utah crouched, ready to free his beast. He saw Spin and Ty do the same.

Lia looked dismayed. Adam didn't.

Utah figured Adam probably thought of this as a win-win situation. If Kione died, Adam got rid of an annoying minion who couldn't be trusted to always follow directions. And if Kione destroyed the five vampires, Adam would have a clear shot at Jude if he wanted it.

With everything at stake, Utah was surprised to see Adam turn to leave. What the . . . ? You'd think Adam would at least make a show of caring what happened to the five vampires. Or maybe he wanted to be able to tell Jude that he couldn't help them because he wasn't there.

And what about Lia? Adam wasn't taking her with him. You didn't just leave a new vampire standing alone. She'd need blood and others of her kind around her. Utah started toward her, but before he could reach her side she waved him off.

"Stay away. Don't come near me." She put her hand over her mouth and stared at him with . . .

Hunger? Not what Utah had hoped to see. He looked closer. Not just hunger, but full-blown bloodlust with a side order of shocked horror. He cursed himself for actually hoping. Had he really thought she might come back unchanged? *Get over it.* She was vampire, and she'd never again . . .

Utah wasn't ready to complete that thought. Not now. He'd think about this after he helped Kione kick some bloodsucker butt. He turned away from her to focus on Kione and the vampires.

The vampire in the middle stepped forward. His long black coat snagged on one of the rose-bushes, but he yanked it free. He pointed one finger at Kione. "No punishment will ever suffice to wipe away what you did to our clan. The curse merely filled the time before we could find and destroy you." A twitch of his lips passed for a smile. "Rejoice, because after this night you need never suffer the curse again." He pushed his coat aside and freed his sword. The four behind him did the same.

Utah was impressed. All five were big men with faces carved into hard lines. He'd bet none of those lines came from laughter. Everything about them was black, from their identical long coats, to their black fingerless gloves, to their eyes. Hate and rage lived in those eyes. Power surrounded them. It wasn't a benevolent power. It reeked of blood and reached out to touch him, promising that he too would die if he decided to interfere. It was an old power, forged from earth and fire, polished by ice and stone. They were one step removed from elementals. Or maybe they just felt that way.

But Utah was still putting his money on Kione. And if Kione needed his help, Utah would have his back. Utah beckoned his beast from its cave.

"I've waited centuries for this moment." Kione began to glow. "I've suffered with your fucking curse, and I added every moment of agony to what you owe me. Tonight your bill comes due. I hope you die hard." His smile would send grown men screaming into the night.

The moment following Kione's last word stretched on and on and on.

Lia looked uncertain.

Not unexpected. The vampires were her people, but Kione was her partner. Utah hoped she had enough sense to stay out of this. She might be vampire now, but these guys were way out of her league.

Ty and Spin moved apart, ready to free their souls.

Utah sensed violence a second before the vampires struck. And as the rose garden became a blur of motion, death stalked the darkness.

Utah took a deep breath and . . . *didn't* free his beast.

CHAPTER TWELVE

There were enough monsters in the rose garden.

Ty and Spin had put lots of space between each other, but still their beasts filled the field, crushing rosebushes and dwarfing everything around them.

Utah didn't often get this perspective because he was usually one of the monsters. But wow, as ancient predators went, Ty and Spin were pretty impressive. He hoped they didn't get so caught up in the killing that they forgot to stop.

He'd stay human as long as possible. He wouldn't be able to marshal all his reasoning powers in his animal form, and at least one person here shouldn't be lost to the bloodlust.

He glanced at Lia. So far, she was just standing there staring.

Everyone that wasn't a T. rex or a Spinosaurus backed up. Kione and the five vampires might fling around all kinds of flashy power, but it all gave way to the sheer physical presence of two predators, each fifty-plus feet long, supplied with all the equipment necessary to kill and to keep on killing. Especially when the supersized killing machines were just about invulnerable in their present forms.

"You would interfere with a fight that is not your own?" an outraged vampire shouted at Utah.

"Doesn't look like the odds are exactly even, bloodsucker. Five of you. One of him. Nope, not even."

Lia seemed to have forgotten him as she stared at Ty and Spin, so Utah edged a little closer to her. Even as vampire, she couldn't compete with the players already on the field. He'd stay nearby in case she needed him. *Face it, the only thing she needs you for now is a quick energy drink, a bloodsucker's caffeine substitute.*

The five vampires needn't have worried about anyone interfering. Kione and the vampires moved so fast that no one could even see them. They were simply shadowy blurs in their dance of death. Yeah, there was blood, but you couldn't tell who had shed it. Ty and Spin stood motionless, ready to grab a vampire if one became visible. Lia still looked dazed.

Utah along with Lia, Ty, and Spin waited, trying to get a feel for how the fight was going, and seeing nothing as the battle raged on and on and on. Utah didn't think he could take it much longer. It wasn't just that he couldn't see Kione or the others, but it was too quiet. A life or death struggle should be filled with shouts, screams, and cries of agony. But there was nothing, just the occasional rumble of thunder. What the hell were they doing to each other? It wasn't natural.

Then everything changed in an instant. A booming crash of thunder shook the ground as five jagged spears of lightning lit the night sky. The sizzle and crack of the lightning as it struck mixed with the scent of ozone, burned flesh, and cloth. When the smoke cleared, the five vampires lay on the ground. They weren't dead, but they were definitely down for the count. Bits of their charred coats still smoked, and each had an impressive hole in his chest. They lay on their backs and stared up at Kione. And once caught in the fae prince's deadly gaze, they seemed helpless.

Everyone stared at Kione. Utah shielded his eyes against the fae prince's brilliant flare. It hurt his eyes, but he couldn't look away, couldn't even shut his eyes to block Kione out.

There was nothing subtle or even remotely human about the dark fairy. He was a blaze of white light so intense that Utah could actually feel it crawling over his body, sinking into every cell, burning him up with its deadly compulsion. *Sex.*

Kione had told them the truth. He wasn't ramping up the sex with them before. *This* was ramping up the sex. Not the fun part of sex, either. Utah's cock was so hard it hurt, the agony building until he doubled over and dropped to his knees. His breaths came in tortured gasps. If he could only breathe he'd scream. He ripped open his jeans and wrapped his fingers around his staff, tried to bring relief, but touching himself brought only more agony.

Along with the pain came the need to screw someone. Nothing emotional about it. Only the mindless compulsion to fuck and fuck and fuck until he was drained and *dead*. But he couldn't move. He could only kneel in the dirt while he hung over the edge of the biggest freaking orgasm of his life. Sweat beaded on his forehead as he strained toward the freefall to end all freefalls. Nothing. He just hung there.

Despair wracked him. No one except Kione could ease his agony. But Kione didn't seem about to ease anyone's pain right now.

That's when he heard Fin's voice in his head.

"I'm going to black out your vision for a moment. When I do, it'll break your connection to Kione. Then look at something else, and don't look back. I can't be there right now. I have something else I have to handle."

Then everything went black. Utah immediately turned his head. And when his vision finally cleared, he knew who he'd be looking at. Lia was staring back at him. Her face was white, her eyes wide with the memory of Kione's compulsion.

"Fin was in your head too?" He fumbled at his zipper, hoping she didn't notice.

Lia nodded. "I didn't know . . . I never thought Kione could . . ." She swept her hand across her eyes. "We have to stop Kione from killing the vampires."

"Why?" He thought the vampires deserved anything they got. Death by sex. Before meeting up with the fae prince, Utah would've thought that was a good way to go. Not now.

"Because they're under Jude's protection. He'll be obligated to challenge Kione. He'll die."

Utah noticed that even as she spoke, she made sure she kept her distance from him. Since when had he become a pariah? Then he tried to think logically. She'd just risen. Lia would probably be leery about getting close to anyone for fear of killing them. Made sense, but it didn't make him feel any better.

Utah turned just enough to see Ty and Spin without looking at Kione. They'd returned to human form and were facing away from the action. So Fin had gotten to them. "I don't know how we can keep Kione from doing what he damn well pleases."

What evidently pleased Kione was explaining a few things to the vampires before he destroyed them. Good. That gave Utah a few moments to figure a way out of this mess.

"You should know the truth before you die. You weren't with your clan, so perhaps you need to see what they did. I'll narrate since I didn't have time to fill in any subtitles. Watch."

Suddenly, images filled Utah's mind. Kione was including everyone in his show-and-tell. A clearing in a heavily forested area. Wooden structures. Lots of men, no women in sight. Utah wasn't a historian, so the men's clothing told him only that this happened a long time ago.

"You'll notice me there. I'm the naked guy chained to the post. Iron chains. Not my favorite metal. Leaves a nasty burn."

Kione's voice was so cold that Utah felt it as a physical layer of ice touching every exposed part of his body. He pulled on the coat he'd taken off earlier, making sure he didn't look in Kione's direction.

"Also notice the lack of women. My bad luck. I knew little about your clan before they captured me. I didn't know that in your clan males lost the ability to have sex as they aged. The ancient ones felt no stirrings at all. They were all ancient here. Your females had left centuries ago. But that didn't mean that they didn't *want* to feel something."

"They discovered what I was, what I could do. And even though they were the most powerful vampire clan on Earth at the time, they wouldn't have been able to capture me under normal circumstances. But I had a fatal weakness. The one and only weakness I've allowed myself during the millennia of my existence. Step into my memories and know why you die tonight."

The scene shifted, and suddenly, Utah was no longer seeing the event from a distant place, a place that allowed him to feel some detachment. He was there, surrounded by the vampires, *one of them.*

The flavor of lust. He rolled it around on his tongue, reacquainting himself with its taste. For so long he'd felt only the one hunger. But no amount of blood could wash away the memory of sexual need, something he'd thought never to feel again. Now he gloried in the hardening of his body, the rush of raw sensation, the *excitement.*

Soon it would be his turn. He'd sink his fangs into the unseelie bastard's neck even as he buried himself in its body.

They'd forced the fae abomination to their will three seasons ago, and he never tired of his explosive release each time he used the creature. He knew only one disappointment. No matter the pain they inflicted, it never cried out. He wanted to hear its screams of agony. He and the others of his clan now competed to see who would be the first to hurt it so badly that it couldn't hold back its cries.

The line moved forward. While he waited for the next male to begin, he stared at the thing's face. Meeting the creature's gaze caused his lust to rise, his body to tighten, his hunger to run unchecked. If his power wasn't so strong, he knew looking at its face would destroy his will. Even now, he had to exert all his strength to keep from falling to the ground and crawling to it.

He glanced at the males around him. Any of them would do for what he wanted, but it was not allowed. They could not take their pleasure with each other, only with the one who had no ties to Earth, who was less than they. Their master was right in his ruling. Once they became lost in sexual frenzy with each other, the unseelie thing might use their distraction to rescue his female and escape.

The male in front of him turned to grin at him. "Thank the gods the fae are immortal. We can take pleasure from it forever."

He snorted his contempt. "Not the gods, but our own hunting party that captured its mate."

A human woman had chosen to love the unseelie animal. She deserved punishment, but they had to keep her alive to ensure the creature's obedience. It had allowed itself to be bound by their magic in return for her safety. But he did not trust that magic or iron chains would hold the creature if it decided to exert its power.

"I like not the look in her eyes. Do you see madness there?"

He wished the male would stop talking so that he could enjoy what was happening at the front of the line. But he did take a moment to glance at the woman.

She stood between two of their guards, as she'd

stood every night since the beginning. It was necessary that she watch each night. The creature needed to see that she still lived. Fury, despair, and love shone from her eyes. But he thought he saw something else in her gaze tonight, something he couldn't identify. It made him uneasy.

Both guards held spears aimed at her heart. One wrong move by her fae lover and she'd die. Not even a creature with its immense power could reach her in time to stop her death. It knew, and the knowing kept it biddable.

"The guards grow lax."

He shrugged. She'd grown weaker. And not once had she attempted to escape. So if one of her guards occasionally left her side for a moment, he could see no harm. He frowned. They needed to feed her better or something. She could not be allowed to die.

Ah, he was next in line. He licked his lips in anticipation as he watched the male who'd spoken to him take his turn. Cuts, bruises, and blood covered the fae creature's bared body, but still it kept its unearthly beauty. The beauty helped him forget that he was reduced to taking his sexual pleasure from one such as this.

He grew even harder as he watched his fellow male flip the dark fairy onto its stomach, free his cock, and drive into its body. The male yanked its head up by all that tangled hair and sank his fangs into its throat. He took the creature in the most savage way he could. Males of his clan enjoyed inflicting pain. Watching another's agony made their climaxes more intense.

But just as the other male finished, making room for him, shouts broke out. He turned to see what was happening. Whatever it was, he would not let it interfere with his pleasure. He'd waited in a long line for this.

It was the woman. The guard had grown too careless. He'd been so busy watching what the other males were doing that he'd taken his attention from the creature's mate.

The woman had thrown herself on the guard's spear. Even with all the blood, he could see it had pierced her heart. Her dimming gaze was fixed on her mate. Her dying words were weak, but he had no problem hearing her.

"You are free now, Kione. Know that I love you."

And that quickly she was dead.

He slowly turned back to the . . . *Gone.* All that was left were its chains. Foreboding touched him, but he pushed it aside in favor of anger that he had missed his turn.

He rubbed at his eyes. What was the matter? He felt as though he were racing backward, the scene growing ever more distant. And then . . .

Utah shook his head and blinked. His mind finally caught up with reality. He was back in the rose garden. Damn. He never wanted to go along on one of Kione's memory trips again. Whatever sympathy he might have felt for the five vampires had disappeared.

Lia. Had she experienced the same thing? God, he hoped not. He looked for her.

She was crying. Lia didn't cry. Ever. It went along with the never-being-afraid thing. Why was she on her knees? She stood, keeping her head down, trying to control the pain she felt for Kione, the hate for his abusers, the sorrow for the woman who'd died to save him.

And when she felt a hand on her shoulder, Lia knew who it was. Utah. She kept her head down, didn't look at him.

"He escaped them, Lia. He's here, he *survived*. And no matter what was done to him, what he lost, he lived. We need to celebrate that, because it's always about keeping on." He massaged her shoulder as he murmured his comfort.

"Maybe he didn't survive, I mean, the part of him that counts. He's never gotten over it." She tried to wipe the tears from her eyes. "God, who could?" Had anyone grieved for Kione, for the unknown woman?

He didn't make cheerful sounds, he didn't demand she look at him, he just gave her his silence. And that was enough.

Lia's instinct was to keep her face hidden until the tears were gone, her traitorous emotions under control. After all, she had a kickass rep to defend. But maybe she didn't want to defend it tonight.

Maybe tonight, with this man, she'd allow herself to be human once more, with a human's unapologetic expression of horror and grief for what

Kione had endured. Sort of ironic that she should turn to her human side when she was no longer human. Dad would applaud.

Lia raised her head and met Utah's gaze. She blinked at the tears blurring her vision. She didn't apologize.

He didn't smile or try to make her feel better. He didn't rush into words meant to take her mind off what she'd seen. He simply wrapped his arms around her and held her. And that was enough.

Slowly, though, something else intruded. Something unwanted, uncontrollable. *Hunger.* A need so powerful she couldn't contain it. Not normal even for a newly made vampire. God knew, after a lifetime spent around them, she recognized what was normal for vampires.

Her gaze fixed on his throat, the pulse beating there. She could hear the rush of his blood, almost smell the coppery scent. Her fangs lengthened even as a killing frenzy gripped her. She opened her mouth and struck.

Utah must've been on his guard because he jerked away from her at the same time he gripped her arms, holding her in place. "What the hell's the matter with you? And don't give me that crap about being newly risen and needing blood. You're stronger than this."

Lia almost tripped in her frantic effort to put distance between them. Utah let her go.

"I don't know what that was about. This feeling just came over me. I knew I had to kill you." She pushed her hair from her face as she tried to calm herself, to think. "Until further notice, I think you need to stay away from me."

Hurt flashed in his eyes just before he wiped all expression from his face. "Sure. No problem." He looked away.

She couldn't deal with this now. Lia forced her attention back to what was happening in the center of the field.

Kione finally spoke. "As you saw, it was tough being the only date in town."

His words might sound light, but Lia heard the layers of hate, bitterness, and heartbreak in his voice.

"I was weak, but when I felt her die, strength came from somewhere. I broke their spell and their bindings. I returned to the unseelie court, where I gathered a force. Then I returned. We destroyed them. But I could not find her mortal remains." He paused, and Lia could feel his despair at not being able to lay her to rest. "I did not love again."

And in that stark statement, Lia heard the depth of what the woman had meant to him.

Kione's attention was totally on his five enemies. "I will free you enough so that you can speak. I wouldn't deny any man his last words."

The vampire who'd been the first to step forward must've been their leader because he was the only one who spoke. "How do we know you tell the truth? You have the power to paint any pictures you want in our minds."

"I didn't expect you to believe me. All these centuries, you thought I'd destroyed all of your clan. I didn't."

Lia could almost feel the collective shock of everyone there.

"There were no survivors." The vampire was adamant in his denial. "We would've known."

"How? We didn't leave enough to identify." Kione shrugged. "I had a lot of hate to vent. Sorry about leaving all those pieces behind."

The vampire didn't answer. Lia supposed he was busy trying to deal with that hole in his chest.

There seemed to be a ripple in the air near Kione, and suddenly, a man appeared. No, make that a vampire. He looked a lot like the five on the ground, except he didn't have their darkness clinging to him or a hole in his chest.

Kione motioned to the new vampire. "For those in the audience, this is Kazan. He was the only one who took no part in what happened during that time. I allowed him to live just in case I ever needed someone to give witness to the truth of what was done to me and mine."

No one made a sound. No one moved.

Kazan spoke. He didn't look at the vampires on the ground. "Kione told the truth. I was there. I did not have the courage to speak out against it. For that, I apologize. I agreed to leave the clan's home and never return. I made no effort to contact any who were not there when the fae attacked. I had no wish to revisit the destruction of my clan or what led up to it. For that I do not apologize."

Time seemed to stretch on forever. Then the spokesman for the five vampires spoke again. "I have discussed this with my clansmen. We agree that you were wronged, Kione. We will remove the curse." He sounded as though giving up his vendetta was as painful as the gaping wound in his chest.

Giving up vendettas. For just a moment, she thought of Utah. How long would he carry his hate for all vampires? She hadn't helped the process along by trying to rip out his throat.

"Aren't you a little too late with your magnanimous offer? All I have to do is kill you to end the curse." Kione sounded anxious for the killing.

The vampire nodded. "I do not deny that you have a right to your anger with all of us."

"Damn right I do." Kione spoke through clenched teeth. "And it was never about what was done to me. It was always about *her.*" All his agony at losing the unnamed woman lived in Kione's voice. Time had not dimmed the memory.

And here Lia had always thought of Kione as emotionless. Maybe he was in other things, but not when it came to the woman he'd loved. *Still* loved.

"Kazan will remain as your clan's only survivor."

The five vampires did not beg for their lives.

"To destroy us is your right." There was acceptance in the vampire's voice. The other four said nothing.

No. Lia couldn't let this happen. "Wait."

Everyone turned to look at her.

"You can't kill them, Kione. This is bigger than your revenge."

Kione didn't comment, so she forged ahead. "I've read about this clan. After the fae attack, everyone thought only these five were left. They were the clan's most powerful hunters. The entire vampire world feared them. If not for Jude, the other clans would've banded together to destroy them. You know this."

Kione remained silent.

"But Jude felt it was unfair to destroy them simply out of fear. He gave them his protection, acknowledged them as his." She took a deep breath before she realized it was no longer necessary. "If you destroy them, he'll be obligated to challenge you. This is one of our rules. And if he fights you, he'll be lost not only to his people but also to the Eleven."

"So you're saying that the survival of the human race is more important than my puny complaint."

She glared at him. "Stop putting words in my mouth. No one thinks your complaint is puny. But they've agreed to remove the curse. They weren't even there when everything happened." Okay, so she was copping out by using a neutral word like "everything." She straightened her back, lifted her chin, and for just a second met Kione's gaze. "When they raped you and caused the death of the woman you loved."

He looked away first.

Lia had no idea what he would've said next, because just then Jude stepped out of the shadows.

"I'm sorry I missed the beginning of the ball. Adam had me doing chores. You know, the usual—sweeping the hearth, waiting on my evil stepsisters, searching for my missing slipper. But now I'm here, and I'm taking my men home." Jude's eyes blazed with the threat of violence.

Kione didn't acknowledge him, just turned his gaze to Utah. "You called me partner. You said you would stand with me. Will you honor that promise?"

Uh-oh. Caught between a rock and a hard case of fae vengeance. Lia looked at Utah, tried to tell him with her eyes that she supported him. But she was afraid that all her eyes telegraphed was: *I want to kill you.* She glanced away.

Utah didn't hesitate. "I'll stand between you and anyone who tries to hurt you, but I can't kill any of these people. All of them have fought beside me." He nodded toward the five prone vampires. "Even them. Remember what I said about loyalty? It still stands."

Lia could count the seconds in years as Kione made his decision.

Finally, he stepped back. "Free me from your curse and then go." Kione didn't sound too happy about the way things had played out.

Kione might've wanted to put a period to his personal nightmare with a good old-fashioned slaughter, but Lia felt limp with relief.

She watched as the vampires stumbled to their feet, hands clutching at chests that still oozed blood. Kazan joined them and helped to support the leader as he gasped out a promise.

"Once we have fed and regained enough strength, we will remove the curse." He hesitated. "We are sorry for . . . her."

From a man who probably had no emotions left for anyone or anything, feeling sorry was about equal to a normal person pounding his chest, tearing his clothes, and shrieking like a banshee.

Kione said nothing. He simply disappeared. Lia glanced around the field. Jude was walking toward his men while Ty and Spin headed toward the SUV. Where was Utah?

Her heart pounded with fear before she took hold of her emotions. He was fine. She was fine. She didn't need to know where he was. Probably as far away from her and her shiny new fangs as he could get. She didn't blame him.

Lia took a moment to close her eyes and just try to clear her mind. Unfortunately, images of Kione's torture played over and over behind her closed lids. They wouldn't be going away anytime soon.

"Do you need help?"

Fin's voice startled Lia. She opened her eyes. "Now you show up." And if she sounded a little ticked, she had a right to.

"I'm sorry." He didn't sound sorry. "I had to keep a lot of humans tucked tight in their beds. And there were a few nonhumans who wanted to join the party. I had to make them understand that this was an invitation-only event."

"Fine. So you couldn't stick around." She scanned the field. Where was Utah?

"I think you should go with Jude and his men."

Surprised at Fin's suggestion, she stopped searching for Utah and stared at him. "Why?" Suddenly, she realized something. She felt no compulsion to attack him.

"You're handling your new-vampire status well, but eventually, your hunger will catch up with you. Jude will have what you need." Fin the diplomat. "And afterward, come back to my condo. We can keep you safe until you adjust."

Safe in his containment room, probably. "Actually, I don't want any blood right now." Of course, if Utah wandered up, she'd probably attach herself to his throat. She needed to find out what was happening there. "I fed from Zero right before we came here." Lia hadn't meant to say that. Fine, so maybe she had. On some level, she'd wanted to upset Fin. Did that make her a mean person?

"Congratulations. I'm sure you're the first. Tell

me if you feel yourself changing into a megalo-maniac." Fin turned and walked away.

Well, that had gone well. Lia continued her search for Utah. Finally, she found him. He was standing beside a tree at the edge of the field. If she didn't have her new enhanced vision, she would've missed him. He stepped out of the shadows when he realized she'd spotted him. But he didn't come nearer.

Lia walked as close as she could, but stopped as soon as she felt the bloodlust rise. "Utah, this isn't about you." She waved her hand in front of her to signal that he should ignore that statement. "No, it *is* about you. *Only* you. I'm not feeling a need to drink from anyone else."

"Should I feel honored?"

Okay, so he had a right to be sarcastic. "I'll figure this out. I'm driving back with Jude, and I'll ask him if he knows what's going on."

Utah looked cold and remote standing in the darkness. Was this the warm and sensual man she'd made love with? Not that she could feel.

"Look me up when you think you can stand being around me." Then he followed Fin away from the field.

Her steps dragged as she followed Jude and his men in the opposite direction. She'd wanted this all her life, so where was the exhilaration? Maybe if Katherine was still around, she . . . She what? *Would love you because you were now worthy? Would respect you as much as she respected her favorite vampires?* Lia pushed the thoughts away. Probably a little too close to the truth. Anyway, she had other things to think about.

She caught up with Jude. "Fin says I should ride with you. Guess he doesn't trust me not to tear out a few throats and make myself a mixed drink. I should've told him I don't drink before breakfast."

Jude laughed as he unlocked a van he'd gotten somewhere. "Hop in. Lucky for you, Reed loaned me his vehicle." He cast her a sideways glance as he went around to the driver's side and climbed in. "Since someone still has *my* car."

She slid into the passenger seat. The five vampires crawled into the back. They didn't seem to be in a talking mood. Kazan had taken off as soon as he'd helped them into the van.

"I'm sorry. With everything happening, I forgot to ask Shen for a loaner."

"Not your fault. You're driving my car because Adam wants to show me he's the boss." His voice vibrated with anger. "Where do you want to go?"

"I need to buy enough blood to get me through a few nights, and then you can drop me off at Fin's. Oh, and I need to borrow a gun. Zero kept mine."

"Sure thing." He stayed quiet for a short time as he drove the dark and deserted Portland streets. "Anything else bothering you?"

She sighed. Jude was too perceptive. "Maybe I wasn't just kidding about tearing out throats."

"Uh-huh." He pulled into the driveway of a darkened house.

"One particular throat."

"Let me guess. Utah's." He turned off the motor and sat in the sudden quiet just watching her.

"It's weird. I understand the issues new vampires have, so I was extra careful. I made sure I wasn't hungry when Zero brought me to the rose garden. I had everything under control." She threw up her hands. "Then Utah came close. I guess what I felt was bloodlust because all I wanted to do was grab him and drink. There was no rational thought connected to it."

Jude nodded. "Not unusual."

"But I didn't feel that way with anyone else. I stood and talked with Fin. Nothing."

"Hmm."

Lia dropped her voice to almost a whisper. "It wasn't just the bloodlust. It was something else." She took a deep breath. "I wanted to kill Utah. I wanted to freaking *kill* him."

CHAPTER THIRTEEN

Fin drove everyone to his condo. Ty and Spin's drivers picked them up and drove them back to their apartments. Utah went directly to his room. There was no sign of Kione.

The last two bothered Fin. Once Kione got rid of his curse, he'd have no real reason to stay. And they needed him. Not many beings had his power. Loyalty? Fin doubted that Kione would think twice about his promise to help track down Seven. With great age came great cynicism. Self-interest ruled the universe. He firmly believed that. Except for his men. He'd chosen them carefully. They had no hidden motives. Sometimes he hated himself for taking advantage of them.

And what about Utah? Ty and Al had found love and married. Love hadn't been part of Fin's long-range plans. He needed total commitment from his men. Love could divide their loyalties at a critical moment. But even he wasn't enough of a bastard to deny them their happiness.

Now it seemed as though Utah was walking down the same path. Fin recognized the signs. Maybe there was still hope, though. Lia was vampire, and Utah might not be able to get past that. Too bad Fin didn't have a close relationship with his men. He could tell Utah that love was a bitch who walked away from you when you needed her the most.

Fin waited only long enough to make sure no one would notice him leaving before heading back to his SUV. He didn't need a vehicle to get where he was going, but he was tired. Driving took less energy. And he had to do this before morning.

Ty and Spin had pretty much torn up the International Rose Test Garden. It was a Portland landmark. Someone would notice. When strange things started happening, people began asking questions. Too many questions, and eventually, someone would come up with an answer.

Fin didn't think about anything during the drive. He was never safe from Zero's probing, so the best defense was a blank mind. Once there, he parked far enough away so that no one would connect the car with the rose garden and walked the rest of the way.

Too bad that someone had gotten there before him.

She knelt in the dirt surrounded by broken and

crushed rosebushes. She might wear a stranger's face, but he knew her soul. She looked up as he approached. Tears filled her eyes.

"They were so beautiful." She cradled one perfect rose in the palms of her hands.

"This was not their time."

"Of course it was their time. I gave them heat. I gave them everything they needed."

"They bloomed out of season."

She made a disgusted sound. "You never had any imagination." Her gaze swept the ruined plants and beyond. "This city is too cold. My parting gift to Portland will be heat, lots and lots of heat." She cast him a sideways glance. "And blood."

"So you'll force your vision on the land." He crouched down across from her. "You were always impetuous and obstinate."

She smiled, and for a moment the smile warmed something eternally cold inside him.

"And those were my good qualities."

"Why are you here with *him*? You weren't one of his the last time he visited Earth."

She shrugged. "Nothing stays the same. Someone was lost to time. I took his place. I thought it was a worthy venture. Humans have misused the planet. Another species deserves a chance."

He decided not to ask if the dinosaurs had misused the planet too. She'd had no part in that, and sarcasm wouldn't gain him anything. "Do you believe the nonhuman population will do better?"

"I have no idea." She placed the rose carefully

on the ground. "Have you come to banish me from Earth?"

"No, that's not my destiny."

"You abandoned your destiny millions of years ago."

Fin smiled. She never changed. "You were always so sure you knew what my future held. Unfortunately, you didn't ask for my input."

She cast him an exasperated look that took him back to so very long ago. Across the millions of years, he still remembered that exact expression. He'd missed it.

"You call us by numbers. I always knew that numbers would consume you one day. Be warned that I won't answer to Seven. I'm Christine for the short time I'm here." She scooped up some soil and let it run through her fingers. "I'll miss the realness of this place."

Fin stood. This conversation couldn't lead to anything good. "I have to put everything back the way I found it." He drew on his well of power, visualized what he wanted, and watched it manifest. Without the flowers. So easy to fix all the snapped and crushed plants, so hard to repair the broken parts of his own existence. "Leave this city, stop recruiting for Zero, and you'll get to stay on Earth until the winter solstice."

She smiled up at him. "I bet he hates you calling him Zero. And no, I don't think I *will* leave this city, at least not until I've done what I came to do."

Tight-lipped, he nodded and turned to walk away.

She called his name. The name he hadn't heard for millions of years. He paused but didn't turn around.

"Come back to me." Her voice was soft with all that had been between them.

The need to turn around, to go back to her, almost won. Then he drew in a deep breath and closed his eyes. "That name belonged to someone from a long time ago. He's gone. Forget it. Forget *him*." And every word dug into his heart—the heart his men believed he didn't have—and he bled.

She didn't try to call him to her again. And when he paused to glance back once he was out of sight, he saw that the rosebushes were once again in bloom.

He should wait until she left and get rid of the roses. He didn't. That was all he could ever give her. Fin walked away.

Maybe it was just his mood, but the drive back to the condo seemed extra long and dark. For a few minutes back in the garden, he hadn't felt alone. He'd been with someone who knew him, understood a little of what he was.

His aloneness sometimes drove him crazy. But he could never share friendship with his men. No one could be allowed to get close because in a moment of weakness he might say too much.

If his men ever found out what he was . . . No, friendship was out.

Fin parked the SUV and headed up to his condo. He found Lia waiting by the elevator in the lobby. She had a small cooler at her feet.

She glanced at the security guard. "He's trying to make up for falling asleep on the job by being extra vigilant. He wouldn't let me go up until you gave the okay."

Fin nodded at the guard and followed her into the elevator. The door closed. He waited for her to break the silence.

"I promise I won't leave holes in all your favorite dinosaurs." She pointed to the cooler at her feet. "I brought my own liquid refreshment. A gift from Jude to celebrate the happy event."

Fin smiled. "Speaking of the happy event, have you told your father?"

She frowned. "Yes. I called him while I was waiting for Jude to get the blood. He wasn't happy about the circumstances. But I was able to convince him not to come here and try to hunt Christine down."

"How did you do that?"

Lia didn't meet his gaze. "I told him I'd be flying home tomorrow."

Fin tried not to show his frustration. He was too tired for this crap. "I think we need to talk."

The opening of the elevator door put a pause to the conversation. But once inside and seated in his office—if he sat on a couch he'd fall asleep—he got ready for a battle that he had to win.

"What made you decide to leave Portland?" Could he be wrong about her feelings for Utah?

"I don't really think you need me to get rid of Christine. No matter what your vision showed, I bet you could do the same thing." She kept her gaze fixed on his hands.

Fin was used to that, but it still got old. Just once, he'd like to yell, *Look at me, damn it*. But that would destroy his reputation as a cold, emotion-less, and definitely inscrutable bastard. Besides, he sensed she wasn't avoiding his gaze because he made her nervous. She probably didn't want him to read anything in her eyes.

"Interesting ring. Any significance?"

Fin frowned. What did his ring have to do with anything?

He glanced down. "No. I just liked the design."

She didn't look as though his answer satisfied her, but she subsided.

"Would you like to tell me the truth now?"

Startled, she finally stared at him. "What do you mean?"

Fin just stared back. And if he allowed a little of his rage that always simmered right below the surface to show in his eyes, so much the better.

"Put the purple away. I'm not intimidated." She sighed. "This is about two things. First, I can't be Utah's partner anymore. Whenever I get close to him, I want to sink my teeth into his throat. We're not talking love bites here. And it's just him. I don't feel like biting you."

"Interesting." He steepled his fingers and studied her. "I could give you another partner."

"I don't want another partner. And I don't want to hunt Christine. Get someone else to do it. And, yes, I sound like a whiny kid." She got up as if to leave.

"Sit down." He put a little compulsion into the command.

Lia sat back down, but she didn't look happy about it.

"Did Zero say anything or do anything to you?"

She closed her eyes. "I woke up. He was there. He talked to me. I don't remember what he said. I slept. When I woke up again, he slashed his wrist and made me drink. Then he brought me to the rose garden." She opened her eyes. "That was it."

"I'm surprised you didn't starve trying to feed from the bloodless bastard." Fin raked his fingers through his hair. He shouldn't have said that.

Lia smiled for the first time. "Well, well, two snarky comments from the great Fin in one night. I like it." She shook her head. "You know, there was something strange about his blood. As I was drinking, I got this crazy idea that the blood was almost a living thing. It was searching for a place to hide so it could wait . . . for something. I know, it doesn't make sense. It was my first bloodlust, and things were all mixed up in my mind."

"Zero is a powerful being. I'm not surprised

his blood affected you." Fin allowed himself a tight smile. "We're all tired. Don't make any final decision about going home until you've had a good day's sleep." He turned to glance at the lightening sky.

She followed his gaze. "I'll miss the dawns." Lia stood and walked to the door. "Sure you don't want to walk me to my room, lock the door behind me?"

"Not necessary. You'll be asleep as soon as your head hits the pillow. Don't forget to make sure the curtains are drawn."

"There are a lot of things I'll have to get used to." And then she was gone.

Fin sat for a while watching the dawn, and thinking. Lia's reactions weren't normal for her. She wouldn't just give up on the search for Seven. It wasn't in her nature. And there was no logical reason for her obsession with killing only Utah. Unless . . .

Zero. He'd have no trouble implanting a few suggestions and then taking away her memory of his doing it. He had no way of knowing how important she was, so he'd simply opted for prodding her into leaving the city. He'd probably pulled her interest in Utah from her mind and used it against her.

This presented a problem, though. Fin didn't know if he could free her. Zero was too powerful. But whether he could or not, one thing was sure. He wouldn't allow Lia to get on a plane back to Philadelphia. Her destiny was linked to Seven, whether she believed it or not.

Utah woke to the sound of someone pounding on his door. When it didn't stop, he crawled from his bed and shuffled over to open it. This better mean the building was on fire. He'd tossed and turned until long after dawn. He got a little cranky when he was sleep deprived.

He flung open the door to find Tor grinning at him. His brother held a covered tray. Utah growled something before turning and shuffling to the nearest chair. He dropped into it and closed his eyes. "What?" He heard his brother settle into the chair across from him.

"Hey, you've slept like the dead all day. Oops, guess I misspoke. Nothing wrong with sleeping like the dead." He scanned the room. "Lia isn't around, is she?"

Utah muttered a string of his favorite curses and attached them to Tor's name.

"You had to wake up sometime, so don't get pissed at me."

Utah opened one eye. "I'm deciding how to kill you." He needed coffee to give him the strength to open the other eye. His gaze fell on the tray. Tor had uncovered it.

Utah opened the other eye. "Okay, you live." He reached for the carafe of coffee. After pouring a cup, he leaned back in the chair. "Talk."

"I've been watching the news this afternoon."

"Yeah?" Was Lia up yet? Utah glanced at the clock. Almost sunset.

"Fin gave us a mental wake-up call this morning to fill everyone in on what happened last night. And according to local news, your rose garden isn't the only thing that's blooming."

Utah was suddenly alert.

"Authorities are worried. Things are heating up in Portland. Almost overnight plants and trees are putting out leaves and flower buds. The ground is getting warmer."

"She always brings the heat. That's what Seir said about Seven. She's crazy about growing things." Utah thought for a moment. "And killing things. Any news about crime levels?"

"Yeah. Homicides are through the roof. The police aren't giving any info about how all the victims died, but at least some of them looked as though large animals had mauled them."

"Seven isn't only drawing vampires to her. What we have is a nonhuman crime spree. And she's cheering them on." Utah put his coffee down and stood. "I don't know what's happening with the ground. Have you talked to Fin about this?"

"No. I came to your room as soon as I got here." Tor picked up the remote from the coffee table. "Go get dressed. I'll wait."

Utah didn't spend much time in the shower. His hair was still damp when he joined Tor. Together they went down to the dining room.

As he walked into the room, he had a fleeting

impression of Ty, Kelly, Al, and Jenna at the table. No sign of Kione. Fin sat at the head of the table. But all Utah really saw was Lia.

Utah hesitated. It was a big table. He had lots of chairs to choose from. He took one step toward the chair next to Lia, and then he saw the panic in her eyes. She dropped her gaze to hide it, but she was a little too late. He wasn't about to make her uncomfortable, so he sat between Kelly and Jenna.

Jenna clucked at him.

Utah stared at her. "Is there a reason for that?"

Kelly poked him with her elbow. "In her own subtle way, my sister is hinting that your backbone is a little rubbery." She turned to her husband. "Speaking of poultry, did you know that scientists believe chickens are the descendants of the mighty T. rex?"

Ty looked outraged. *"Chickens?"*

"Cross my heart." Kelly laughed.

Jenna leaned close to Utah. "You should've sat next to Lia."

"She doesn't want me near her."

Jenna shook her head. "Beautiful but clueless."

Okay, he wasn't going to sit here and take this abuse all through his meal. Utah stood and went around the table to sit next to Lia. Jenna's laughter followed him.

Lia offered him a quick smile.

"Will you be all right with me sitting here?" He noticed that she leaned away from him.

She shrugged. "If I go for your neck, throw your

glass of water on me. Fin blessed it right before he parted the Willamette River. It was spectacular."

Utah smiled and tried to relax. "Do you still want to kill me?"

"Very much."

"Then why don't you ask me to move?"

Lia finally turned her head and met his gaze. "Because I want you near me more than I want to kill you."

Utah forced back his instant surge of hope. Fate had a way of squashing him when his expectations bypassed reality. Besides, he hadn't decided how he felt about her as vampire yet. *Who're you trying to kid? You still think about her all the time. You still want to make love to her. Looks as though her fangs haven't slowed you down much.* Self-knowledge was a bitch.

He decided to drop the subject as Greer put a plate of bacon, eggs, and sausage in front of him. Breakfast didn't have a set time at Fin's. Utah paused as he noticed the silence beside him. He glanced at Lia.

"No, don't let me stop you from eating." She kept her gaze on the food. "I just can't believe I'm not hungry for any of that stuff."

"Do you have blood here?" Utah decided he might as well say the B word.

Lia slid her gaze over his body until she reached his neck. "Sitting right next to me." She must've sensed his startled horror because she laughed.

"Lighten up, raptor. I've already fed. Jude supplied me with lots of blood. It's in the fridge."

Utah nodded and tried not to look relieved. Wasn't much he could say to that. He glanced to where Tor had just finished talking to Fin. Probably filling him in on the latest news.

"I need your attention for a few minutes." Fin rose and pushed back his chair. He picked up his coffee and walked over to the bank of windows. Then he stood staring out at the darkness.

Utah tried to focus as Fin told everyone what Tor had discovered. It was tough. He didn't have to be looking at Lia to be aware of her. Her scent—vanilla and sensual woman—clung to her. She must've just showered. That thought immediately led to images of warm water flowing over her naked body, her skin gleaming, her . . .

He took a deep breath and forced his attention back to Fin.

"I knew Seven a long time ago, before she joined Zero." Fin kept his back to the table. "I've already told you this, but you . . . forgot."

You could almost hear the collective intake of breaths. Utah wasn't surprised at the news. He just wondered why Fin felt a need to admit it.

"I'm telling you this so you'll accept what I say next as true." Fin's voice held no inflection. "Seven is working up to something big. I think she's almost finished with Portland. And she always liked to celebrate. I'd guess that in the very near

future she'll call all her recruits together for a go-
ing-away party. Unfortunately, her idea of a good
time will mean a bad time for Portland."

"What are we supposed to do?" Ty's voice was
tight.

"Keep your ears to the ground. Literally." Fin
finally turned to look at them. His eyes were flat.
"She's obsessed with plants and the earth. If she
decides to make a statement, that's where it'll
happen. Report back anything you hear or observe that has to do with an earth change. And
she's a chaos bringer, so she'll enjoy upping the
killings to throw the general population into a
panic."

He stopped talking, and the silence dragged on
and on until Lia spoke.

"This is a little off-topic, but I really want to
know. You didn't answer me last time I asked. You
knew Seven. The rest of your men didn't. There
seem to be lots of differences between you and
your men. So I assume you weren't a dinosaur
like them. What were you sixty-five million years
ago?"

Instinctively, Utah braced himself for the stabbing pain in his head and the brain fog that wiped
everything away. He didn't have any proof, but he
suspected he wouldn't even remember her asking
the question. *She* wouldn't remember asking it.

Nothing happened. Fin walked back to the
table and sat down. "I wasn't a dinosaur. That's
all you need to know."

Shock seemed to keep everyone quiet. Fin had never openly offered insight into his past. Sure, he'd hinted at some things to a few of the guys one-on-one, but never like this.

Fin glanced at Lia and Utah. "When you're finished, I'd like to see you in my office." And without a backward glance, he left the room.

Ty looked thoughtful. "Maybe it's time to get a few things out in the open." He glanced around the room. "We were something else before our souls ended up in predators. Some of us know for sure, and some of us just suspect it. As part of our wedding ceremonies, Fin gave both Kelly and Jenna glimpses into the before time."

"He gave me a little of my memory back too." Al reached out for Jenna's hand. "Not enough to know what was going on, but enough to scare the shit out of me."

Jenna nodded. "It was a nightmare world. I think Fin feels obligated to keep it from you guys." She took a deep breath. "And he *is* keeping it from you."

"Guess he's loosening up a little then, because you know he's in our heads now, so he knows what we're discussing." Ty glanced at Kelly.

Kelly nodded. "He could stop this little trip down memory lane anytime he wanted."

Utah worked hard to hold on to his temper. "And you never saw fit to tell the rest of us any of this?" He didn't need to look at Tor to know his brother felt the same anger.

Ty tensed, his T. rex reacting to Utah's challenge. "What good would knowing that little bit do? It would just confuse everyone, take their focus away from Zero. And you might think you're big and bad enough to force Fin to tell everything, but your head would be looking for your ass if you tried."

Kelly laid her hand on his arm, a calming influence. "I think Fin is slowly giving us more information. I don't think getting in his face and demanding to know everything would work with him."

Al shrugged. "What are our options? Get mad and walk away? Where would that leave humanity?" He gazed at Jenna, all his love for her there for everyone to see. "Where would that leave *us* if humanity fell?"

Lia stood. "Maybe I should've kept my mouth shut, but it just bothers me that he doesn't have confidence in your ability to handle the truth. I mean, how bad could it be?"

No one offered to answer that, so Utah stood too. "Fin's waiting for us." He aimed a pointed stare at Al, Kelly, and Jenna. "When we have some downtime, I'd like to talk about what Fin showed you." Maybe between here and Fin's office he'd get control over his need to knock his leader on his ass.

They left the others still sitting there. Lia didn't say anything as they walked to Fin's office. He

called them in before they had a chance to knock.
Utah opened the door.

They sat down—Lia pulled her chair as far
away from Utah as possible—and stared at Fin
across his desk. Nothing cluttered the huge expanse. Utah wondered what he did in this office.
From the look of things, it didn't involve paper-
work.

Utah decided to strike first. "Trust is a two-way
street. Someone needs to cuff and ticket you, because you're crossing a lot of lines."

"Think you can do it, raptor?" Danger filled the
room, a dark blanket of dread.

Since suicide wasn't an option, and attacking
Fin would definitely qualify, Utah reined in his
fury. "How can you expect us to trust you when
you don't tell us the truth?"

Fin shrugged. "That's for you to figure out. I do
what I think is best for everyone, given the circumstances."

Lia jumped in. "You have incredible powers, a
lot more than your men. I still don't see why you
can't get rid of Christine."

Utah could almost hear Fin's patience snap.

"If I could do it by myself, I wouldn't be sitting here listening to this crap. I would've taken
her out at the rose garden. Get this through your
head, Lia, you're the *only one* who can send Seven
home. Why? How the hell do I know? Maybe it has
something to do with you drinking Zero's blood.

I don't think he's ever shared it before. Some of his power could've come with it. But that's only conjecture. All I know is that my visions always show the basic scenario, even if some of the details might change."

"It all comes down to you and the number seven. I've sat here for days trying to figure out what form the seven will take." He drew in a deep breath. "I guess the universe will just have to manifest it."

Lia leaned back in her chair. She radiated frustration. "Well, I hope the universe lets me in on the secret before I go mano a mano with the queen of buds and blood."

She took a deep breath. "But that won't happen anytime soon because I'll be flying back to Philly in about four hours. Dad is taking care of it. A friend of a friend has a private jet all decked out for safe travel in daylight. He'll take me home."

No. Utah bit back his impulse to shout the word. His face must've shown what he was thinking, though, because she started to reach out to him, then paused. Sighing, she dropped her hand.

"I'm no use here." She focused on Utah. "You'd never know when I might lose control and attack you."

"I can handle it." He knew he sounded a little desperate, but he couldn't help it. She couldn't leave . . . *him*. When had she become so important? The thought shook him to his soul. And his soul growled its need to force her to stay. There were some things about the good old days he missed.

"Besides, I can't seem to work up any energy to fight Christine." Confusion filled her eyes. "I don't know what the hell's wrong with me."

"I do."

Fin had Utah's instant attention.

"I've had time to think about it, Lia. I'd guess that Zero planted a few compulsions, then made sure you wouldn't remember him messing with your mind." Fin shrugged. "It worked. He wanted you to abandon the battle, and you have."

Startled, her eyes widened. "Why go to all that trouble? Why not just kill me?"

"Dead trade bait loses its value."

"Okay, so if he went the compulsion route, why not plant the suggestion that I kill all of you, not just Utah?"

Utah could see her turning over Fin's statement, examining it from all angles. Whether it was true or not, he hoped she'd believe it, because it might convince her to stay.

"The larger the scope of a compulsion, the more energy it takes. Zero needs every bit of his energy, so he planted only what he thought necessary to achieve his goal. Luckily, he doesn't know how important you are. This whole thing was never about you killing any of us; it was about scaring you into running."

"I don't run." She radiated outrage. "I'm leaving so I won't hurt Utah."

Fin went on as if she hadn't spoken. "Besides, he probably thought if he went small with his suggestions, no one would guess he'd compromised your mind."

"I. Don't. Run."

"Running is running no matter what the reason." Fin's voice was soft, but he might as well have been shouting.

Lia's glare had all of her old fight in it. "That bastard. How do I get rid of his crap?"

"I don't know."

"Not the answer I want." Lia balled her hands into fists.

"He's too powerful." Fin's words seemed dragged from him. "I'll need time to work on it." He rubbed his forehead, a rare expression of frustration for Fin. "I might need help."

"What about Kione and Jude? Even Adam?" Utah would use the devil himself if he could help Lia.

Fin shook his head. "Not powerful enough."

Utah met Lia's gaze. "Stay. I'll help you. Leaving won't cure the compulsions, it'll just put them on hold." Was he begging? You bet.

She closed her eyes for a moment, and Utah swore he didn't breathe during the whole time.

Finally, she opened them. "I'll stay." Her smile didn't quite reach her eyes as she looked at Utah.

"But if you end up a dry husk in a ditch somewhere, don't say I didn't warn you."

Utah exhaled deeply. Thank God.

If Fin was relieved, he didn't show it. But that was just Fin being Fin. "Now for the reason I asked you here. Adam contacted me. He wants to see both of you as soon as you can get there. I don't know what this is about."

Not something good. Utah wasn't looking forward to the meeting. "Have you seen Kione?"

"No. The vampires must've freed him from the curse by now. He's probably long gone."

Lia looked a little sad. "You don't have much trust in the goodness of people, do you?"

Fin returned her smile, only his was a lot colder. "I have no reason to."

"Guess we'd better get going. Don't want to keep Adam waiting," Utah lied. He'd love to keep the bastard waiting. Forever. But he wanted out of this room. And he was sort of curious about what Adam would say now that he knew Seven was taking his vampires.

"You need a driver now that Lia isn't human. Greer will take over that job until further notice. He's about as human as you get around here." Fin smiled, and this time it reached his eyes. "I hope you appreciate the sacrifice I'm making. I'll have to cook my own meals. It's hard to look godlike when you're burning the bacon."

Fin waved them out the door. "Greer's waiting

for you in Utah's new car. And yes, I remembered that neither of you had a vehicle. Tell Jude he can pick up his car here." He met Lia's gaze. "Stay strong. Utah can help you fight the compulsions."

They didn't speak on the way down in the elevator.

When they finally stopped beside the car, Utah asked the inevitable question. "Where do you want to sit? You in front, me in back, or vice versa?"

"Let's try both in back." She waved off his attempt to interrupt. "I have to work on my control. If I let Zero dictate how I live my life, then he wins."

He nodded, and they climbed in.

Greer headed for Old Town. "Hope you don't mind, but I drive fast and hard. It's the only power trip my tiger ever gets."

"The faster the better." Lia sounded fierce.

Utah loved that about her.

"What do you think about Kione?" She sat pressed against her door.

Utah gave her all the space he could. "Don't have a clue. I can't read him." He hoped he got a chance to see the fae prince again.

The conversation lagged as awareness reared its sexy head, at least for him. Lia's tension might have a lot to do with her urge to slide across the seat and sink her fangs into his neck.

Logically, he knew she was vampire. That should translate to hate in his mind. Well, his mind wasn't getting the message. It along with the rest of his body thought she was fine in whatever form she wore. No use fighting the inevitable. He thought Rap would understand.

Luckily for all concerned, Greer's driving was insane. Couldn't concentrate on much of anything when death waited for you around every curve. They were soon parked behind the art gallery.

Greer turned to look at them. "Fin wants me to wait out here. Better that way. Don't want the bastards to be picking their teeth with my bones and drinking to each other's health with my blood. Times like this I wish I was a real shifter, none of this a-tiger-in-my-heart shit."

Utah clapped him on the back. "Stay safe." Then he and Lia climbed out.

Reed still waited like a fanged goliath by the door, but someone else waited too.

Kione stepped out of the shadows.

CHAPTER FOURTEEN

She was glad to see Kione. That surprised Lia. Maybe seeing how he'd suffered, how he'd *loved*, made him more . . . human. Or not. You couldn't judge someone's humanity on a sliding scale. And being human didn't guarantee goodness and light. Besides, she didn't qualify as a judge of humanity anymore. She should change her wording. Seeing how Kione had suffered made him seem more *vulnerable*. And vulnerability softened some of his sharp fae edges.

Oh, and she was also glad to see him because he could act as a buffer between Utah and her.

"Where the hell have you been?" Utah's grin balanced out his gruff words.

"I had to make sure my vampire friends did what they promised." Kione's cold eyes seemed to warm a little as he reached them.

"Did they?" She hoped so. No one deserved to live with that kind of pain.

"Yes." For a moment, Kione looked almost disbelieving. "I'm free."

"From *everything*?" Utah tensed.

Kione laughed. A rare sound. "Don't worry, I'll keep my promise to Fin."

Utah relaxed. "Good. I'd hate to have to break in a new partner."

Lia interrupted. "Guess we'd better go see what Adam wants. It probably won't be good."

As usual, Reed had nothing to say as they entered the building. Another silent vampire opened the door to the tunnels. Utah took the lead as they walked down the dark corridor toward where the tunnel opened to a slightly larger area, and Adam sat with his vampires grouped in a semicircle around him. Candles cast shadows across their still faces. The play of light and dark highlighted Adam's perfect face, accented his golden eyes, and chilled her blood.

There were a lot more vampires this time. They waited, silent, with unblinking eyes that gleamed black in the candlelight. Adam stood as Utah reached him.

Uneasiness poked at Lia. There shouldn't be this many vampires here right now. This was prime hunting time. In front of her, Utah tensed. He felt it too.

"You wanted to see us?"

Utah sounded relaxed, but as Lia stepped up

beside him, she could see his narrowed gaze scanning the semicircle of vampires. Behind her, she knew Kione would be doing the same.

"Have a seat." Adam smiled, but his eyes stayed hard.

"No." Utah didn't waste words.

Adam shrugged. "I won't need your services anymore. Christine and I have come to an agreement."

From the corner of her eye, Lia could see the semicircle closing a little. Behind her, Kione hissed a quiet warning. She nodded to let him know she'd heard.

"So your deal with Fin is off?" Utah moved a few inches so that Kione could fit between Lia and him.

"That's about it." Adam abandoned even the semblance of friendliness. "She made me a better offer. I join my forces with hers, and then when she leaves I take over everything."

Lia couldn't keep quiet. "You're already *our* leader, so what did she offer you beyond that?" This was bad. If Adam was able to deliver the whole vampire nation to Seven, the Eleven and humanity were in deep trouble. Jude wouldn't go along with it, so Adam would have to destroy him and any other regional leader who didn't cave.

Adam's eyes glowed with excitement. "She's leading more than just vampires. Once she's gone, I'll control all the shifters, demons, and other nonhumans she's gathered together." He licked his lips. "I'll control the world."

"That's right, think big." Kione's murmur broke the stunned silence.

Lia chose not to point out that Zero had other people out there recruiting, and that not all of *their* nonvampire recruits would follow Adam. She'd let him keep his illusions of world domination. No need to tick him off with a dose of reality.

"Guess we need to leave then." Utah backed up a step. Lia and Kione backed with him. "Where do we pick up our checks?"

Adam looked apologetic. "Sorry, but there won't be any severance pay because . . ." He smiled. "You'll be dead."

"Adam, you are such an optimist." Lia decided her former leader wasn't as smart as she'd thought he was. "Have you really thought this through?"

The strange connection she had with Utah told her his beast was close to the surface. She glanced up—about seven feet clearance right here. Lia hoped that would be enough. His twenty-plus-foot length would fit, but he wouldn't have any maneuvering room. The tunnel was probably twenty feet wide plus whatever width the cells gave it. Enough for him to turn, but not comfortably. And no way would he be chasing anyone. She'd bet these tunnels narrowed in spots.

"I always think things through." Adam drew a gun. "Please don't move. I'm very good at head shots. Even if I don't kill you, I'll put you down

long enough for my friends to finish you off."
Adam smiled, and there was real enjoyment in
his smile. "I'd enjoy watching that."

"Fin will hunt you down." For once, Lia hoped
Fin was monitoring her thoughts.

Adam seemed unconcerned. "Christine promised I'd be under Zero's protection. Checkmate."
He glanced at his watch. "We've wasted enough
time. First I get rid of my dark fairy." He stepped
aside so they could see the circle on the floor.

Then Adam rattled off some words in a language Lia didn't understand. From his gestures,
she figured he was saying something like: "Get
your ass into the circle."

While Adam was speaking, his vampires
closed in around them. Lia glanced at Utah. They
were surrounded.

Fin's voice in her head almost drew a startled
yelp from her.

*"Adam's been trying to get into your mind since you
entered the tunnel. He failed because I'm shielding you
and Utah. I think Kione can take care of his own mind.
None of the Eleven's beasts will fit in the tunnels, so I'm
sending in Shen. I'll keep Zero from interfering."*

Shen? What could he do? Then she stopped
thinking about Fin's assistant as she watched
Kione move toward the circle.

He was obeying a little too easily. Didn't Adam
see that? Guess he was too caught up in his own
power trip. Lia edged away from Utah. She could

almost hear the howl of his beast. Any second now . . .

Kione stepped into the circle and stood waiting. He looked bored. "Say your words, vampire."

Adam frowned. He liked creating fear, and Kione wasn't cooperating. Lia slipped her hand into her coat pocket and gripped the gun Jude had loaned her. Zero still had her sword, but she now had all her shiny new vampire skills to make up for its loss.

Adam's arrogance would bring him down. He wanted to drag out their deaths, play with them. A major mistake. You didn't give your enemies time to prepare.

If Adam thought Utah would stand quietly until it was his time to die, he was stupid. Maybe he thought he and his vampires could react fast enough to keep Utah from releasing his beast. Maybe he even thought Utah wouldn't take the chance of becoming raptor in the confined space of the tunnel. If that's what he thought, he was wrong on both counts.

Utah waited until the moment Adam's attention switched to Kione. That moment was all he needed.

Adam had never seen how fast Utah could change. Utah leaped, and by the time both feet hit the ground, he was raptor. The vampires were a second too slow. Adam's bullet slammed into Utah, but Utah in raptor form didn't even flinch.

Lia's fighting instincts kicked in. She knew better than to get in front of Utah. Adam might have trouble killing *him*, but she'd make an easy target. And getting caught between the raptor's huge body and the tunnel wall was asking to be flattened. So she ran behind him. Way behind him. As a few of the vampires were learning, his tail was a lethal weapon all on its own.

Gunshots echoed through the tunnel again and again. Then she heard the click of Adam's empty gun. The candles flickered out. The darkness was a blanket settling over her—suffocating and totally black.

Something savage and eager woke in her. Even without light, she could see the shadows of Adam's vampires moving in to attack Utah and her. Where was Kione? She curled her lip to expose her fangs. Bloodlust flooded her, burned through her body, screamed its need to tear, and kill, and feed. Lia launched herself at those shadows.

For the first time in her life, she fought as vampire.

Blood. Nothing else mattered. She forgot about her gun. She would rend flesh with her bare hands, sink her fangs into soft throats and drink from spouting rivers of blood, bathe in the warmth flowing over her hands, her body.

Lia loved it. She'd never felt this alive when she was human. Had she ever been human? She couldn't remember what it felt like, couldn't remember anything that came before the *blood*.

Her enemy was all about speed, strength, and fangs. He thought that was enough. Lazy, stupid vampire. Didn't he know that she'd kill him because she wanted it more—the blood, always the blood. Lia realized she was laughing wildly. Why? Didn't matter why. It felt so good, why shouldn't she laugh?

Even when something flung her to the floor, she kept on laughing. Her hands slipped in the puddle of blood collecting around the head of one of Adam's vampires. She didn't know where his body was, didn't care. She had to get up to kill some more. More blood. She needed more damn blood.

Something slithered past her. It felt like . . . a snake? What would a snake be doing in the middle of this?

Before she could think about that, someone yanked her to her feet. Lia leaped at him . . . and immediately ended up back on her ass. She tried to puzzle through the reason for this, but she couldn't think past the scent of blood all around her. *Bloodbloodblood—*

"The bloodlust has you, Lia. Fight it."

The whisper sounded familiar, but she couldn't think. In front of her, the dark mass that was her beast methodically tore apart vampires. He wasn't even trying to drink their blood. That puzzled her. Wait, *her* beast? Why was he *her* beast?

The reason eluded her. Lia turned her attention back to the killing. But there were no more moving shadows. Everything was still. No, it couldn't be over. She could smell so much blood, and it just made her want more. More death. More, more, *more*.

"The battle's over. Adam has fled. He was the only one to escape."

Fled? Who the hell said fled? Did real people talk like that? Lia scrambled to her feet. Nothing knocked her down again, so she looked around. Everything was quiet. No more moving shadows. And her beast was gone. Where? Frantically, she looked around. For some reason, it was important that she find him.

Candlelight flickered on, and in its dim light stood a figure. It had a head, body, two arms, two legs, and a *neck*. Prey!

She launched herself at the figure and hit it with enough force to send both of them to the ground. Lia bared her fangs and struck at his throat. Only his throat wasn't there anymore. He'd moved his head aside and was gripping her shoulders to keep her away from him. How did he have the strength to hold her like that? Furious at being denied all that hot sweet blood, she slashed at his arm, the only part of him she could reach.

Lia barely got to lick his blood from her lips before that unseen force slammed her off him and onto her ass again.

"Newly made vampires are tiring. Piglets at the trough. No self-control." The voice sounded resigned.

The man she'd attacked rose to his feet. He leaned toward her.

She bared her fangs and tensed for the leap.

"Lia."

The word was a hand pressed against her heart, freezing her in place. No, it wasn't the word, but the voice that stopped her. She knew the voice. Utah?

The driving need to kill eased, the crazed blood chant quieted, and Lia was left standing alone with her horror. She stared down at her blood-drenched coat and hands, and knew the blood coated her face too, could smell the coppery scent of it everywhere.

She looked up to meet Utah's gaze. The quiet sadness there made her glance away. Lia drew in her breath. Blood trickled down his arm from an ugly gash. Had she done that? She couldn't remember. *Yes, you can.*

She scraped her hair away from her sticky face. "I lost it, didn't I?"

"Gloriously and completely." Kione didn't seem overly upset about it.

She dared a quick glance back at Utah. The sadness was gone from his eyes, replaced by . . . nothing.

"We need to bandage that arm." She looked around for something that wasn't already soaked in blood.

"Never mind. The bleeding's almost stopped. I'll take care of it later." Utah didn't sound mad.

She would've preferred mad.

The corners of Utah's lips tipped up in a humorless smile. "I hope you've had your rabies shots."

"Not funny, Endeka." She took a deep breath and really looked around her.

Bodies of vampires lay everywhere. "Did the three of us kill all of them?"

"We had some help." Kione nodded toward a shadowed alcove.

Lia frowned. A snake stared back at her. Brown, about six feet long. Looked unassuming.

"That's an inland taipan, also known as the fierce snake. One bite has enough venom to kill one hundred adult humans." Utah walked toward the snake.

"Don't." She couldn't hold back her warning.

Utah glanced over his shoulder. "This is also Shen's shifter form. He can wiggle into small spaces, and the enemy never sees him coming." He grinned at the snake. "He'd return to human form, but he left his clothes upstairs."

Lia sighed. Of course it was Shen. What else could she expect from an assistant to Fin? As she watched Shen slither back up the tunnel, a thought occurred to her. "You keep your clothes when you go from one form to another. Why?" Not a really important question, but she needed a few minutes to put the pieces of her psyche back together again.

Utah glanced down at his still-bleeding arm. "That's because my human form never goes away.

It's not lost to my beast. If we'd been fighting in bright sunlight, you would've seen the shadow of my human form within the beast."

"But the opposite isn't true." Kione seemed intrigued.

"No, my beast stays hidden until I need it. Fin seems to think it's because my humanity is stronger than my beast, that someday my soul might be completely human." Utah shrugged. "I hope that doesn't happen soon. My beast is keeping me alive."

Lia changed the subject. "Adam escaped?"

"He bailed when he saw his vampires going down. Guess he figures they're expendable. Bet he has a lot more where they came from." Utah took one last look around. "Let's get out of here. Fin will send in a cleanup crew."

Lia didn't wait to see who was following her. She was outta here. Now. She could hear Utah's footsteps close behind her as she strode down the tunnel. "I'm surprised you'd get this close to me after what happened." *That's right, rub salt in your wound.*

"You seem okay now. I think you're a lot like me. You have your own beast, only it doesn't have a separate form like mine."

"I'm nothing like you." But even as she rejected his comment, she was thinking about it.

"Yes, you are." He'd moved closer. "You were crazy with bloodlust back there. Your beast was in control. I know the feeling. I've been there."

Talking about bloodlust. "Don't get any closer." Even now, she could feel the compulsion to turn and kill him tugging at her. "Oh, and so we keep my killing urges straight, what I'm feeling now is Zero's compulsion. What I felt back there was just a new vampire's killing high." She made an impatient noise. "I always thought I could control the bloodlust when I became vampire. Shows what I know."

"You were fighting for your life. The adrenaline rush tipped you over the edge. Understandable."

"But I *enjoyed* the killing." That's what she couldn't forgive in herself.

"Welcome to the predators' club." He didn't back off. "I think in a calmer situation, you'll be able to handle this."

She knew her laughter sounded harsh. "You have more faith in me than I have in myself." Time to change the subject. "That rabies crack was mean."

He chuckled. "I was pissed. You're lucky. Most vampires that try to rip out my throat end up chasing their heads down the street."

She fell silent. The vampire thing still stood between them. Oh, he accepted her as a partner, but she couldn't see how he'd ever again accept her as his lover. And that realization hurt. It hurt a lot.

By the time they'd reached the door to the cellar, Kione had caught up with them. They climbed the stairs to the art gallery. Tor, Q, and a fully dressed Shen waited there.

Shen grinned. "That's the most fun I've had since Philly. Oh, and next time watch where you put your big feet, raptor. You almost got my tail. I've never tried to bring down a dinosaur. Might be fun."

Utah didn't rise to the bait. He was too busy worrying about Lia. She looked like she was thinking serious thoughts. He hoped those thoughts didn't involve changing her mind about going back to Philly. "Time to head home. I know I've had enough for one night."

"Go without me. I have some things I want to check out." Kione didn't elaborate.

"If you need a ride, Fin can—"

Kione waved Utah's offer away. "I don't need a car. I *never* needed a car." He proved his point by simply disappearing.

They walked to where Greer still waited in Utah's car. Lia climbed into the back. Utah didn't give her a chance to argue. He slipped in beside her and closed the door.

Greer handed her a few packets of hand wipes and then pulled out of the parking lot. He cranked up the radio. Utah figured he was signaling that he wouldn't be listening to anything they said. Good. Because Utah had lots to say.

"Stop beating yourself up over what happened tonight. It's over. We move on from here."

"*We* move on?" Once again, she'd pressed herself against the far door, putting as much distance as possible between them.

She scrubbed at her face and hands with the wipes hard enough to take off a layer of skin. He could tell her to stop, that the stain was gone, but he knew that wasn't what she was really trying to get rid of. The memory of blood stayed a long time.

"Yeah. You're my partner, but you won't be much help if you're fighting Zero's freaking compulsions." Utah knew she wouldn't appreciate sympathy, so he appealed to her sense of duty. "Let's figure out how to get rid of them."

She narrowed her gaze. "How?"

How? A good question. "Fin said he'd need someone to help him, someone with more power than Kione. Who do we know that would qualify?"

It didn't take her long to come up with a name. "Seir."

"He gets my vote too. So all we have to do is find a way to contact him and then convince him to help the brother he probably hates by now."

She closed her eyes. "That's assuming he's not working for Zero, in which case he won't do squat for any of us."

When she kept her eyes closed, Utah figured she didn't want to talk. He left her alone for the rest of the drive home. After Greer parked the car, and they walked into the lobby, Lia signaled for Utah to let Fin's assistant go up in the elevator alone.

"What do you have in mind?" Utah knew what

he had in mind, but he supposed it wasn't going to happen. He'd had time to think about it, picture it, all the way back from Old Town. He must have a death wish.

"Maybe this is crazy, but Seir has waited outside Fin's condos in three cities. Is there a chance he's still waiting?"

"After the way Fin treated him?" But he glanced toward the door.

"There's one way to find out." She must've seen his hesitation because she rushed to explain. "You're right. I can't work with you like this. So we either get Seir to help, or I get a different partner."

"You fight dirty, lady."

She smiled. "It's called desperation."

They walked back out into the night. Utah led the way. "We're only staying out here for a few minutes. If anything looks off, I mean *anything*, don't try to fight it, just run back into the building. I don't think even Seven would take a chance entering Fin's space."

Lia nodded as she scanned the darkness. "Seir?"

Utah tensed. He hoped to hell nothing else was out here.

"Fin's going to lock you in your rooms and never let you out again. He's a control freak, and you just keep doing things without telling him first." Seir's mocking voice sounded right behind them.

Utah spun, a growl rumbling in his throat. Lia simply gasped. Seir stood only a few feet away.

"Did I startle you?" Seir looked amused.

"Why the hell are you still hanging around here?" True to his predator nature, Utah got aggressive when someone surprised him.

"Why the hell are you out here calling my name?" Seir mocked him. Then he took a close look at Lia. "You're wearing a whole blood bank. Must've been a hell of a vampire coming-out party."

Utah couldn't keep his mouth shut. "We just got back from clearing out Adam's nest of vampires in the Shanghai Tunnels."

"Hey, bet you loved that, raptor." He looked from Utah to Lia. "But maybe you don't hate the bloodsuckers as much as you used to. Maybe you've decided that not all vampires are the devil's spawn. Maybe you even—"

Utah sprang at him. He didn't bother to call out his beast. He wanted the satisfaction of planting his fist in Seir's grinning face. He really needed to do this.

Only Seir wasn't where he was supposed to be, and Utah ended up punching air. "Hold still, you bastard." He turned to find Seir standing by Lia.

Fin's brother laughed. "I'd think about why what I said made you so mad, Utah."

"Stop it, both of you." Lia focused on Seir. "We need a favor."

Seir's smile turned savage. "And why should I do anything to help my loving brother?"

"Not to help Fin, to help Lia. She's picked up a few compulsions she wants to get rid of." Utah hated to ask for anything, but he wouldn't hesitate this time.

"I want to kill Utah, and I don't want to hunt Seven." Lia looked uncertain about Seir's reaction.

Seir shrugged. "Doesn't everyone want to kill Utah? I wouldn't blame that on Seven."

"I feel a compulsion coming on to kill *you*." Utah sympathized with Fin.

Lia looked exasperated as she pushed her hair from her face. She glared at Utah before turning back to Seir. "Seven didn't do this, Zero did."

Seir stilled.

She pressed her advantage. "Look, I don't know what's going on between you and Fin, and I don't really care. Call me selfish, but right now, all I want is this thing inside my head gone. I want my free will back. How would you feel if someone made you their puppet?"

Seir glanced away.

"Fin said he can't take away Zero's compulsions alone. He needs someone even more powerful than Kione to help him. You're the only one we know who fits that description. Please, help me."

Utah clenched his hands into fists. He sensed how hard it was for her to beg. He'd put his fist through Seir's smirking face if he made fun of her plea.

Seir exhaled deeply. "I'll probably regret this, but I'll help. Get this straight, though. I'm doing this only for *you*." He held up his hand to stop her words of thanks. "A few conditions. We do it out here. My brother isn't getting me back into his condo. And we do it now."

"Out here?" Lia glanced at Utah.

"Done. I'll contact Fin." Utah wasn't giving Seir any time to reconsider. He opened his mind to his leader.

"You have to come outside." Utah tried not to make it a demand, but Fin had to do this.

"What's happening?" Fin sounded sleepy.

Funny that Utah never thought of Fin as needing sleep. *"Seir has agreed to help get rid of Lia's compulsions, but he wants to do it out here, and right now."*

Fin cursed quietly and then went silent. Just when Utah thought he couldn't wait another second, Fin spoke.

"I'll be down."

Utah almost slumped with relief. "He's coming down."

Fifteen minutes later, Fin strode from the building. He took his good old time reaching them. Utah knew Fin could be wherever he chose in the blink of an eye; then why . . . ?

Seir's lips smiled. The rest of his face? Not so much. "God, Fin, you're turning into more of a human every day. Keeping me waiting because you're pissed at my conditions is so human it's scary."

Fin's smile looked almost real. "If it annoyed

you, then it was worth it." His smile faded. "Why did you agree to this?"

"You don't believe I'm capable of sympathy?"

"I think you're capable of self-interest. What do you want?"

"I want you to go to hell." Seir started to turn away.

"Oh no, you don't." Utah wasn't letting him leave. He grabbed Seir's arm to stop him. It felt as though he'd grabbed a live wire. A flash of white-hot energy whipped through his body. Utah could only gasp as he yanked his hand away.

"Don't go." Lia had enough sense not to grab Seir too. "I need you." Her last words were almost a whisper.

Utah turned on Fin. "And you stop being an ass." He froze the moment the words left his mouth. No one spoke to Fin like that.

Fin's eyes swirled purple. "You dare much, child."

Huh? Child? That didn't even sound like Fin. Utah backed away as Lia gripped his hand.

Seir laughed. "See, that put me in a good mood again. Get over yourself, brother. Utah called it. You're acting like an ass. Own it."

Shit. We're all going to die. Utah frantically searched for a way to get Lia to safety.

Suddenly, the tension was gone. Fin's eyes returned to silver. "It's cold out here. Let's get this done."

Utah wasn't deceived. They'd come close to something deadly. "Do you need anything for the ritual?"

"There is no ritual." Seir was suddenly serious.

Lia leaned into Utah's side. "So how do you do it?"

Fin moved close to his brother. "We join our powers and remove the compulsions."

Seir clenched and unclenched his fists, a strangely nervous gesture for him. "We have to be touching."

Utah suppressed a shudder at Seir's words. What the hell was wrong with him? "And?"

"When we touch, things could get weird." Seir glanced at his brother, no hostility in his eyes. "We haven't touched in millions of years."

"If this is dangerous, maybe you shouldn't try it." Lia looked worried.

Fin shook his head. "No, Lia, you deserve to be free. You were helping me, and I take care of my own." His eyes never left Seir.

"Not always, brother, not always." Seir's voice was flat.

Utah needed to know what to expect. "What could happen?" A little ground shaking, a few broken windows, it wouldn't be that bad.

"Half the earth destroyed, or nothing." Fin's expression said he didn't expect *nothing*.

"Wait!"

Lia barely got the word out before Fin clasped Seir's hand.

CHAPTER FIFTEEN

S cary was the unknown, that I-don't-know-what-will-happen-next-but-I-know-it'll-suck feeling. Battling vampires wasn't scary because she'd done it before. This, on the other hand, was not only scary but bordered on oh-my-God territory.

She clamped her fingers around Utah's hand as fog formed. It crept between trees, phantom fingers plucking at branches and leaves. It swirled around her, damp tendrils of misty terror sliding over her exposed flesh, looking for a way in. Small cracks crisscrossed the ground in a growing spiderweb pattern. Holy shit.

Fin's and Seir's clasped hands glowed.

She shivered. Cold. Ice crystals would form on her eyelashes at any moment. Utah started to wrap his arms around her, but she shook her head and moved away. Her compulsion was alive and well, urging her to forget about the scary stuff and just tear his freaking throat out. Wasn't going to happen.

Lia wanted to shout at Fin and Seir. *Stop, stop. Whatever the hell you're doing, just stop.* Too late.

She stared in unblinking horror as ghosts leaked from the cracks and drifted up and up until they merged with the mist, only to be replaced by more spirits. They came, filling the air—laughing, crying, screaming. Emotions beat at her—joy, sorrow, fear, anger—until she wanted to close her eyes and clap her hands over her ears.

And overriding everything was her fright. Yes, she admitted it, ghosts scared the hell out of her, had scared her since she was a kid. She'd even avoided Casper. Obviously, becoming one of the undead didn't cure her human fears.

Wait. She'd never been a fearful child. Insecure, but not fearful. *Yes, you were.* Lia closed her eyes. She'd swept all that fright under her personal rug and tried to forget about it. But the bump was still there, waiting for the moment when she'd have the courage to lift the edge to see what was beneath it.

She hadn't dared look under it until now because the daughter of Katherine wasn't afraid. And her mother's opinion had ruled her life.

Lia opened her eyes. Not anymore. Someone else's opinion now mattered more. She lifted the rug, laying bare all her fears—of high places, of fire, of never loving, of dying alone, and so many more.

She looked up at Utah. "I'm afraid of lots of things."

He didn't make a big deal of it. "Me too."

Lia smiled. He was lying, but he was doing it to make her feel better, so it was okay.

Suddenly, her smile died. Her head felt funny, as though something was being pulled from her mind, something ugly attached to a long string. Whatever it was exited with a popping in her ears. The compulsions? She moved close to Utah. No urge to kill. Lia thought about Seven. She wanted to start hunting the bitch right now. She sighed. They were gone along with the ghosts, mist, and cracks.

Fin and Seir dropped their hands and the glow faded.

For a moment, Lia stared at their hands. Their rings had the same design—three connected spirals. She already knew that. But there was something else, something important she should remember about the rings, something just out of reach. Then Fin spoke to her, and the thought was gone.

"You're free now. No more compulsions." Fin stepped back from his brother.

Seir glanced from Utah to her. "Unless you really want one. I have a few you could take for a test drive. Just sensual enough without being too much." He looked hopeful.

"Stop trivializing everything. You'd get more respect if you took things seriously." Fin frowned. "Besides, Kione is their partner. They've seen the dark side of sexual compulsions."

"Take things seriously? Like you?" Seir shrugged. "You're wound too tight." He smiled at Utah and Lia. "Forgive my brother's eternal gloom. He has intimacy issues, and holding hands with me was tough for him. He covers his discomfort by going all judgmental."

Fin shook his head. "See, that's why we need millions of years separating us."

But as Fin turned to walk away, Lia noticed a smile tugging at his lips. She sort of thought Fin needed Seir's banter once in a while.

They were silent as Fin walked away. And if he'd taken the time to glance back, he would've seen how serious his brother could be.

Lia didn't miss the sadness in Seir's expression. She decided to take a chance. "If you love him so much, why do you always try to irritate him?"

Seir looked startled for a moment and then smiled. "It's what he expects from me. He assumes I'm not capable of any kind of deep feelings, so I let him keep his illusion. It makes him happy."

He started to turn away, then paused. "I noticed that the ghosts bothered you. Don't let them. They were only residual images, a playback of past events. The earth holds the energy of all the people who lived and died on this spot since the beginning of mankind. Think of the ghosts as recorded memories. We disturbed the earth and those memories. What you saw wasn't an intelligent haunting. It was simply like a movie image. Not real."

Lia watched him disappear into the night before looking up at Utah. "I think there's actually a kind person inside that gorgeous but sometimes annoying exterior."

Utah raised one brow. "Gorgeous?"

She tried to keep from grinning. "Okay, so I've seen more gorgeous."

"Let's go inside." He kept his arm around her waist all the way to her door.

Lia stood there, indecisive. She wanted to ask him in, but what if he turned her down? She was vampire and he still hated vampires. The killing compulsion might be gone, but he'd gotten a front-row view of her out-of-control bloodlust. What if he turned her down? What man would want to wear an iron collar every time he went near a woman? *What if he turned her down?* She sighed. Fine, so she didn't handle rejection well.

"Going to ask me in?"

"Sure." What the hell, she'd take her chances with rejection. He was worth it.

Once inside, he took off his coat before dropping onto her couch. "You take a shower first." He turned on the light beside him.

She nodded. "I can't stand the blood smell anymore." *Translation: I don't want any hint of blood to trigger my hunger.*

Lia left him reading a magazine. Her shower was short, hot, and fraught with worry. Once dry, she tried to choose between the clothes she'd brought in with her—a nightgown or fresh jeans and a top. The nightgown wasn't sexy, but it still carried a different message than the jeans. She took a deep breath and pulled on the nightgown.

When she emerged, he didn't stare. He simply put down the magazine and headed for the bathroom. Only after he shut the door behind him did she realize he didn't have fresh clothes to change into. She hated that he'd have to put his dirty clothes back on.

He didn't. A short while later he came out wearing only a large towel draped low on his hips. He sat down next to her on the couch.

God, did anything smell as good as a man fresh from a hot shower? The scent of soap and clean warm male triggered a lust that was a welcome change from what she'd felt in the tunnel. She controlled her need to slip her fingers beneath that towel and—

"Why did you ask me to make love to you?"

Well, that was a slap in the face with a cold washcloth.

"Does it matter?"

"I think it does." He rubbed his hand across his still-damp chest.

She followed the motion until she realized he was watching. Then she looked away. He deserved the truth. "I'd agreed to become vampire. I knew you hated vampires." The rest was obvious.

Evidently, he didn't think so. "You're not finished."

Anger sharpened her voice. "Fine, so you want me to say it? I knew you wouldn't want to make love with me once I was vampire." This was going to be harder than she'd expected. "But *I* wanted to make love with you, so I decided to take my chance before the change." She shrugged. "I should've told you the whole story, but I wanted you as my last gift to me as a human." She waited for his anger.

"You were probably right. I wouldn't have been able to overlook that you'd agreed to become vampire."

His admission was a shot to her heart. There were times when being right wasn't fun.

"But something happened between then and now." He captured her gaze, held it.

She couldn't blink, couldn't look away. Funny, but she'd never stared into the eyes of his beast. Maybe that was because she was busy trying to stay alive when his beast was around.

Now, though, she knew exactly what was looking back at her. It was primal, dangerous, and touched the newly born predator in her.

"I want you, in every way possible." And his eyes promised that she'd love every one of those ways.

"I . . ." She tried to summon all the logical reasons that he couldn't want her. She could remember only one. "You saw what I became back in the tunnel. What if I lost control again?"

His laughter was soft and so sexy she wanted to wrap her naked body around it.

"I was in that tunnel too. Remember what *I* became."

Lia found it hard to recall anything because her gaze had dropped to focus on the broad, muscular expanse of his bare chest.

He put his finger under her chin and tipped up her face until she was again caught in his mesmerizing stare. "Pay attention." But he sounded pleased by how easily his body could distract her. "All of the Eleven except for Fin have to fight their beasts for supremacy every day . . . and every night. Sexual excitement is a perfect trigger. So don't give me any of that I'm-a-deadly-vampire-so-be-afraid crap." He leaned forward until his lips were barely touching hers. "Instead of denying who we are, let's explore our predatory natures."

She smiled as she cupped his cheek and brushed her lips across his. "Sounds exciting. But I don't want to hear any whining when you're sticking pieces of tissue all over your luscious body to stop the bleeding after I'm finished with you."

"Luscious body, huh?" Without another word, he stood and then scooped her up in his arms. She had only a moment to savor the feeling of her body pressed against his chest before he deposited her beside the bed. He reached down, gripped the edge of her nightgown, and slid it over her head. Somewhere between the couch and the bed, he'd lost his towel.

"Climb into bed while I get the light." He turned and strode to the lamp.

Those few strides widened her eyes and redefined the meaning of "fine" for her. His smooth, perfect back was a given, but his beautiful bare ass in motion went a long way in erasing the horror of the tunnel.

Sexual hunger licked its lips, and she had every intention of satisfying it tonight. *What if the bloodlust*— No, she wouldn't ruin this time with Utah. She would control what needed controlling and let everything else fly free.

She'd barely settled down before he climbed in beside her. He propped himself up and leaned over her. His hair fell forward to shadow his face, and for a moment, she was reminded of how much she didn't know about this man.

But then she dismissed the thought. She knew the important stuff. He cared enough for her to put aside his hatred of vampires, and she . . . ? Was she willing to say the word yet? She didn't know.

He smiled. God, he had a beautiful smile. She reached up to trace his lips with the tip of her finger. This would be a slow, wonderful lovemaking building up to—

He nipped the end of her finger. "I don't know if you've looked at the clock, but we'll have to race the dawn."

Damn. Well, she'd simply modify her expectations. "I was planning on hours of foreplay, so now we'll just compress things, make every move count."

"Fast and ferocious?" His smile turned feral.

"Oh yes." She grabbed his hair and yanked him down to her. Then she took his mouth with a savagery that surprised her. Did she want him that much? Definitely.

He buried his hands in her hair as her tongue tangled with his. God, she'd walk across hot coals for the taste of him, the scent of him, the drugging *need* for him.

It wasn't until she felt his tongue trace the length of her fangs that she realized vampire Lia had come out to play. Did that mean she was losing control? She started to pull back.

He held her in place while he slid his tongue over each of them. And when he finally broke the kiss, he held his finger against her lips to keep her quiet. "Shush. Your fangs are a part of who you are now. What's happening is natural. Hey, you've seen my beast. I know about teeth."

"What do you know about vampires?" She smoothed her hand up and down his arm, feeling the bunched muscles, the tension.

"I asked Jude a lot of dumb questions when I knew you'd be coming back as a vampire." Utah kissed a line along the bottom of her jaw and down the side of her neck. He paused at the base of her throat. "He told me that vampire orgasms included taking blood."

She shuddered, desire and anticipation at even the thought fueling a delicious heaviness low in her belly. "I wouldn't expect you to—"

"It isn't about what you expect, it's about what I want to do." He rolled one nipple between his thumb and finger while he flicked the other with his tongue.

She couldn't suppress a low moan. "Wow, I love a man in command."

His soft laughter fanned her skin, setting off more seismic activity down below.

"Just remember that, woman."

"Mmm." She slid her hands down his back and over his butt, property that she was considering laying claim to for at least a long-term lease. Lia squeezed his cheeks, feeling them flex beneath her fingers. Then again, everyone said buying was a good investment. And she'd have lots of pride of ownership if she moved in here.

While she'd been thinking about mortgage payments, he'd moved on. He licked a path over her stomach, and she clenched around the slow, hot glide of his tongue across her flesh and the cool fan of air against her damp skin.

Lia knew where he was headed and totally agreed with his travel plans, but she had a few out-of-the-way places she wanted to explore first.

She tugged at his hair to get his attention. "Hey, move over. I want to drive for a while."

He raised one brow. "You'll wander down every side street. I like the direct route."

Lia glared. "Too bad. I'm taking control."

She wrapped her arms around him, rolled him over, and climbed on top of him. Preternatural strength was amazing. She was queen of the whole freaking universe.

"Not so fast." He was on top again.

Before she knew it, Lia was wrestling with him. But somewhere between the neck scissors and the octopus hold, playfulness gave way to heat and intensity.

He'd propped himself up against the headboard while she knelt between his legs. His hair was tousled and his skin was damp from his exertion. His eyes gleamed with laughter. Right now, he didn't look like a guy with the soul of an ancient predator or humanity's last chance for survival. He looked young, gorgeous, and as sexy as a man could look.

She didn't say anything as she nudged his legs farther apart. Lia met his gaze and watched his eyes lose their laughter as they darkened with something hot and hungry. She knew her own eyes must look the same.

Dawn was near. Urgency whispered in her ear. *Now, now, now.* She had to cram all the touching, the tasting, the *everything* into such a short time.

Almost feverishly, she skimmed her fingers up

the inside of his thigh, felt his muscles flex, and leaned forward to slide her tongue along the same path her fingers had taken. When she reached the top of his thigh, right where she could hear his life force pulsing just below his skin, the blood hunger struck. She resisted. And the denial of her need was a sexual thing in itself. Lia dared dance in temptation's path as she twirled the tip of her tongue over his skin at the exact spot where his blood flowed strongest.

He smoothed his fingers over her hair with hands that shook. "If you keep that up, the dawn won't be the only thing coming."

She didn't acknowledge his complaint. Instead, she ran her tongue around each of his sacs and continued up the long, hard length of his cock.

He shuddered, and the shudder became her own.

She closed her lips over the head and then swirled her tongue around and around and around. She closed her eyes to savor the tactile sensations—smooth, warm, male.

He groaned, and she deepened the sensations, taking more and more of him, and then retreating. Imitating the rhythm of sex, she felt the slide of his hard flesh in and out, in and out.

The rhythm took her, drove her. She wanted more, had to have more.

He gripped her hair and tugged her away from him. "It's time."

"You've been strangely compliant." Her words

felt thick in her throat, her twin hungers surging, her mind twisting into heated coils of need—for his body, his blood.

"Not compliant. *Waiting.*" He made a move to pull her under him.

"No." She pushed him back. "This is my time, my ride." Leaning down, she whispered in his ear. "The hunt calls, raptor. Come hunt with me." To soften her demand, she moved so that her breasts just skimmed his chest.

He sucked in his breath even as the pleasure-pain of her sensitized nipples rocked her. Mmm, it felt so good that she did it again.

Utah's patience came to a sudden end. With a muttered curse, he introduced her to the wild ride. Clasping her bottom in his big hands, he lifted her onto his cock.

"Wait, wait." When he returned control to her, she lowered herself until she could just feel his cock nudging between her legs. Moisture made her slick and ready. The heavy feeling softened, opened her.

"Not waiting much longer." He muttered his threat through clenched teeth.

She lowered herself onto him, feeling the stretching, the filling, the incredible sense of another's body inside hers, *his* body inside hers.

Suddenly, her bloodlust's howling demon grabbed her, shook her, and growled its demand. She barely held it at bay as she pressed herself down on Utah, taking more and more of him, grinding herself against him. And if she screamed at the almost unbearable friction, the sense of her muscles clenching around him, it was preferable to the alternative—burying her fangs in his throat.

But her bloodlust wasn't the only one doing some shaking. Utah had grabbed her arms and was shouting at her.

"Look at me. Freaking *look* at me." He punctuated each word by shaking her.

She was trying, damn it, she was trying. Lia forced herself to meet his gaze, to drag her senses from between her legs and her unblinking stare away from his throat. Were her eyes black? God, she hoped they weren't red. Not that it mattered. Right now, her thoughts were jumbled, bouncing around in her head with each shake.

"I want you to feed, Lia."

She blinked. Had she heard him invite her to drink? Was it all a figment of her fevered imaginings? She must've looked blank because he said it again.

"This is everything. No yesterday, no tomorrow, just *now*. Drink."

"I can't, I . . ." *I might not be able to stop. I might kill you.*

He ran a shaking hand over her shoulder, between her breasts and down her stomach. She sucked in a breath she no longer had. He touched her right above where they were joined, rubbing his finger back and forth across the nub that was already way too excited. She jerked and moaned low in her throat at the same time she tried to pull his hand away.

Words were flying away from her as fast as she thought of them, but she had to make him understand. "Afraid. Losing control."

"Look. At. Me."

She did.

His beast's eyes stared back at her. Filled with a primitive hunger that had never known limits and a violent need to satisfy that hunger, his gaze seared her—a heated knife's edge ready to slice away all that remained of her resistance.

Lia surrendered . . . and released her vampire. Baring her fangs, she rose off him until only his head remained inside her, and then she slammed back down, driving him deep, deep inside her.

No thoughts interrupted her drive to completion. She was working on primitive time. Rise and fall, the slide of his cock inside her ruling every sensation, dragging every gasp and wail from her.

At some point, she realized he was helping, driving up into her. She increased her speed, his penetration, until she felt the wave building and building. No, no. Too soon. Let the dawn catch her. She was going up in flames anyway.

The wave crested. The world stilled. She hung there at the top of it all, able to feel the universe in that one moment.

Then she lowered her head and drove her fangs into his throat. She drank.

She was sliding down, down the back of the

wave as it rolled toward the shore, powered by spasms that killed her with each clenching. Blood, rich and sweet, filled her.

As the frenzy eased, and the spasms weakened, something else filled her. *Love.* Yes, she could think the word. And because she loved, she was able to push back the bloodlust and stop drinking. It was as simple as that. Who would've thought?

She slid her tongue across his neck, healing the wound, then just lay with her head on his chest listening to the slowing of his heartbeat. And wondered what the hell she was going to do with her discovery.

When his whisper came, she wasn't prepared for it.

"I love you, vampire. Make sure you understand what I'm saying. I love *you*, all of you, and that includes your crazy dental setup."

She believed him. Tears slid down her cheek, because she loved him so much it hurt, and because she'd have to wait to say the word back to him. He wouldn't appreciate her reason for withholding the word, but he hadn't lived his life with Katherine.

Lia wrapped her arms around him and hugged. She'd never be close enough to him. "You're more special than anyone I've ever known."

"But not *that* special?"

His voice didn't accuse, but she felt the sadness in it.

"Wait for me. Just a little while."

"Why?"

She rolled off him and lay on her side facing him. "I have to work through some things first."

"You either love or you don't love."

He was trying hard to sound reasonable, but she'd bet his beast was laying waste to the civilized part of him, demanding that he knock her over the head and carry her off to his cave. She almost wished he would. It would lift the decision from her slumping shoulders.

"Understand me, raptor. My mother used love to manipulate. She said she loved my father, but all she wanted was a live-in lackey. She never even tried to love me because I could never live up to her standards. The only thing she ever loved was power, with a little left over for her favorite vampires, the ones who were vicious enough to live up to her expectations."

Utah was wise enough not to interrupt her.

"I tried so hard to make her love me. When you and I first met, I was still trying. Even in death, she didn't lose her power over me." She reached across to cup his face and felt his jaw clench. This was as hard for him as it was for her. "You helped me break that cycle of need. But now I have to be sure I'm giving my love for the right reason."

He nodded. "You're right. I'll wait."

And that quickly, he accepted her explanation. She hated herself for keeping the real reason from him. Soon she would face Christine. Her gut told her she wouldn't survive the meeting. She wouldn't chain him to a dead love as her mother had chained her. Lia just wouldn't.

Sleep tugged at her. Dawn was here. She glanced over to make sure the drapes were tightly closed. "I know you must want to get to your room."

"Do you want me to go?"

"No." She was being selfish, holding him close when she had no right. But she wouldn't lie about this.

"Then I'll stay."

The last thing she felt as the day sleep claimed her were his arms tightening around her.

CHAPTER SIXTEEN

The pounding on the door woke Utah. For just a moment, he wondered where the hell he was. Then he remembered. Lia. She was snuggled up against his back.

He'd gotten up during the day and then returned to her bed an hour before sunset so she wouldn't wake alone. Okay, so he was hoping they'd have a chance to make love again. He was a self-serving bastard.

Must've dropped off to sleep, though, because a quick glance at the clock showed it was time for her to rise.

He cursed as he climbed from her bed. Whoever it was had lousy timing. Pulling on his jeans and shirt, he walked to the door and pulled it open.

Shen stood with his fist raised ready to start a

new round of pounding. He didn't look happy. "Good. You're here. Fin wants all of the Eleven in the media room as soon as possible. Bring Lia with you."

He didn't even give Utah a chance to curse him out before striding away.

Well, crap. Utah raked his fingers through his hair as he returned to the bed. Lia was awake but still looking a little groggy.

"A meeting? What's that about?" She sat up and stretched.

Utah followed the motion with intense interest and explosive hunger. God, she was beautiful. He was glad she didn't feel the need to shield her breasts from his gaze.

"Don't know. Must be important, though." He forced himself to concentrate on the night's business, otherwise he'd start thinking about her refusal to say she loved him.

Too late. He was already thinking about it. *Hey, stupid, maybe she won't say she loves you because she, well, doesn't love you. You're not the most lovable guy in the world. Accept it.* Too bad he was lousy at giving up on what he wanted. But maybe he needed to start thinking in terms of what *she* wanted. He'd always thought he was a patient hunter, but not with Lia.

She leaned down, scooped her nightgown from the floor, and pulled it on. As she climbed out of bed, the nightgown rode up her long legs and smooth thighs. Utah swallowed hard. If he stayed in the room much longer, he was going to do something stupid like ignore Fin's orders in favor of making love with her. But as tempting as that thought was, he knew Fin wouldn't have called all of the Eleven together if there wasn't an emergency.

Utah had to get out of here before temptation reeled him in. "I have something I have to do. I'll meet you in the media room." She looked disappointed. Good.

He stopped in his room to freshen up and change into clean clothes before going to the media room, where most of the Eleven were already lounging around on couches and chairs. Tor waved him over to a couch he shared with Lio.

Utah grinned as he joined them. "How do you get the blood out of all those expensive clothes, Lio?" He'd never seen Lio dressed in old jeans and a T-shirt. The Liopleurodon was always camera-ready. If Fin ever had to make a statement to the press on short notice, Lio would be his choice to do it. That said, Utah couldn't fault the guy for his love of clothes, because when Lio hit the water, there wasn't another creature on earth that could challenge him.

Lio laughed. "I don't. I just throw them away and buy new ones. Fin has deep pockets."

As Utah settled onto the couch, he kept his attention on the door. When Lia entered the room, he waved her over. It was a tight fit, but she was able to squeeze in next to him. Utah admitted to being a jealous jerk, because he'd made sure she was wedged between him and the end of the couch. No one else was getting a chance to touch her. And wasn't that pathetic. He didn't have ownership papers for her, and she wasn't making any I'm-yours-forever noises. But pathetic or not, he was what he was. He'd keep her to himself as long as he could.

"Know what this is about, Tor?" Utah did a quick count. Everyone was here. His gaze snagged on two men who stood near the door. Kione and Jude. He wondered why Fin had asked them to be present.

"No idea." Tor nodded at Fin, who'd just entered the room. "No one else does either."

"I wonder why Fin didn't just put out a mental news flash to you guys. Would've been a lot faster." Lia spoke to everyone on the couch, but her gaze never left Utah.

He forced himself to concentrate on her words as opposed to everything else about her. Utah hoped he sounded cool and detached, not intense and possessive. "Mental messages take energy. If this is something big, he'll have to conserve his power so he can keep Zero busy while we battle the big bad."

He wanted this to be huge. Utah needed to work off his frustration by beating the hell out of something. A primitive reaction, but it worked. He glanced at Lia. She glanced away. Yeah, he needed a good fight.

Silence fell as Fin spoke. "I got word a short while ago that the mayor is about to order the evacuation of Portland."

Talk about a bombshell. Utah took a deep steadying breath as he looked at Lia. She stared back at him from wide, shocked eyes. He guessed she was thinking the same thing he was. Seven.

After a moment of stunned silence, everyone started tossing questions at Fin. "Why? How did you find out? What do we do?"

Fin held up his hand for silence. He got it. "The how is that I know people who know people." His smile was grim. "I've found humans are susceptible to offers of large sums of money. The why is because Portland's volcanoes don't seem to be as extinct as everyone thought they were."

"What the hell?" Spin spoke for all of them.

Fin glanced at his watch and then clicked the TV remote. He tuned in to a local station. "The news should be breaking any minute now."

They all watched in silence. And when the announcement came, Fin kept the TV on only long enough to verify that, yes, Portland was being evacuated. He turned it off as they were listing evacuation routes.

"We don't need to know the evacuation routes because we're not leaving." He set down the remote before wandering over to the windows. "Here's a rundown on recent events. The temperature of the ground around the cinder cones has been rising. The cones have begun to swell.

Seismologists have recorded a growing number of small tremors." Fin turned to face them. "And two hours ago steam started rising from them." He shrugged. "All of which are impossible because the volcanoes are extinct."

Utah spoke up. "Is this Seven's going-away party?"

"Yes." Fin sounded definite. "I'd say she's doing this all on her own, though. Zero would want her to keep a lower profile." His smile looked almost admiring. "But she's never been about low profiles." His smile faded. "And that will be her downfall."

Lia nudged Utah. "The steam is probably the smoke Fin saw in his vision."

Fin turned his attention away from the night sky. "Here's what's going to happen. There are several cinder cones within the city limits, but Mount Tabor is the largest. Seven would always choose the biggest. Q will fly out to make sure her people are gathering there."

"What if someone sees me?" Q stood.

"Not likely. It's nighttime. Besides, most people will be concentrating on getting out of town. Go." Fin didn't watch as Q left.

Utah's exultation at the thought of battle turned to sudden fear. The time when Lia would have to play her part in sending Seven home had somehow seemed further in the future. Now it was in his face, and he was terrified for her. He had to find a way to protect her.

"What about Zero?" If Lia was nervous, she didn't show it.

"Zero will be angry, but that doesn't mean he won't try to protect her." Fin moved to the nearest chair and sat. He looked troubled. "I'll try to keep him away from Mount Tabor. It won't be easy. I've used up lots of energy on him lately." He looked at where Jude and Kione still stood. "Kione has agreed to add his power to mine. We'll see what happens."

That didn't sound very comforting to Utah. "Have you asked Seir for help?"

"No." Fin's expression said to drop it. "Jude and his five vampires have agreed to help. We'll need them, because you can bet that Adam will be there with his vampires."

Damn his pride. Utah didn't care what Fin thought, if he could contact Seir, he'd beg for his help.

"So what's the plan?" Car looked ready to tear someone apart right now.

"As soon as Q gives the word that we have the right place, we head out. We'll keep to the back streets to avoid the evacuation routes. Once there, Gig, Ty, and Spin will close in on one side while Utah, Tor, and Lia come in from the other. Jude and his vampires will go where they're needed."

"Hey." Car sounded outraged. "What about the rest of us? We don't get a shot at them?"

For just a moment, Fin looked weary. "I never commit all of you to the fight. I can't take the chance of everyone getting wiped out at one time. There always has to be some of you left alive to fight them at another time and place. You know this."

"Seems like the more of us there are, the better chance we have of winning."

Al sounded as though he was trying to be reasonable, but his resentment showed. Jenna put her hand on his arm. Utah figured that she'd just breathed a huge sigh of relief.

Purple swirled in Fin's eyes. "If Zero gets past me, every one of you that's standing on Mount Tabor will die. He's one of the few beings who can destroy you in your predator form. You can't fight him, you can't defeat him. He *will* kill you." He looked away. "I won't chance losing all of you."

Utah filled the silence following Fin's announcement with frantic thoughts about how to keep Lia safe.

Lia evidently had her own doubts. "What do you expect me to do? Even if I manage to get close to her—which looks pretty impossible right now—I still don't know what I'm supposed to use to touch her."

Fin frowned. "You'll have to improvise."

"Hey, good plan, O Lord of All Wisdom. I should've thought of that." Lia was in full sarcastic mode.

The walls shook, and there was a sudden crash as a large mirror fell to the floor. Fin stared at Lia. "You annoyed me. And I liked that mirror." It was an unusual expression of frustration for Fin. "I don't know what to tell you. But something will be there."

Lia looked as though she wanted to go another round with him, but then she sighed and swallowed her comment.

Fin nodded. "Car, you and the others who won't be part of the battle will drive. You'll stay with the vehicles until you hear from me." He paused, his thoughts seeming to turn inward. "Once we leave this room, every one of us has only one goal—to get Lia within touching distance of Seven. Do whatever is necessary to make that happen." Left unsaid was that "whatever is necessary" might include dying.

His gaze swept the room. "Now we wait for word from Q."

Lia couldn't believe two hours ago they were sitting in Fin's condo talking. Normal humans doing normal things. Okay, maybe not so normal.

Now she was climbing up a steep path that wound among towering Douglas-fir trees—to face God-knew-what with some as yet to be determined weapon. She was so going to die tonight.

Lia glanced at Utah walking beside her in the darkness. At least she'd die near the man she loved. She really needed to tell him that, but not right now. That admission would bring on the kind of emotional scene guaranteed to make her lose focus on Christine. She'd tell him after this was all over, if she lived. And if she died? He'd probably forget her more easily if he thought she'd never loved him.

He moved closer. "Let me do this, Lia. I don't give a damn about Fin's vision. In Philly, he saw Jenna ringing the bell, but I'm the one who actually did it. No big deal. Eight went home just the same."

His words were a whispered temptation. It would feel so good to unload this whole thing onto someone else's shoulders.

"Do what? If you know, please tell me." Lia sighed. Sarcasm wouldn't help. "Evidently, Fin's vision means I'm the only one who'll recognize the mysterious something meant to get rid of Christine. The powers-that-be have a lot of faith in my ability to think on the fly."

Utah made a frustrated sound and kept walking.

Ahead of them, Ty, Spin, and Gig ghosted from shadow to shadow. It was amazing to Lia how men who morphed into such huge beasts could move so silently as humans. And somewhere behind them, Tor watched their back trail.

Jude and his vampires were out there too. Lia tried to take comfort in the powerful forces backing her up, but the bottom line was that she'd have to face Christine alone.

The silence worked on her nerves. She had to say something. "I'm surprised the city didn't put police around here to keep gawkers away."

Utah shrugged. "If they did, Seven took care of them."

Silence descended again. She glanced around at the leafy trees, the grass, and the *flowers*. "Christine's been a busy girl. This could be the middle of July."

Before Utah had a chance to answer, Lia glanced into the darkness beside the trail. She controlled a startled gasp. Seir stood beside one of the trees. She prodded Utah to get his attention.

They stopped as Seir stepped onto the path in front of them.

"Live volcano, psycho immortal, wacko followers. Not a great place to take your date, Utah." Seir wasn't smiling.

"Yeah, well, some of us care about more than just running our mouths." Utah stepped closer to Seir.

Lia wanted to grab his arm and yank him back. "I'm glad you showed up, Seir. I think Fin could use some help holding off Zero while we take care of Christine."

"Should I care about what my brother needs?"

Seir's body language said relaxed, but Lia sensed tension thrumming just below the surface.

Utah made a visible effort to control his aggression. "Sorry about going off on you. I'm always strung tight before a battle." He tried to smile. "I appreciate what you did to get rid of Lia's compulsions. I'm just afraid . . ."

Lia could see him struggling with how much

it was safe to tell Seir. After all, Seir's loyalties were murky at best. But Lia believed there were times in everyone's life when you had to trust your instincts. And her instincts were telling her Seir wouldn't betray them. If she was right, it was an epic win. If she was wrong, she wouldn't be around to bemoan her stupidity.

She laid it out for him. "I have to get within touching distance of Christine. Fin's trying to make that happen."

Seir looked intrigued. "I'll have to see this. I assume it all has to do with kicking Christine back out into the cosmos."

Utah moved closer to Seir, his expression intent. "If Seven stays, those volcanoes will blow and people will die. Officials can't evacuate a city this size fast enough to beat an eruption. And once she's finished here, she'll go on to some other city to spread her poison."

"Hmm. So what I'm hearing is that both of you want me to help so that humans will survive."

"Yes." Lia glanced at Utah when he didn't answer immediately.

Seir's smile was slow and wicked. "Truth, raptor."

Utah kept his face averted from Lia as he answered. "No, damn it. Okay, so I do want humans to survive, but I want Lia to survive more. If Fin can't hold off Zero, she'll die."

"Well, well. Self-interest rears its beautiful head." Seir looked gleeful. "And if I agree to help?"

Utah exhaled deeply. "I'll owe you."

"A favor owed. I love it." Seir nodded. "You have a deal." He stepped back before fading into the darkness.

Utah shook his head. "Tell me I didn't just make a pact with the devil."

Lia held up her hands. "I'm staying out of this." But she couldn't leave it at that. "Thank you for caring so much about me." She didn't try to keep the softness out of her voice.

He smiled. "Always, vampire, always."

They were getting close to where Q had said Christine was, so they moved more quietly. Lia could feel the heat buildup. And as they neared the summit, she could see the trail of steam above the trees. They weren't as far from the crater as she'd like to be. The air felt dense, stifling. She didn't know whether to blame the volcano or Christine's evil miasma for that.

She didn't have to guess where Christine was because she could hear shouts and laughter coming from someplace ahead.

Suddenly, Ty emerged from the darkness. They waited for him. Silently, Tor joined them.

"The park has a bunch of reservoirs. Number five is just ahead. Q said that Seven and about sixty of her followers are in an open space near it. We caught a break. She didn't bring everyone, probably just her main people. Q saw Adam there. He has about ten of his vampires with him."

Caught a break? Lia had to call him on that.

"Maybe you count differently than I do, but the last time I checked my fingers, sixty was a lot more than twelve."

Ty's grin flashed white in the darkness. "We fight big, sweetheart."

Utah looked worried. "Don't forget that Seven can return us to human form. Without our beasts, we'd be in deep shit."

Tor spoke up. "Let's hope she can't *keep* us in human shape. Once she's distracted, we can regain our predator forms."

If you're still alive. Lia silently prayed that Tor was right.

"Spin, Gig, and I will head around that way." Ty pointed. "You come in from the opposite side. Jude and his guys are already in place. They're hiding up in the trees. They'll be ready when we attack." The thought of Jude sitting in a tree seemed to amuse Ty.

"The plan?" Lia was getting nervous. The more she stood around, the more time she had to think about what could go wrong.

"Right. As soon as I know you're in place, I'll attack with Spin and Gig. Once Seven is focused on us, you, Utah, and Tor can make a run at her. At the same time, Jude and his vamps will come out of the trees. It'll be total chaos."

Utah didn't look too in love with Ty's plan. Lia wasn't either. She would've liked something a little more organized.

Ty must've sensed their doubts because he hurried on. "You're vampire now, Lia. If you put on some speed, you'll just be a blur. Everyone will be concentrating on the rest of us. They probably won't even notice another vampire until it's too late." He threw up his hands. "I know it's not perfect, but we didn't have much time to put something together. We had to act fast. When Seven shuts down this party, she's outta here. And you already know how she'll celebrate leaving town. This volcano along with the others in the city will blow."

Lia didn't need a reminder of how urgent the situation was. She didn't want to be a Debbie Downer, but she had bad feelings about this. What if she got in front of Christine and there wasn't a seven in sight? Should she just wave and say hi?

"Let's go kick some immortal butt." Ty's voice was a hushed rallying cry.

Then they were running. Utah leaned close. "Tor and I will be with you every step of the way."

Lia smiled up at him as she pulled the hood of her jacket over her head. She loved him so much it hurt, and she truly hoped he wouldn't be with her every step of the way. Not if those steps took him too close to Christine, too close to death.

Events were moving so fast she couldn't think straight. Lia didn't believe in putting her life in fate's hands, because fate was a clumsy bitch who stumbled and dropped things a lot. But that's what Lia was doing tonight.

They stopped among the trees, watching the

large open area where Seven and her followers laughed, drank, and generally whooped it up. The vampires had brought their own wet bar—a bunch of terrified humans trussed up in the back of a pickup truck. It wasn't tough to spot Christine in the middle of all the partygoers. She wore a long, flowing white gown. Trying to recapture her lost virginity? Or maybe she thought of this as her wedding night. The bride of blood and death. *Okay, getting way too melodramatic about this. Focus.*

Utah watched Lia's changing expressions— worry, determination . . . And when she looked at him? Love? It didn't matter. He loved *her*, so she was family now. He'd protect her better than he'd protected Rap. *And those others he couldn't remember.*

Tor interrupted Utah's thoughts. "Where are Seven's guards? They should've stopped us before we got this far."

Utah snorted his contempt. "If she had guards, Jude and his vampires probably got to them. But she's full of her own power, overconfident. She knows Zero is out there, so she thinks it's safe to party hard."

Everything would be over soon, one way or another. But as Utah waited for Ty, Spin, and Gig to crash Seven's party, he realized something. Life had never been so important. Lia and he *had* to survive. He loved her too much to believe they'd have no more tomorrows. And Tor? Utah *wouldn't* lose his only remaining brother. He called on his beast, and his beast screamed its readiness to make sure Lia and Tor lived.

As though in answer to that silent cry, the T. rex, Spinosaurus, and Giganotosaurus broke from the darkness. Utah just had to admire the jaw-dropping effect of a combined twenty-two tons of angry predators charging into the clearing. A real holy-shit moment.

Evidently, Seven's followers thought so too. There was lots of yelling and cursing. But these were nonhumans. It took them only a few seconds to regroup and attack. Once the shifting was done, a pack of bigass werewolves launched themselves at Ty and the others. Adam's vampires moved with blurring speed, fangs bared. The demons in the crowd had their own styles—strange but deadly. There were even a few entities that Utah didn't recognize.

"It's time." Utah resisted the urge to pull Lia into his arms. Not now, but afterward . . . He made do with sliding his fingers along the side of her face and felt her jaw clench, saw her will harden beneath his gaze.

"Stay safe, raptor." She placed her hand on his chest where his jacket gaped open.

He absorbed the warmth of her touch for one last moment before she withdrew her hand. Taking a deep breath, he became raptor.

Utah's beast knew he must protect Lia, understood that he couldn't lose himself to the blood-lust. He swung his head to make sure his pack mate was on her other side. Then they leaped from concealment.

She moved with a vampire's speed. That speed kept her alive now as she raced beside him. He and his pack mate flung aside any who tried to attack her. And no matter how much he wanted to savage the ones who dared try to touch her, he kept moving.

From the corner of his eye, he saw the vampires that were his allies leaping from the surrounding trees onto their enemies. Even though he recognized them as friends, he still would've attacked them if given the chance. Only the spark of humanity within his predator's body kept him under control, stopped him from trying to kill anything that moved.

Except for Lia. Even with bloodlust pushing at him, he knew he wouldn't kill her. She was . . . special.

He turned his head to watch the wolves swarming over the enormous beasts he called pack mates, at least for now. The wolves were losing. They lay, broken and bleeding, and he wanted to scream his pleasure at their defeat. But he knew he must not call attention to the woman he guarded, so he remained silent. He burned to take part in the kill, to sink his teeth into living flesh, but he couldn't because—

As he returned his attention to Lia, he realized his mistake. While he'd watched the wolves, a vampire had appeared in front of her with lip curled back to expose its fangs. He prepared to leap at it.

She waved him away. "I'll get this." She pulled out her gun and shot it. The vampire went down. "Did you see her expression? Looked insulted. Guess the vampire code of ethics frowns on using anything but fangs in battle. Tough shit. She might not be permanently dead, but a few bullets will take her mind off of me for a while." She grinned up at him before continuing to fight her way forward.

His beast felt pride in her. She'd make a worthy pack mate. The human in him murmured that she'd make a fine *mate*. Forget the pack part.

The whole place had become a bloody tangle of churning bodies. It was getting harder to make headway. They'd caught a break, though. As the fighting escalated, the predators worked themselves into a frenzy of killing and then reverted to their true natures. Everyone turned on everyone else in a supernatural free-for-all. He wanted to be part of the fun, but he stayed close to the woman.

Worried, he watched her almost lose her footing on the ground now slippery with blood. She kept scanning the area, searching for something. His beast's mind wasn't sure what she was looking for, but he'd see that she lived to find it.

Suddenly, a wolf sprang past him to clamp his teeth onto the woman's arm. She muffled a pained yelp.

The wolf had hurt her. Fury drove him. He leaped

onto the enemy. And even as he disemboweled the wolf, three others charged him. They had abandoned their larger prey. Perhaps they thought he'd be an easier kill. Their mistake.

The wolves' ferocity drove him to the ground. For the next few minutes, he showed his attackers what a raptor's teeth, tail, and claws could do to their flesh.

When he had finished, he was surrounded by dead wolves, blood, and . . . a yellow flower. He stared at the small bloom that had managed to survive being crushed beneath dozens of struggling bodies. Blood dotted the petals, but that's not what caught his attention. There was something important about the flower, if he could only concentrate.

Thoughts whirled through his mind. *Get up. Protect the woman.* He gathered himself. He'd tear apart any others who threatened her. Then he paused.

Lia would want the flower. The flower was important.

He couldn't process all his thoughts. His beast wanted to forget the flower and get on with the slaughter. But he knew the woman needed the flower, needed *him*.

Beast warred with human. Humanity won. Utah returned to human form even as he reached for the flower. Not much could take the place of opposable thumbs. He plucked the flower and struggled to his feet. He had to find Lia.

Utah was vulnerable now, but that's not what drove him as he forced his way through the fighting masses. *Where was Lia?* Luckily, the nonhumans pretty much ignored him in human form. They were too busy trying to tear each other apart.

He glanced around. Tor was locked in battle with two of Adam's vampires. Seven was just visible through the mob. She faced Ty, Spin, and Gig. He drew in a sharp breath as all three winked out one after the other. Damn. She must've returned them to human form. At least, he hoped that's all she'd done.

He couldn't help them now, couldn't help Tor either. Fear—an unfamiliar emotion—choked him. *Where the hell was Lia?* He tried to stem the adrenaline surge urging him to action, *any* action. His pounding heart threatened to kick a hole in his chest if he didn't do something *now.* He forced himself to slowly study the crowd.

There. She'd almost reached Seven. Holding the flower above his head, he slipped through any openings offered. But just when Utah thought things were swinging his way, Seven turned to face Lia.

No, no, no! Determination gave him strength he'd felt only in his beast's form. He fought his way toward her, beating back anyone who got in his way.

Lia missed her sword, but she'd been right to leave it back at the condo. It would've hampered her

movements in this mob. Besides, she didn't have
time to take any heads. She had to reach Christine
with . . . Well, that was the problem. She didn't
have seven of anything yet. Urgency snapped at
her heels. She forced one foot in front of the other
and tried to keep hope alive. Her time with Utah
would *not* end with her flat on her face in front of
Christine.

Glancing up, she saw Ty disappear. It took her
a moment to realize that Christine had returned
him to human form. Panicked, she watched the
same thing happen to Spin and Gig. God, let them
survive in human form until they could find their
beasts again.

Lia looked behind her. She couldn't see Utah.
Two vampires kept Tor busy. *Where was Utah?* Fear
for him almost paralyzed her. She took a deep
breath, forced herself to concentrate on Christine.

Lia was on her own. Somewhere beyond the
trees, she heard a series of explosions, followed by
brilliant flashes of light. Fin and Zero were getting physical this time. She hoped Kione and Seir
could help Fin and still stay alive.

Christine started to turn when Lia was about
twenty feet away from her. Oh no. Lia looked
frantically around for a seven—buttons on a shirt,
anything. Where the hell was the freaking seven
Fin had said she'd find?

Lia was now ten feet away from Christine and
closing, but the other woman had spotted her.
Christine smiled, a smile that promised her that

death would be swift and not particularly pain-
less.

She wasn't going to make it. Beyond Christine,
she saw that Ty, Spin, and Gig had regained their
predator forms. Relief flooded her. Lia hoped
she'd be tonight's only casualty. She wanted to
turn for a possible last glimpse of Utah, but the
press of bodies kept pushing her forward.

Christine waited, an immortal spider certain
that her prey was firmly caught in her web. "So
brave, but so foolish. Did you honestly think you
could make a difference?" She glanced down at
the gun still clutched in Lia's hand. The gun disappeared.

Christine seemed annoyed rather than fearful
as the battle raged around her. Of course, she had
the advantage of being indestructible.

Suddenly, Lia heard someone shouting her
name above the din. Utah? She looked behind her.
He was back in human form and fighting his way
toward her.

God, no! He'd die in human form. She tried to
wave him away, but he ignored her. Lia watched
in horror as he pressed forward.

Then she noticed something. What the . . . ? Lia
stared. He was waving something above his head.

Christine laughed. "How sweet. He's bringing you a flower. We'll put it on your grave." Her
laughter faded. "I could've destroyed all of your
little attack party if Fin hadn't used some of his
power to protect you."

This was news to Lia.

Christine pouted. "This little setback is inconvenient, but it'll hardly stop me." She seemed to perk up. "But Zero is draining Fin's power, so I'll be able to kill *you*." She glanced past Lia to where Utah drew closer, still waving his flower. "And *him*."

No. He was risking his life to bring her a flower. Lia tried to wave him away, but Utah stretched his hand out to give it to her. She reached past a bunch of bodies to grab it from his fingers. He was trying to tell her something, but there was so much noise that even with her enhanced hearing she couldn't understand him.

As she took it, she met his gaze. The last time she'd see him. Her final chance to say what she should've said last night when they made love. Bloody tears trailed down her face. She swept them away with her hand.

"I love you." She mouthed the words. There was nothing more to say. She didn't have time to watch his reaction. *Please free your beast and stay safe.*

Lia glanced down at the flower. It didn't have seven petals. A beautiful parting gesture but not the hoped-for miracle. She turned back to Christine.

A Christine who watched her from narrowed eyes. "You and your friends have ruined my party. I'll make sure to give the eruptions extra punch to express my anger. A lot more humans will die because of you."

Just what Lia needed, a whopping dollop of guilt to pile on top of her already mountain-sized sense of failure.

"Time to die, little vampire." Christine took the steps needed to reach her. "I could destroy you neatly without getting any messy stains on my gown, but you know how I love the scent and taste of fresh blood. First, I think I'll rip out your heart and lick it." She slid her tongue across her lips, a strangely erotic gesture.

Lia shuddered. This was it then. Her dying time. She wouldn't go down without a fight, though. In the end, she was Katherine's daughter. She got ready to make Christine regret taking the bloody path in killing her.

Her mind was way ahead of her, imagining the pain, the final moment, the rending forever of her connection to Utah.

Suddenly, her thoughts ground to a halt. Her mind rewound the last few seconds. She'd missed something important. Lia wasn't sure what it was, but . . .

She looked down at the flower again. It seemed as though everything faded away—the fighting, the screams, the hopelessness—until only one thing existed in her entire universe. *A bright yellow flower.*

And as Christine reached out to take her heart, Lia scooped up the ladybug with its glorious seven spots from the flower's petals and placed it on Christine's outstretched hand. "There. A go-ing-away gift from me to you, bitch."

Christine's eyes widened in horror. She dropped the ladybug, but the damage was done. She began to shimmer.

"No! I don't want to leave." Christine's frantic gaze was fixed beyond Lia. "Help me."

Lia turned to see whom she'd appealed to.

Fin stood at the edge of the tree line. He was pale and looked as though he could barely stay on his feet. He stared at Christine. Some power-ful emotion passed between them. Then he shook his head. And turning away, he disappeared back into the forest.

Lia's respect for the Eleven's leader took a giant leap. Fin really cared for Christine. But he'd chosen humanity over her. He wasn't afraid to make the hard choices.

Lia looked back at Christine in time to see her disintegrating into glowing particles. It was all over within a matter of seconds. At the end, all the glowing bits coalesced into a whirling ball of light and disappeared into the night sky.

Only two thoughts filled her mind. Utah and relief that made her legs go all rubbery. Her gaze automatically went to where she'd last seen him. *There.* He'd shoved his way almost to her side. Other than a bloody cut on the side of his face, he looked okay. *Thank you, God.* Something stretched tight inside her slowly relaxed. He was safe.

Only then did Lia realize complete silence had fallen. She looked around. Most nonhumans were pretty pragmatic. Their leader was gone, and they'd ended up trying to beat the crap out of each other. They realized their union wasn't going to happen.

Lia could see Adam moving among them trying to rally them, but only his vampires paid any attention. The other nonhumans melted away, leaving the vampire leader furious at his lost opportunity for world domination.

Adam was crazy out of control when he spotted Lia. She didn't like the look in his eyes as he started toward her. Lia had no doubt there would be only pieces of her left if he reached her. She tensed to run. That's when Utah stepped up beside her.

Not in front of her. *Beside* her. Even with her life on the line, warmth flooded her. He acknowledged her fighting ability without saying a word. Lia wondered if he recognized the importance of his gift.

Adam stopped about ten feet in front of them. He almost vibrated with his need to kill. "Too late to call your beast." His smile was twisted, filled with hate as he stared at Utah. "I can reach you before you even think about it."

Utah shrugged. "I don't need my beast for this."

Lia nudged Utah. No need to enrage Adam to a frothing frenzy. And why *hadn't* Utah called his raptor? Invulnerability was a good thing.

"You think not?" Adam curled his lip, exposing his fangs.

"Lia is one of your regional leaders. She's vampire now, so her people will feel even more loyalty to her. Your power base has eroded, Adam. Look behind you." Utah seemed calm, confident.

Unwilling to take his gaze from Utah, Adam glanced quickly over his shoulder. His remaining vampires had faded into the forest.

Adam's furious hiss promised death and dismemberment to those who'd run away.

Utah continued. "So I'd say you need strong regional leaders on your side. And I bet if you showed Lia some respect, she'd be willing to work with you again."

Hell wouldn't be freezing over anytime soon. But Lia didn't share that fact with Adam.

Utah threw out his final argument. "Get weak enough, and someone else will be waiting to jump in and take over."

"Jude." Adam's snarl showed he knew where the danger lay.

Utah shrugged. "I bet there're others." Reaching out, he took Lia's hand and turned away from the angry vampire.

They walked toward the forest, and Lia felt Adam's hate-filled gaze on her back every inch of the way. Utah only paused long enough to make sure Tor was okay and then he led her into the shelter of the trees. Relief flooded her once they were out of Adam's sight.

He kept walking until they reached a clear spot that opened to a view of Portland's lights far below them. Beautiful and somehow a fitting ending to this horrendous night.

"You took a big chance." She tightened her grip on his hand, her only admission of how much he'd scared her back there.

"Not really." He pulled her close and wrapped his arm around her waist. "I get the feeling Adam isn't universally loved by his people. I don't think many bloody tears would be shed if we killed him. And I bet Adam knows that. He's all about staying in power, even if that means sparing your life."

"When we first met you would've just killed him and forgotten about it." Now that Christine's heat had faded, Lia could feel the night's chill. She snuggled closer to him.

His smile flashed white in the darkness. "You've corrupted me. I'm listening to my human side too much. That means probably overanalyzing things. If we killed Adam, it might make him into a martyr with his people. We still need the vampires to help us."

Lia didn't want to talk about Adam. She wanted to talk about—

Utah turned her to face him. He pushed her hood back from her face with fingers that didn't seem quite steady. "Did you really say, 'I love you' back there?"

She stilled. Here it came. Her admission. What

did she know about love? She loved her father. She'd tried to love her mother. That hadn't worked out well. And that was her total experience with love. Until Utah. Lia gazed up at him, into those eyes that shone warm for her even in the darkness. Experience or not, she knew what she wanted.

Lia tipped her head up as he lowered his head. She feathered a kiss across his lips before whispering, "Oh yes. That was definitely an 'I love you.'"

Burying his face in her neck, he exhaled deeply. Then he kissed the spot where her blood beat strong at the base of her throat. "I thought I might be twisting the words into what I wanted to hear." His husky laughter heated her flesh. "You could've just been saying, 'I love Chinese takeout.'"

She pulled her head back to grin at him. "Nope. I love you so much I want to write it in giant letters across the sky."

His gaze heated. "Then marry me, Lia. Right now. Right here."

She opened her mouth to point out how impossible that was, but something else entirely came out. "Yes."

CHAPTER SEVENTEEN

Lia thought he'd kiss her then. He didn't. Instead, he stared at her grimly. Not what she'd expected. No good news went with that expression. To cover the uncomfortable silence, she rushed into speech. "Can Fin perform marriages? Do you want all the guys here?" Maybe the tightness around his mouth was simply an oh-crap-what-did-I-just-say moment. "We don't have to do this right now."

He smiled at her then, and she relaxed a little.

"No one needs to be here, just the two of us. But I'd like Tor to witness the ceremony."

Witness the ceremony? Sort of formal wording to describe two people exchanging a brief vow to love each other forever.

He led her to a nearby picnic table. They sat. "And yes, it has to be right now." Some of that grimness crept back into his face. "I don't want to waste a moment of my life with you."

He bent down to trace her lips with the tip of his tongue. Then he deepened the kiss. She was vampire now, and her senses flared to life. Along with the taste of heat and desire, she felt his sadness, vague and unfocused, a leftover from a time he couldn't remember. She silently promised to bury those memories with years and years of love and happiness.

She shivered. They weren't all phantom memories. Rap's spirit would stand with his brothers tonight. Was any of that sadness hers? She didn't think so. Thoughts of Katherine sparked nothing—no anger, no resentment. There wasn't room in her heart for that anymore. All because of Utah.

He broke the kiss to study her. "You're thinking." His smile shattered her gloomy thoughts. "Forget sad. We own the world tonight. Seven is gone, and we have each other. Forever." He said the last word with an intensity that wiped the smile from his face. "There is one thing we have to talk about." He glanced away.

"What's the matter?" She cupped his jaw, forcing him to meet her gaze.

"It's our mating ceremony. It's a little different from a human wedding."

If the stiffness in his shoulders meant anything, it was a *lot* different. "So it's not just me promising to love, honor, and maybe obey if the situation warrants it?"

He looked back at her, and what she saw in his eyes scared her.

"No. It's more involved than that. There's a . . . ritual any woman who agrees to marry one of the Eleven has to go through." He held up his hand to stop her questions. "Yes, this comes from the time I can't remember. It must be so embedded in our psyches that even Fin can't make us forget."

"I don't need a ritual. I don't even need any words. But if that's what you want, we'll do it." Lia's anger was aimed directly at Fin. How dare he steal his men's memories. She could see how much this small bit of Utah's past meant to him. She ached for what he'd lost.

Utah raked his fingers through his hair. "Look, marrying any of us comes with a shitload of ugly baggage. Any woman who loves us should understand what she's signing up for, and then decide if she's willing to make a lifetime commitment. During the ritual, you'll see some of my past—the good, the bad, and the oh-crap stuff." He smiled as he touched her lips. "Because you know this, Lia, we *will* be bonded forever. I'll never let you go."

Even after he'd removed his finger from her lips, she could feel the pressure, the texture of his skin against hers. "So this ritual might fill in some of the blank spaces in your history?"

Utah nodded. "At least that's what Kelly and Jenna said."

"Good. Bring it on. I want to know everything about you." *So that I can share it with you.*

His smile turned rueful. "Hold those thoughts. To marry me, you have to walk into the heart of my beast and claim a part of my soul."

"Symbolically?"

"No. Really."

"Okay, officially confused. Explain." She slipped her hand into her pocket to touch the yellow flower she'd somehow saved. It was real, *this* was real, no matter how down-the-rabbit-hole it seemed.

"My love for you creates a physical response that opens me to you."

"You do know that what you're describing has a major ick factor." She tempered the words with a smile.

"What I meant is that my body becomes incorporeal so that you can enter."

She nodded, trying to understand, to accept, to *trust*. "Like walking into a ghost?"

"Sort of."

"And once I'm in, what happens?"

"You'll become a part of my past. You'll see and feel what I saw and felt as raptor and . . . before. Then you'll decide whether to accept or reject me." His expression tightened.

"I'll *never* reject you." She was fierce in her denial.

He didn't comment on her vow. "If you accept me, you'll take a part of my soul that I freely give."

"And that does what?"

"We both become more. You'd be immortal if you weren't already. It bonds us as mates forever."

"How do you know all this?"

He shrugged. "Ty and Al have shared some things. But mostly it just feels . . . right. Like I've done this before. But I can't remember." He closed his eyes, but not before she saw his pain. "I can *never* remember."

"It doesn't matter." She stroked his face. "I love you so much I'd dance naked over hot coals. A virtual trip into your past isn't going to discourage me. All I have to do is get through the walking-into-the-heart-of-your-beast part." And once she'd returned, she'd be able to at least give him a peek into that before time.

He opened his eyes and gazed at her. His lips tilted up. "Dancing naked. Now that image is burned into the back of my lids forever."

Utah might be smiling, but she felt his relief. "Why don't you find Tor? I'll wait here."

He hesitated for a moment before disappearing into the darkness. She spent the next few minutes staring down on Portland and marveling how love could make the night come alive in a way that had nothing to do with her vampire senses. And as she absorbed the fact that she really was going to share her life, her love with Utah, the scabs that had formed over Katherine's memory slid away, leaving only shiny new hopes behind.

She turned as Utah and Tor emerged from the darkness. Tor hugged Lia. "He's a good man, and a great pack mate. You won't see anything in his past to contradict that." He glanced at his brother. "Rap would love her. Go for it, bro." He clapped Utah on the back and then stood back to watch.

Lia nodded as she swiped at her damp cheeks. Dumb tears. She hadn't cried when she was a kid, but she was sure making up for it now. "Let's do it."

Utah walked a short distance away and then turned. He stared at her, all his love and promises for the future there for her to see. "If you want to escape at any time, turn around and go back the way you came. I'll understand."

He became raptor.

Lia started walking. Only her enhanced vision allowed her to see the faint form of the man within the beast. She focused on his shadowy human shape. When she took that last step, she resisted the urge to close her eyes and trusted that she wouldn't go splat against his body.

She passed through and into his predator past.

Lia didn't have time to feel fear. As vampire, she had her own predator roots. Silently, she circled around herds of massive plant-eaters while she kept watch for any more dangerous animals. She didn't allow herself to dwell on her aloneness in this strange landscape of grass, trees, and rocks that seemed to go on forever.

But when she finally spotted Utah and his pack, she couldn't stop her surge of primal fear. Her instincts understood the danger.

She recognized him even though his raptor had

no identifying human form within it. This was a savage killer. He wouldn't know her. She'd be nothing but prey to him.

Lia crouched and held her breath until the pack spotted a herd animal lagging behind the others. Relieved that she wouldn't be a raptor meal today, she followed the chase at a safe distance. And when the bloody takedown and kill happened, she forced herself to watch.

The Utah she loved would expect no less. He'd want her to know the worst as well as the best of him. What he still might not believe was that his worst made no difference to her love.

Reluctantly, she finally moved on. She didn't have a clue where she was going, but she knew she had to keep traveling.

Night fell, and the darkness was a black shroud, unrelieved by any modern lighting. So she wasn't aware that everything around her was changing.

Suddenly, explosions rocked the night. The ground shook, and the sky turned red as fires raged. In their glow, she saw alien buildings so tall they seemed to pierce the crimson sky. Destruction and death surrounded her.

Her heart pounded, a drumroll of primal panic and unreasoning dread. Her breaths came in panicked gasps. It didn't matter that a vampire should be beyond those human reactions. She'd been human a lot longer than she'd been vampire, and in this time of terror, she reverted to instinct.

Distant screams filled the night, and she felt

death creeping closer. But it wasn't the sight of bodies strewn everywhere or the unseen menace peering from every shadowed alley that terrified her. It was her almost uncontrollable need to turn and race back the way she'd come.

No. She wouldn't cut and run. Lia pulled up an image of Utah in her mind and kept going. There was something she had to see just ahead.

Beyond the horrors of the bodies and blood—she'd seen all that before—was the sheer *strangeness* of this city. It had nothing of 2012, nothing of Earth's time—past or present—about it.

If only she could see the enemy. Something out there was killing and destroying, but at least on this street, there was only silence. And that all-pervading sense of doom.

Just when she thought she couldn't go any farther, she *saw* him. Utah stood amid the carnage outside what must have been some kind of house. Hard to tell now because it was mostly gone.

She knew it was Utah even though his face wasn't the same, human but subtly different. Lia would always recognize him, though. He could never hide from her. Around him lay about eight people. Two men were struggling to their feet. Rap and Tor?

Utah ignored everything as he knelt beside a woman lying on the blood-soaked street. Lia knew she was dead. Horror piled on horror as she realized the woman had been pregnant.

No. Lia looked away. She didn't want to see his

pain or put a name to the dead woman and her child. But then she forced herself to look back. She owed it to Utah to witness his loss, his grief, and then make it part of their shared memories.

The Utah of this time looked up at the two men who'd stumbled over to him. "They killed my wife, our child." His voice was harsh with layers and layers of pain and fury.

Caught and buffeted by his agony, she didn't take time to wonder how she could understand him. He wasn't speaking any language she recognized.

One of the men turned away to walk among the other bodies, searching. "Parents. Grandparents. Sisters. Dead." He spoke in a strangely emotionless monotone, as though he were talking about strangers. "All of our family. Gone." Suddenly, shock released him and sobs brought him to his knees.

"I'll kill them. I don't care how long it takes, I'll kill every fucking one of them." Utah's whispered promise faded away as he turned back to his dead wife. He smoothed the dark hair from her face before lowering his head and crying.

Lia scrubbed at her own tears as she slowly backed away. It was time to go. She couldn't change his past or comfort him here. When she was far enough from the men, she turned to continue her journey to . . . She wasn't sure. All she knew was that out there somewhere was the Utah she knew. Lia had to reach him.

Then she saw the man standing in the shadow of a burned-out building. He was watching Utah and his brothers. She couldn't see his face, but the gleam of silver hair caught her attention. Fin? No, it couldn't be.

She shouldn't stop. Interacting with anyone could be dangerous. But she had to know. Calling herself a fool, she strode to where the man waited silently for her.

"Fin?" Lia didn't go too close. She could run like crazy if she had to.

"No. But it's a good name. Perhaps I'll claim it." His smile held secrets. "Someday." He studied her from those strange silver eyes. "I've seen you in a vision."

She didn't know how much to tell this Fin, so she opted for questions. "Who are you? Why are you watching them? What happened here?"

He remained silent for so long she thought he wouldn't answer.

"I'm a visitor, like you." Then he glanced away from her, turning his attention back to the brothers. "A time cycle ended today. This is always a period of great change. Unfortunately for these people, it was a catastrophic change." His tone grew thoughtful. "There are always those who believe they know what is best for others, and sometimes they are powerful enough to enforce what they believe. A group of ancient immortals decided that the old must be destroyed so the new might flourish." He shrugged. "In a few hours, they will have obliterated all signs that a great civilization once existed here."

"But you're going to save them, right?" She looked back at Utah and his brothers.

Fin seemed to consider the possibility. "Perhaps I will. They didn't deserve this. Some species have needed killing, but not this one. The carnage . . . bothers me."

She got the feeling not much "bothered" him. "You seem a little disconnected from everything."

"Oh, you have no idea how connected I am." Then he turned away from her.

She understood a dismissal when she heard it. Besides, she had to find *her* Utah. Just thinking his name drove her onward. And only when she was blocks away did she realize Fin hadn't answered all her questions.

Lia raced up and down darkened streets. The fight still raged on some of them, but most were deserted except for the stench of fire and death. Panic pressed her to run faster, to get to where Utah's soul waited.

Soon she was out of the city and running into the total darkness again. She couldn't see, couldn't hear, could only *feel*. He was *there*. Just ahead.

Suddenly, she burst from the darkness. Utah stood bathed in a circle of light. He smiled and held his arms wide for her. With an inarticulate cry, she flung herself into them.

Was this his soul then, this light surrounded by darkness? Well, she intended to widen his little patch of soul-shine. She wrapped her arms around him and hung on tight. "I went, I saw, and it scared me witless, but I still want you, raptor."

He felt the moment she claimed her share of his soul. It was a completion, a fulfillment he knew he'd always searched for, one he never thought to find. No matter how many lifetimes he'd lived or would live, there would never again be a joy like this.

It was over. Utah closed his eyes. He'd always thought his soul was raptor, but it had welcomed her in human form. Tonight, for *her*, he'd wanted it to be human.

When he opened his eyes, they were both standing in the clearing with Tor looking on. Lia's expression mirrored conflicting emotions—love and joy along with a memory of horror. He pulled her closer.

Without warning, words came. Words he hadn't thought but knew he had to say. "You touch my soul, Lia. You touch what I am, what I once was, and what I will be."

"I accept what you share with me tonight—your love, your soul. I give my love and my soul in return." Tears shone in her eyes.

He touched her lips with his. "Take what is mine, and let it join us forever."

Silence hung between them until Lia finally spoke. "Those words were beautiful and fitting, but they weren't my words. Where did they come from?"

Utah shook his head. "I don't know, but Ty and Jenna said the same words. I was there."

She smiled up at him. "It doesn't matter. They were the right words."

The night should end with those words. They'd triumphed over evil and found love. *Leave it. Ask her tomorrow.* But he couldn't. He had to know now. "Something in my past scared you." He took a deep breath. "Tell me."

"Wait."

Tor's voice startled Utah. He'd almost forgotten his brother was there.

"Congratulations, and I love you guys, but I'm outta here." Tor's smile looked strained. "I choose not to know. *This* is my time. I don't want a past to haunt me that I can't even remember. Sorry. I'll wait for you back in the other clearing." He turned and walked away.

Maybe Tor was right. With Zero and the rest of his immortals still out there, Utah had enough complications in his life. He thought about it for all of two seconds. "Tell me."

Lia met his gaze. "I think Zero and the others destroyed your civilization—the one *before* the dinosaurs—the same way they're trying to destroy ours. I ended up in a really strange-looking city. It was burning and its people dying." She seemed to be thinking about what to say next. "I saw you . . . and your family." She hesitated.

His heart clenched. "Go on."

"You were kneeling by a dead woman. Your wife. She was pregnant."

Dead. Wife. Pregnant. The words pounded at him, hammer-slams to his gut, his heart. All he could do was nod.

"There were other bodies scattered around you. Two men—I guess they were Rap and Tor—were still alive. One of them looked at the bodies. The dead were your parents, your grandparents, and your sisters."

He fought to slow his racing heart, to calm his breathing, to keep his emotions under control. "Did you see anyone else?"

"Fin was watching you."

Utah wasn't surprised.

"He said the immortals were responsible for what was happening to your world."

History repeating itself. But this time they were taking it to the bastards. Fierce joy filled him. "Fin say anything else?"

Lia shrugged. "Just that he and I were visitors there. Guess that proves he wasn't one of you guys. Oh, and he explained the whole end-of-time-period thing that we already knew."

Who was Fin, and why didn't he want to talk about his past? But those were thoughts for another day. Right now, only Lia mattered.

"You okay with all this?" She looked worried.

He wasn't used to anyone worrying about him. He liked the feeling.

"Yeah, I think I am. Don't get me wrong, I'll always wonder about the woman who was my wife, and I'll mourn our unborn child. But that was a long time ago." He hugged her tighter and buried his face in her windswept curls. At least he now understood his obsession with avenging Rap along with his flashes of memory. Subconsciously, he'd known. Family was precious. "I love *you*. In *this* time, in *this* place."

She moved back, and he let her go. "You've lost too many family members. We're going to do something about it."

He could tell her that when she got a militant gleam in her eyes she was beautiful, but she wouldn't appreciate it. She'd rather think that her determined expression cowed anyone who got in her way. So he'd keep his thoughts to himself. "What's your plan?"

"Come with me." She strode back to where the others were.

Only they weren't there anymore. Tor sat on the ground with his back against a tree, waiting as he'd promised. Fin stood alone in the middle of the clearing. He was almost swaying on his feet. What the hell had he done to himself when he fought Zero?

Lia's gasp pulled Utah's attention away from his leader. He followed her gaze to what lay behind Fin. Then he looked back at Fin. "Why'd you kill Adam?"

"He needed killing. He intended to find Zero or

one of the others and offer them the same deal he offered Seven."

"How do you know that?" Lia shifted her gaze from the dead Adam to Fin.

"His thoughts on the subject were clear."

"Do you stay out of *anyone's* mind?" Lia seemed more outraged over Fin's mental breaking-and-entering than about Adam's death.

"Not if they have something I want." Fin's was the voice of cold reason. Emotion would never warm it.

"Won't that make a martyr of him?" Utah's beast thought Fin's solution made perfect sense. The human part of Utah thought that Fin might've found a less drastic solution, like wiping out Adam's memory of ever meeting Seven.

"Not if a better qualified leader takes charge. Jude comes to mind." Fin's gaze sharpened as he studied them. "You've gone through the ceremony."

"Lia is my mate." He met Fin's stare, daring him to disapprove.

"And you're going to give us a wedding gift, Fin." Lia ignored Utah's raised brows. "You're going to restore Rap to his brothers."

Fin didn't look shocked, but Utah knew that Tor and he did. Out of the corner of his eye, he saw Tor stand.

Utah rolled the idea around in his mind. Even a chance at getting Rap back excited him.

Lia spoke before Fin could think of a reason

that he couldn't make it happen. "You need a body. There's one right behind you. It's in great shape. I don't know how you killed him, but I don't see any obvious wounds." She hurried on. "Adam had skills that Rap could use to help the Eleven. He could see the short-term future, and he had thousands of years' worth of knowledge about vampires."

"Tempting." But then Fin shook his head. "I don't have the power. Zero drained me. And even if he hadn't done a job on me, I couldn't afford to use the power it would take to put Rap in a new body. I have to stay at full strength in case I need to yank someone's ass out of the fire."

Sometimes Utah hated Fin's cold logic. And yeah, he'd had to save the Eleven a few times.

Lia went into negotiating mode. "Think of the possibilities, Fin. Rap could control the vampires, and no one would know it wasn't Adam except for us. You need the vampires."

Fin didn't immediately reject the idea.

"We can feed you power. We did it with Kione, we can do it now. I want my brother back." Utah realized that this could really happen, and he fought for Rap like he fought for everything—aggressively and with a threat of violence. "Make it happen."

Fin tensed. Purple flooded his narrowed eyes.

"Hey, I hear that you gave Ty and Al gifts to celebrate their weddings. Rap would be the ultimate gift. Think about it. Utah would owe you. Bet he'd never disobey an order again."

Lia was trying to sound cheery and oblivious to the danger, but Utah felt her fear. He never wanted her to be afraid of or for him, so he forced back his need to challenge Fin, tried to think logically. He wouldn't do Rap much good if he was dead.

"Never disobey an order again? When he's dead, maybe." Fin still sounded pissed, but some of his tension seemed to recede. He turned to glance at Adam's body. "I don't know. I don't want to bring him halfway here and then strand his soul where I can't find it."

"I'll help." Tor walked to stand beside Utah.

Fin just nodded. He knelt beside Adam. They all did the same. Utah clasped Fin's and Lia's hands. Tor took Lia's other hand. Then they waited.

Fin stretched his free hand over Adam, palm up. He closed his eyes.

Utah thought the sensation would be the same as he'd felt when they took Kione's pain. It wasn't.

It was worse. It felt as though everything inside him was liquefying and then oozing out through his pores. He broke into a cold sweat. Nausea made him close his eyes and concentrate on not humiliating himself.

Beside him, he heard Lia's small whimper.

To hell with his promise not to go all protective on her. She was his mate, and she was suffering. He visualized a steel door closing between them. Then he sealed that door so tight that nothing could get through it, not even the liquid fire that was now a river of agony racing through his veins. He tightened his grip on Fin's hand and opened himself to more and more and more . . .

Lia punched him. Hard. He grunted his surprise.

"Don't you dare do that. We share everything—love, happiness, *pain*. Don't cheat me out of any of it."

"She's damn right." Tor growled his agreement. "You cut her off, and you cut me off with her. She's pack now. We bring Rap back together or not at all."

Utah said nothing, just swung the door open. Then he concentrated on getting through this without screaming.

Suddenly, a small ball of light appeared in Fin's palm. Lia gripped his hand harder as Fin lowered the light to Adam's eyes. The light disappeared.

Still on their knees, they waited.

Dread pulled at Utah. Finally, when he felt he couldn't stand it another minute, Adam blinked.

He looked at each of them in turn, and then Adam smiled. "Jeez, I never thought I'd see your ugly mugs again." His gaze stopped at Lia. "Except for you. You're not ugly, and I don't know you." His grin widened. "But I'd like to."

Lia returned his grin. "I'm Utah's mate. Welcome home, Rap."

Rap. He was back. The realization sucked all the breath from Utah's lungs. Tor jumped to his feet, dragged Rap after him, and then pulled him into a bear hug.

Utah and Lia rose to their feet more slowly. He felt a little wobbly as he wrapped his arms around his brother. He should be saying something emotional, but instead, he put all his feelings into the hug.

Rap punched his shoulder, but Utah didn't miss the wet sheen in his eyes. "Wow, a mate. I go away for a little while and look what happens." Then he hugged Lia. "You take care of him."

Lia wrapped her arm around Utah's waist. "We'll take care of each other."

Rap grinned. Then he frowned. "I'm not in the same body. What do I look like?"

Lia studied him. "You've got dark hair, gold eyes, and a perfect face. Women will love you."

Rap looked relieved. "Good. Women are important."

Tor dragged Rap toward the trail leading down from the volcano. "Let's head back to Fin's condo. I'll catch you up on the way there. We have things to celebrate tonight."

Utah watched them walk away, then looked over at Fin. He was gazing up at the night sky. What did Fin see in that sky? Was he thinking about Seven? Because Utah figured there was history between those two.

Utah and Lia joined him. Utah looked at the sky

too. He could see plenty of stars now that the volcano had settled down. No more steam. He lowered his gaze to the city lights spread out below them. People could return home now.

Utah coughed. "Look, I want to thank—"

"Don't thank me. Don't *ever* thank me."

Utah sensed bitterness behind those words and wondered.

"What is Rap now?" Lia leaned into Utah.

"He's more than he ever was. He took Adam's nature, so he's vampire. But his soul is still raptor." Fin never dropped his gaze from the sky.

Lia looked thoughtful. "I spoke with you during my journey to Utah's soul. You never told me who you were."

"I never did, did I?" Fin looked away from the sky long enough to smile at her. "Go celebrate your marriage and Rap's return, and forget about unanswered questions for the night."

"Sounds like a good idea." Utah took Lia's hand and headed away from Fin and all his mysteries.

Hand in hand, they walked silently for a while before pausing in a small meadow. The flowers were already dying without Seven's heat.

He had to make things clear to her. "I'll be tough to live with. I'll always have to fight my beast. Sometimes I'll need him, but other times he'll just be a pain in the ass."

She laughed. "You don't think living with a newbie vampire will be a treat, do you? I'll have a steep learning curve."

Lia turned and walked into his arms. He lowered his head and traced her bottom lip with his tongue. She tasted of night, sex, and love.

"I'd make love to you right here, but it's too cold." She slid her fingers into his hair and pulled his face closer. "Not that we wouldn't set the woods ablaze once we started."

He wrapped his arms around her and slipped his hands beneath her top. Her skin felt cool and smooth. He kissed the sensitive skin behind her ear and whispered, "I think we should skip the party, hmm?"

"Sounds like a plan to me."

Her soft laughter stirred his hunger. He grabbed her hand and hurried her to the car.

She settled into the seat and remained quiet while he drove. Probably frozen in terror. He was breaking sound barriers tonight.

Finally, she spoke. "You know, I think I've figured things out."

"Uh-huh." One mile to Fin's.

"It's all about perspective."

"Sure." A half mile to Fin's.

"Most people think 2012 is an ending. Generates lots of negative energy."

"Right." He roared into the parking garage, pulled into a space, and hit the brakes.

Lia put her hand on the dash to stop her forward momentum. "But I don't think of it that way."

He leaped from the car, ran around to the passenger side, ripped open the door, and scooped her up in his arms.

Laughing, she flung her arms around his neck and held on as he suffered through the hour-long elevator ride up to Fin's floor; rushed past an astonished Ty, who opened the condo door; and finally set Lia down on her bed.

She stared up at him. "A hundred years from now, I'll look back at 2012 as—"

He dropped onto the bed beside her and gathered her to him.

"The beginning."

Next month, don't miss these exciting new love stories only from Avon Books

Scandal of the Year by Laura Lee Guhrke
Julia always knew that Aidan Carr, the oh-so-proper Duke of Trathen, had a bit of the devil in him—a devil who secretly yearned for what he could not have. So when she decides she needs to be caught in a compromising situation, Aiden is the answer to her prayers.

Night Betrayed by Joss Ware
The Change that devastated the earth did not destroy Theo Waxnicki, it made him something more than human—eternally young...but not immortal. When he dies on a mission, he's lost in darkness...until a miracle lady brings him back.

Burning Darkness by Jaime Rush
Fonda Raine, a government-trained assassin, has her sights locked on her latest target: Eric Aruda, a rogue Offspring—a pyrokinetic who can create fire with just a thought. But Fonda has awesome powers of her own—and her ability to be in two places at one time enables her to put herself exactly where she wants to be...in Eric's bed.

Tainted by Temptation by Katy Madison
To escape the cruel false gossip of London, Velvet Campbell accepts a governess position in remote Cornwall. But when she finds, to her dismay, that her new employer—the darkly handsome Lucian Pendar—is himself the subject of whispered insinuations, she wonders: *has she found a kindred spirit, a destined love...or placed herself in peril?*

Unforgettable, enthralling love stories,
sparkling with passion and adventure
from Romance's bestselling authors

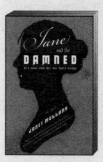

At Avon Books, we know your passion for romance—once you finish one of our novels, you find yourself wanting more.

May we tempt you with . . .

- **Excerpts** from our upcoming releases.

- Entertaining **extras**, including authors' personal photo albums and book lists.

- Behind-the-scenes **scoop** on your favorite characters and series.

- **Sweepstakes** for the chance to win free books, romantic getaways, and other fun prizes.

- Writing **tips** from our authors and editors.

- **Blog** with our authors and find out why they love to write romance.

- **Exclusive content** that's not contained within the pages of our novels.

Join us at
www.avonbooks.com

AVON

An Imprint of HarperCollins*Publishers*
www.avonromance.com

Available wherever books are sold or please call 1-800-331-3761 to order.

FTH 0708